As The Sparks Fly Upwards

RICHARD STAMP

Published in Australia by Sid Harta Publishers Pty Ltd,
ABN: 46 119 415 842
23 Stirling Crescent, Glen Waverley, Victoria 3150 Australia
Telephone: +61 3 9560 9920, Facsimile: +61 3 9545 1742
E-mail: author@sidharta.com.au

First published in Australia July 2011
This edition published July 2011

Cover design, typesetting:
Chameleon Print Design

This is a work of fiction. All the places mentioned and all the characters are entirely fictional and do not portray any individual, living or dead. However, most of the incidents in the book do have some basis in fact. Descriptive terms and modes of address are those which were in use at the time in which the book is set.

Stamp, Richard
As the Sparks Fly Upwards
ISBN: 1-921829-35-4
EAN13: 978-1-921829-35-2
pp284

FOREWORD

This is storytelling at its best, in the great tradition. *As the Sparks Fly Upwards* is the kind of writing that will never go out of fashion, because it connects with some of the elements that lie deep within the human spirit. We enjoy stories that touch on the human condition, that show us and our neighbours as we are, and we especially warm to stories that have at their heart a true love of humanity. The rule applies, whether we are talking about the wry humour of Yiddish folk stories, the affectionate observations of Irish tales, the dry humour of Australian bush yarns, or any one of thousands of other narratives found the world over.

"Life is a comedy to those who think, a tragedy to those who feel." Richard Stamp walks the line between the two. He writes with an intimate knowledge of bush people and an obvious respect for them. Through the eyes of his naive protagonist the remote areas of Australia are peopled and brought to life in a way which gives true delight.

Those who read *As the Sparks Fly Upwards* are placing themselves in the hands of a master storyteller.

—John Marsden

CHAPTER 1

Breaking In

The Tin Hare, two carriages and definitely not air-conditioned, rattled its way westwards across the plains. Under the drumming wheels the miles unfolded, the line a strand of DNA encoding both its own destination and my future.

Brother Edwin from Blaxford had rung me the week before.

'I suggest you catch Monday's train up here. That will give you time to settle in and visit some parishioners during the week so that some of them will know who you are before you front up to them in church on Sunday.'

Brother Edwin was a big man physically. When he suggested, it was wise to comply.

I had met him at the annual gathering of all the brothers, just after I arrived from England. It was February and the year was 1962. Now I was travelling inland to work with him. Somewhere, deep and visceral within me, my youthful sense of excitement and adventure was trying not to collide with an undigested sense of unease about what I had let myself in for.

Monday proved to be a stinker. It was hot and close and thunder rumbled. Lightning flashed all day on the western horizon. I stared out of the train window at a landscape of mesmerising sameness and was surprised at how many large trees there were. Back in England I had imagined an interior of hot sand and sparse scrub. The sand was hot enough and red in colour. It gave way in the afternoon to black soil as the small, intermittent sandhills disappeared and an all pervading flatness spread out in every direction, except in the north-west where one grey, hunchbacked hill pulled itself over the rim of the world like something struggling to be free. There was a lot of sky. The heat was like hot brass laid across my forehead.

In the late afternoon the engine gave an exhausted sigh as it slid into Blaxford Station at the end of the line. The train not so much stopped as collapsed with a final rattling of hot metal. I could identify with how it felt as I picked up my bags and stepped onto the platform. Five other weary travellers also alighted. They glistened with sweat and homecoming anticipation, climbed gratefully into five waiting vehicles and disappeared, leaving a trail of dust hanging in the air.

Of Brother Edwin there was no sign. So much for his promise to meet me! I stood at the station entrance and looked out at what I could see of my new posting.

The main street into town stretched out at right angles to the railway. Square weatherboard houses pulled tin roofed verandas over their eyes and tried not to blink into the sunlight which now slanted increasingly from the west under the receding thunderclouds. There had obviously been sound and light but not much rain with the thunder. Small volcano-like craters from the few rain spots speckled the dust of the station forecourt. Round the end of the building came a whirling wind that picked up sticks and dust in a choking vortex, then travelled past me and blustered down the main street like a ruffian looking for trouble.

Where was the man? I could feel anger rising within me. He could at least have been on time. I waited. I stood tired and lonely at the end of the world and I had no idea which direction to go, no idea where the rectory was that would be home to me from now on. In the end came another cloud of dust which resolved itself into a battered old ute out of which stepped a lanky youth wearing jeans and a torn shirt.

'Brother Edwin had to go out bush. Someone died and he's gone to see the family. Won't be back until tomorrow. He asked me to pick you up. My name's Glen. You must be Brother Mark.'

We shook hands and he hoisted my luggage into the back of the ute and we were off down the street and round a couple of corners. We pulled up on the river edge of town in a short extension of a street that seemed to be composed mainly of tin sheds, garages and agricultural implements.

The rectory was old and well settled into its block of ground. It was built of rammed earth with a corrugated iron roof and a front veranda that sloped alarmingly from left to right. Glen pushed open the front door and hauled in my luggage. He was obviously at home in the place.

'Brother Edwin said you could have this room,' he said as he shoved at a sticking door and placed my bags on a newly made bed under a circular hoop made of bamboo and from which hung a pure white mosquito net. The net was loosely knotted ready to be unfurled for use at night. An old electric ceiling fan straight out of *Casablanca* hung from the middle of the ceiling.

'Are you staying here with Brother Edwin?' I asked. I was not sure where he fitted into the scheme of things.

'Me? No, not really. Brother Edwin gives me a bed for the night when I'm in town every now and then. My gran's in hospital and I came in to visit her and to stock up on a few things. I'll be away in a moment. I'm fencing about eighty miles north of here. Got an early start in the morning.'

'Fencing?' I asked. I had mental images of swordplay which somehow didn't seem to fit.

'Yeah, there's about twenty miles of fences still to be replaced on O'Grady's place. They got burned in the fire last year.'

'Well, I'm really glad you're here to see me settled and thanks for meeting me at the station. I hadn't a clue where to go.'

'That's okay. Brother Edwin says there's cold meat and other stuff in the fridge and he'll see you in the morning sometime.'

I noticed a huge crack in the bedroom wall. It was big enough to put a fist in. Already clouds of mosquitoes seemed to be making forays out of its dark recesses.

'What do we do about mozzies?' I asked. 'That crack looks as though it could let in a herd of elephants let alone a few insects.'

'Yeah the cracks are a bit of a worry,' said Glen. 'The whole place is built on black soil, which moves. Build anything round here with brick or concrete and its soon going to crack.'

'Does that include the church?' I asked.

'Too right,' he added with a bit too much enthusiasm for comfort I thought. 'There's a huge open crack in the church sanctuary. You'll notice it soon enough.'

'Sounds dangerous,' I said.

'No, not really, but the breeze comes through it pretty strong. Blows the candles out on Sundays. The building replaced the old wooden one and when they built it they put twenty-foot pillars down until they hit rock. They made them boat-shaped so the ground moved past them.'

'Clever thinking,' I said.

'Yeah, that was the idea and mostly it worked ... but not quite.' His voice trailed off as if so much talking had exhausted him. Then another idea worked its way through the cogs of his brain.

'As for the mozzies, there's citronella oil for rubbing on and you'll find the mosquito net keeps out most of them. Make sure you tuck it well under the mattress. The little blighters soon suss out anywhere they can get in.'

Glen went off and left me to it. After a while he put his head round the door and said, 'I'm away, then. See you around.'

I unpacked my few belongings and headed for the shower to get rid of the dust and sweat. An hour later I was sitting, the inner man satisfied, after some slices from a cooked leg of lamb and a couple of potatoes with a salad which had been washed down with a bottle of cold beer that I found in the fridge. Then I wandered over to the church to have a look around and get my bearings.

The church was a newish brick building with not much

to recommend it architecturally. The west end wall was weatherboard and it looked as if it had never been finished. True enough, for I found a duplicated and dusty pamphlet inside the door saying just that. It was meant to be longer, but same old story. They had run out of money and it was left in its truncated state. I found the great crack in the sanctuary and again clouds of mosquitoes had made it their main entrance. I didn't think they were coming in to pray and I made a mental note to buy some repellent and to cover myself in it on Sunday, a wise precaution as it turned out.

Outside the church there were some neat bits of garden with really green lawns of buffalo grass, hard on bare feet, but it covered the ground and kept the dust down. I was to discover later that the town water was pumped from the river and that the filtration plant was not up to its expected task. This meant that the water was often so cloudy with silt that it top-dressed the gardens for free. The church stood on a corner, the intersection of a street that crossed the one in which the rectory stood. Across this side street were two brick-faced buildings. One had metal lettering across it, high up for all to see: OLD AND SILVERTON. STOCK AND STATION AGENTS.

Next door, in sombre red brick and obviously older, was the local branch of the Central Bank. On the diagonally opposite corner there was a small, parklike area of grass and immediately opposite the rectory was a garage of the kind that mends cars but doesn't sell them. There was nothing flashy about it though it did have some interesting vintage petrol pumps in front of it. A faded sign said simply: 'SIMMO'S G' before the right-hand edge ended abruptly in a jagged line that suggested it had been ripped off by the wind. Presumably it had once said 'GARAGE' as well. What struck me was how isolated the church and rectory were. Nobody actually lived within a block of the place.

The evening was still warm; the thunder of the afternoon had done little to clear the air. I went back to the rectory, switched on the bedroom fan and turned in for an early night. I must have gone to sleep pretty quickly, for I remembered nothing further until I woke suddenly. It was about two in the morning. What had woken me was a strange sound, a sort of sibilant *whoomph* like a sudden short gust of wind, not very loud.

I sat up in bed and listened to the aftermath of the sound, which sounded like the falling of a child's set of play bricks, just one or two. After that it was eerily quiet, so I settled back to go to sleep again. Then came the moaning. There was nothing for it but to get up and investigate.

I pulled on a pair of shorts and looked out of the front door. Nothing seemed to be amiss. The moaning, however, continued, so I walked to the corner near the church. There seemed to be a fair amount of dust in the air which was not the usual sort ransacked by the wind from the topsoil of the surrounding country. This was grittier and dryer somehow. Then I saw why. Across the road the whole front wall of the stock and station agents had simply fallen out and lay flat on the pavement. The moaning was coming from a solitary figure sitting right in the middle of where it had fallen. I ran across the road to see if he was okay.

I found the man to be of middle age and sitting in front

of where the front door had been. He had an unruly mop of red hair with stubble to match. The door was, or had been, a glass shop door. Remarkably, when the wall had fallen the door seemed to have shattered over the man, leaving him apparently unscathed, sitting in the middle of a pile of broken glass. There was no blood as far as I could see.

'Are you okay?' I asked him. The reply came in a thick Scottish accent through rich and smoky fumes of whisky. Whatever he'd been drinking smelt as if it had come straight out of burning peat with just a hint of dental decay.

'Aye,' he said, 'some bugger hit me on the head.'

'What do they call you?' I asked.

'Dougal,' came the thick reply.

'Well then, Dougal. Let's help you up. Mind you don't cut yourself on all this glass.'

I held out my hand and he grabbed hold of it and levered himself unsteadily to his feet. There was a tinkling sound, as of fairy bells, as a small shower of tiny glass pieces fell from his clothing. It was an odd association of ideas. You'd look at this fellow a long, long time before you were reminded of Tinkerbell.

'Can you make it across the road? You could just sit down awhile on that seat in the church gardens and recover a bit,' I said.

And taking his arm I guided him across the road and sat him down on a bench inscribed to the memory of some long lost soul called 'John Henry Eccles, Public Benefactor. Died 1889'. Dougal was obviously made of stern stuff. He seemed to be none the worse for being hit on the head by a falling wall and door, testament, I imagined, not only to a strong constitution but also to the anaesthetising effects of good Scotch whisky. I began to breathe a sigh of relief.

'Where's my Jack?' he suddenly piped.

'Who's Jack?' I asked with some alarm as it struck me that someone else might be buried underneath the fallen wall.

'Ma wee doggie, Jack,' moaned Dougal. 'Where is he?'

I looked across the road and could see no sign of a dog.

'I'll just go back and have a look for him,' I said and returned across the road to the shambles on the other side. I briefly took stock of the damage. Up and down the street, where the houses began, there was not a light to be seen. The whole town was asleep and I was left alone with the situation. The fallen wall was almost intact as it lay there, horizontal. Perhaps it got tired and wanted a rest, I thought. I noticed that it had been keyed into the brickwork of the bank next door and when it fell it didn't want to let go. It was still holding hands with some of the bank's bricks which had pulled out, leaving a bit of a hole in the bank wall, not a large hole but large enough as I soon found out. Then there was the smallest of movements over to my left.

A few fallen bricks began to heave and a white paw appeared, followed by a spotted body, as a Jack Russell shakily emerged. It must have been knocked cold by the wall and who could blame it? Its powers of recovery were remarkable and immediate. It took one look at me and bolted, somewhat uncertainly at first, but it soon got up steam and ran around in circles trailing a rather scuffed looking leather lead. I thought, if I don't catch it now it will be off, so I made a lunge at the lead which turned out not to be the best of strategies. The dog had its own ideas about where to go and as I lunged it took off straight into the hole in the bank wall. At the very last minute my outstretched fingers tangled with the lead and what with the dog pulling and me lunging towards it, my arm got dragged into the hole and there it stuck, tight. To make matters worse, a few more hanging bricks decided to come down and wedge my arm in place, just in case I should think of escaping.

The silence of the town was now broken by a shrill wailing that was designed to wake the dead. The lead had slipped from by fingers, my arm was jammed tight and inside the bank Jack was galloping around. He must have set off the burglar alarm. There was nothing I could do but wait, trapped there as the town came alive. People in nightwear tumbled out of the houses up the street, women with their hair in rollers crowded round for a good look and before long came another wail as the local police car careered round the corner and came to a stop.

Out got a constable with cocky self-assurance evident in every step. He looked with disbelief at the mess on the pavement and the open front of the stock and station agency. Rolls of barbed wire glinted in the lights of the police car. Cans of sheep dip and metal star posts stood to attention as if mounting a guard of honour.

'Anyone see what happened?' inquired the copper to no one in particular. There was a murmur of negativity.

'Okay, son, what's your name and what have you got to say for yourself?'

'My name's Mark,' I said, 'and the wall fell down.'

'Just like that?' asked the policeman in obvious sarcasm.

'And what are you trying to reach inside the bank? I suppose that's a coincidence,' he said, still in obvious disbelief.

'I'm not trying to reach anything,' I said. 'It's just that my arm's stuck. I was trying to get hold of the dog.'

'Whose dog would that be?' said the constable with a hint of interest.

'His dog,' I said, pointing with my free arm across the road. But Dougal had apparently melted from view when the police car arrived.

'Anyone know who this bloke is?' asked the law of the assembled crowd. Another round of head-shaking ensued.

'Look here, Constable,' I pleaded. 'Can't you see my arm's jammed and it's painful and can you find someone with a hammer or something so that you can knock a couple of bricks loose and free me?'

'All in good time, son,' he said. It was beginning to irritate me the way he called me son. It wasn't so much the word as the way he said it, as if I was some idiot offspring that he didn't want to acknowledge and who should have been shut in a cupboard away from public view. The burglar alarm wasn't helping either as it still shrieked into the night.

'Okay,' said the policeman, turning once more to the growing crowd, 'anyone got a crowbar or a hammer close by and can somebody nip round to the bank manager's house and get him to turn off this damned siren? I suggest the rest of you go on home back to bed. Your police force is well able to handle things from here.'

Two or three men duly ran off and the onlookers began to shuffle away.

'Have you got anyone who knows you and can vouch for you?' he asked me.

'There's Brother Edwin,' I said, 'but he's away for the night.'

'Oh very convenient,' came the heavy sarcasm again. 'Now, look at things from my point of view, son. It looks to me that this is a bank job gone horribly wrong for you. No one knows you. I find you with your arm reaching inside the bank through a hole in the wall that wasn't there yesterday. How did you do it? What explosive did you use? Too much by the look of it, or was it stuff from the stock and station agents that you were after? Either way you haven't been very clever, have you?'

He paused in his litany of apparent crimes I was intent on committing as two men came back with a six-pound hammer and a crowbar. They both got to work, not too gently, on the bricks around my arm and in no time they were loosened enough for me to extract my arm which by now had gone rather numb and blue looking. I thanked the men for their efforts and began massaging the numbness out of my arm.

There was another minor episode as the bank manager arrived with tousled grey hair and opened the front door. He reached inside and flicked a switch on the wall and, mercifully for us all, the banshee was abruptly silenced. Then the manager left as abruptly as he had arrived, but not without first giving me a look that would curdle milk. I took it that he wasn't too keen on being woken up.

Everyone forgot about the dog, me included, until too late and the bank manager had gone. However, there was no further sound from the bank building, so I assumed the dog must have gone to sleep.

'You'd better come round the police station while we sort this out,' said the constable as he grabbed my arm and led me to the police car.

The police station was situated on a corner just opposite the courthouse. The courthouse was a nineteenth century extravagance, built when bushrangers needed to be reminded of the majesty of the law. I later learned that it had been designed for some West African town of the same name as Blaxford, but someone had got the names mixed up and the plans and instructions to build were sent to Australia by mistake. It looked out of place where it was, but I could see that on some palm-fringed shore with the Union Jack flying proudly above it, it would have been the very epitome of colonial architecture. Here its cool verandas provided shade for lounging under on a hot afternoon.

The police station by contrast was a twentieth century monstrosity. I could understand the constable's truculence if he had to work daily in a place like that. It was built of hard-edged red brick with yellow quoining in a style not unlike many a public lavatory. Its barred windows suggested to all and sundry that once inside it might be hard to get out again.

I was led in the front door and the constable, who was the sole lawman on duty overnight, took off his hat and then picked up an imposing bunch of keys. He led me down a corridor out to the back where there were two concrete block holding cells.

I made one last tired attempt to explain.

'Look, Constable,' I said. 'Can't you see that I'm not a would-be bank robber? I only got into town today and I'm exhausted. Can't you just let me go back to bed? This is clearly all a mistake.'

He was obviously tired too and wanted the easy way out.

'You can sleep on things in here,' he said and pushed me into the cell. 'The sergeant will process you when he comes on duty in the morning.'

There was nothing else to do but take his advice.

I stretched out on the iron bed. There was no mosquito net here. Insect protection for the night was achieved by biological control. Across the window was stretched a huge spider's web with a large grey spider at its centre. Four other webs adorned the corners of the room high up near the ceiling.

I went to sleep and dreamed of Robert the Bruce sitting in a bank vault. From the roof a spider was lowering itself on a silken thread. When it reached the floor it turned into a dog named Jack.

A key rattling in the lock was the next thing I heard as a shortish, round and kindly looking sergeant came in with a mug of steaming tea in one hand and a clean towel and soap in the other.

'Here, drink this,' he said. 'My name's Sergeant Hughes and I think you and I better have a chat, don't you?'

He sat on the end of the bed and I recounted to him my story; who I was and what had happened. I told him too that I had tried to tell the constable last night, but he had seemed to have his own ideas stuck in his mind and didn't really want to know.

'Ah yes, Constable Gorman,' said the sergeant. 'He hasn't been with us long. Came here from Redland down in the city. He's very keen but hasn't yet realised he's in the bush now. Tends to see big crime round every corner. He'll mellow in time. Meanwhile, how about some breakfast? We get an allowance for feeding prisoners. May as well use some of the government's money in giving you a decent meal. What would you like. Eggs, a couple of chops, tomatoes, mushrooms and toast and coffee sound all right to you? Meanwhile you may as well freshen up.'

'So you believe me?' I said.

'Sure,' he replied. 'That wall was put up six months ago without proper foundations. Typical decision from the firm's head office in the city. They didn't even bother to ask for local advice. We've all been wondering how long it would be before it fell down. And Dougal McLashen is well known to us. His wife died a while back and he gets on the whisky every now and then, but he's harmless. I'd better check on what's happened to his dog though. Oh, I'll obviously need to have someone officially verify who you are. I'll get in touch with Brother Edwin as soon as he gets back. You should be out of here by midday.'

And that's exactly what happened. I enjoyed the best breakfast that I'd had since arriving in the country. Brother Edwin came in at last and laughed like a braying donkey. The sergeant released me and later in the day we learned on the grapevine that the bank manager had gone into work early and, as he unlocked and opened the bank's front door, something like a miniature tornado hit him around the legs and bit deeply into his calves before racing off down the street, its lead still trailing. The manager had to go to the hospital and get twelve stitches in the wound. I remembered his withering look and, just for a moment, the unworthy thought flashed through my mind, 'Vengeance is mine saith the Lord'. The dog must have gone straight back to Dougal, for I saw them both down the street the next day.

On Wednesday a woman with a camera came to the door. She was, she explained, from the town's weekly newspaper, *The Inlander*. She said that it was the custom to take a photo of clergymen new to the town and to write a short piece about them when they arrived, as a kind of welcome to the community. This seemed fairly routine and harmless, so I readily agreed. It would do no harm for folk to recognise my face at least. The paper came out early on the Friday of each week.

Friday morning dawned fine and clear. A cool change had blown in from the south overnight and the birds were out on the topmost branches of the trees instead of skulking in the undergrowth. Brother Edwin said that I might as well make myself useful by going up the main street and doing the weekly shopping for food. Friday was the day when most folk from the country further out came in to do their shopping and I might meet some of them.

'A morning spent meeting folk down the street on a Friday is worth a month's parish visiting,' he said sagely.

We made out a list and he told me where each shop was, who ran it and who charged more than the others. So up the street I went. As I turned into the main shopping block I was suddenly the celebrity of the moment, or so it seemed. My fame, apparently, had gone before me. Old ladies waved to me, stockmen driving past in utes honked their horns and each shopkeeper was most solicitous in attending to my needs. I couldn't have attracted more attention if I'd been a pop star. 'G'day, Brother bank robber,' was a greeting I got more than once.

I spent quite a long time being accosted and spending the time of day with folk who went out of their way to stop and have a chat. It was a couple of hours later when I eventually got back with the shopping, which included the local paper. I could see that Brother Edwin was a bit edgy. It crossed my mind that perhaps there was a touch of jealousy there.

'I don't know how you've done it,' he said, 'but people have been calling all morning with bits and pieces of food. It's been, "I've brought a cake in to welcome Brother Mark" and "I wonder whether Brother Mark is partial to smoked cheese. I've just been and got some for him". There's a pile of produce on the kitchen table big enough to stock a stall at the market. You needn't have gone shopping at all. There's enough here to feed us for a month.'

I laughed and handed over to him the copy of *The Inlander*. There on the front was a full-page photo of me and the headline above it screamed: NEW BUSH BROTHER MISTAKEN FOR BANK ROBBER.

I said, 'If you ever find yourself running short of food you could always take up a life of crime, Brother. Oh and by the way, I don't think you'll have to work too hard on that speech of introduction for me on Sunday morning. I'd say I'd arrived.'

Brother Edwin said nothing, but volumes were written across his face. I got out of his way … fast!

CHAPTER 2

Reaching Out

The punch landed on my upper left arm. It was one of those so-called male bonding expressions – half an act of affection, half a means of punishment. This one hurt, I suspect, more than was intended, for Brother Edwin didn't appreciate his own strength. The surprise of it caused me to swerve and nearly took us into the table drain.

'What was that for?' I asked with some heat.

'You're riding the clutch,' was Edwin's terse reply. 'Who taught you to drive?'

My mind went back half a year to the narrow cobbled ways and steep hills of the ancient university town in which I had learned to drive in preparation for coming to the Brotherhood. My instructor had been a mild-mannered man in his early forties. The car he used for teaching was equipped with dual controls so that in any emergency, when his pupils did the wrong thing, he could immediately take control. It was testament to his iron nerve that, all through the time that he taught me, he never ever resorted to using any of the alternative controls, not even once. Mind you, his foot wavered near the brake pedal once or twice and he went pale in the face on one occasion and gripped the seat with tense hands, but for the most part he was content to murmur confidentially such things as, 'I think we might brake, yes, and a little harder ... harder yet, yes and even more firmly' and then loudly, 'Put your foot down hard NOW!'

On one memorable occasion he advised me to change gear as we were driving up a steep cobbled hill and we came, quite literally, to a grinding halt with an awful grating noise. As we sat in the middle of the road with the traffic swerving round us, he turned and quietly said, 'Well, my friend, we appear to have found reverse.'

I eventually passed the driving test on the first attempt, but not before our final outing during which he boosted my confidence enormously by saying, just as I was trying to negotiate a narrow bridge with a sharp bend at the end of it, 'It isn't your wild speed around the corners that particularly bothers me, but at the moment, the car is out of control.'

Now, as Brother Edwin and I sped into the gathering dark along a raised welt of a road, lashed across the convict back of the ancient landscape, I realised that nothing had prepared me for driving on gravel interspersed with mud and dust, depending on the season. Nobody had warned me about corrugated roads that shook the living daylights out of you and loosened every carefully tightened nut on the car, or of the tendency of six foot tall kangaroos to hop into the glare of the headlights just at dusk when it was virtually impossible to see them. I had a lot to learn and Brother Edwin knew it.

For a month we had been making some far-ranging forays out into the parish so that I could get to know its geography and some of the main church families and where they lived, the folk who made up the Anglican presence in about twenty-five thousand square miles around Blaxford. The country fascinated me. Huge, treeless, black soil plains alternated with red rolling sandhills which were lightly covered in dryland timber and bushes. Occasionally there reared up a few flat-topped mesa-like hills in the east while a hundred miles further west there were outcrops of broken rock which stood up saw-toothed against the sky. The hills could be seen for miles. They appeared at first as a low smudge on the shimmering horizon and gradually turned from blue to grey-green as we got closer.

The roads could be hypnotically straight for miles on end and, though we occasionally passed a steel gate with its roadside mailbox standing on perpetual duty, there was rarely the sight of any house or other building. Often there was not even a fence or a gate, simply a lonely pair of wheel tracks leading off into the bush, the only indication that this was the entrance to someone's property being a drunkenly leaning wooden post weathered to silver and sandblasted to the sheen of satin by the wind and years of ancient topsoil. An old oil drum nailed on the top served as a receiver for the mail and whatever else the mailman delivered. Sometimes we would rattle over a cattle grid set in the road where a fence line cut across the landscape.

We had been out on every weekend and held services in the places of worship. There was only one actual church building and that was in Blaxford itself. All other worship locations were in tin halls, outback pubs, people's living rooms, indeed anywhere else where folk could be gathered together for convenience.

When Sunday worship was over we were invited to stay the night at someone's property, sometimes sleeping on the back veranda or in the shearers' quarters down at the shearing shed. I soon learned that breakfast was a serious matter for these working families whose staple was the meat that grew on the hoof all around them. To a stomach that had grown used to starting the day on a bowl of cornflakes and some toast there was a certain challenge to the question at daybreak, 'Two eggs or three with your chops, Brother?'

The road on which we were travelling had deep table drains on either side to take away surplus water when it rained. It was impassable even when only a few points of rain were in the rain gauge. We were on black soil, which ground down to dust as fine as talcum when it was dry and clogged up into a sticky mud when it got wet, so sticky that it would fill up the space between the tyres and the wheel arch and make the vehicle undriveable. Since it hadn't rained for five months our wheels were putting out two fine plumes of thick dust behind us.

Brother Edwin was keen on getting out and around the parish and visiting. He echoed what I had had drummed into me at theological college. 'A visiting priest makes a churchgoing people'. Much later on in my ministry I was to come to appreciate some of the truths behind this statement. Right now I had my doubts. There seemed to me no pat formula for ministry that would automatically convert the world and its wife to a love of the Lord Jesus and cause it to live on the highest spiritual plane. Nonetheless, I was soon to discover that folk expected to see you. Non-Christians and Christians alike would look out for the brother when he was known to be in the area. I guessed that it was a result of isolation and that deep need of fresh company which most of us possess. Brother Edwin's insistence on being seen around the parish, however, went hand in hand with his insistence that there must be a reason for every journey.

'You need to remember that the parish is paying for the vehicle and for every drop of petrol you use,' was a theme he seemed to harp on frequently.

I could see the responsibility in that approach but found it hard to justify some of my visits simply on a hard cash basis. Such a practical view seemed to me to ignore the promptings of God's Spirit when he put into my consciousness, and indeed into my prayers, the needs of particular people at particular times. At such moments the thought that 'I must visit this person some day' turned on the fulcrum of spiritual awareness into the more urgent imperative, 'I ought to visit that person right now'. I was beginning to realise that when I followed God's promptings then, upon arrival at the person's doorstep, there seemed to be ground already prepared for my visit. Such phrases as, 'It's funny that you should call today, Brother, because I really need your help with ...' were commonplace when my visit came out of my prayers.

As my ministry progressed I was constantly to discover that God has a way of timing things that have little to do with human economics. But all of that was to come later in my experience. For the present I was being disciplined by Brother Edwin to justify my journeys. It was to prove a useful block in the early foundations of a lifelong involvement in parish ministry. But at the time I fretted away at the apparent difficulty of being outwardly responsible and inwardly honest to my calling. I kept remembering a wartime poster during my childhood. It was displayed everywhere from railway stations to doctor's waiting rooms. 'IS YOUR JOURNEY REALLY NECESSARY?' it proclaimed. I mentioned it to Brother Edwin.

'Exactly. Don't forget it,' was his terse comment.

Now I was getting tired after driving for the past couple of hours. For the last half hour I had been wrestling with the uncertain light of the setting sun. Things were getting increasingly hard to see as we traversed the zone when daylight declined but not enough for the headlights to really make any difference.

'Watch out for kangaroos,' said Brother Edwin unnecessarily and annoyingly. My eyes were already aching from constantly scanning the road edges ahead.

'I'm trying to,' I answered somewhat testily and then braked hard as a large, scruffy bag of feathers with long legs padded suddenly out of the bush and swerved around the front of the car.

'Watch out for emus too,' said Edwin.

The light had now gone and we got going again, but not for long for, in the far distance something was seen to flicker.

'Did you see that?' I asked

'Looks like fire,' said Edwin. 'We'd better see what it is,' he added. What was it about his voice that gave me the impression that he already knew and expected to find it?

We pulled up beside a telephone linesman's camp. Parked well off the road, in a patch of straggling timber, was a square metal box on wheels, the standard linesman's caravan. Two men sat on logs in front of a good fire on which was a boiling billy of water.

'Just in time for a cuppa,' said Edwin as he got out of the car and stretched his legs.

'Thought you were never coming, Brother,' came the reply from Tim Cordman. I recognised him as someone I'd seen at church in Blaxford. He had a wife and a couple of school-age children.

His companion was like an old ship's tank; square, covered in rivets and going rusty. His head was crowned with a dumpling of a hat with a floppy brim, oily from years of use. Underneath he sported at least two days' worth of ginger stubble. He stood up, mug in hand, and offered the other hand to me. 'Bob Jouster's the name,' he said.

'Brother Mark,' I answered. 'How long have you been out?' I asked.

'Three days, checking this line,' said Tim. 'Back in Blaxford tomorrow when we turn into respectable citizens again.'

Edwin was busy dragging his swag out of the back of the car, then a couple of tins of stew which we carried in case we got caught out overnight.

'Looks like we're expected,' I said to nobody in particular.

It was Bob who answered, in a gravel-bottomed voice. 'Brother Edwin said we might see you when you were out this way. Thought you might've been along yesterday.'

Obviously Brother Edwin liked to spring surprises. I had noticed it once or twice before. He would say things like, 'Hop in the car.' And when I asked, 'What for?' or 'Where are we going?' he would answer, 'You'll see.'

I had smarted at it only a couple of weeks before. We had gone out to take a service in a small local shed of a community hall. Brother Edwin was supposed to be preaching that day, except that he didn't. When it came time for the sermon he suddenly sat down and said to me, 'You can preach.'

I stood up completely unprepared and managed a short few words about the scripture reading we had all just heard. I was furious at what he'd done.

'That was uncalled for and not fair on these folk who have gathered to hear something which has been carefully prepared,' I said afterwards, 'and you seem to treat it as a joke.'

'Lesson number one,' he replied. 'A brother has to be prepared for anything at all times, and especially prepared to speak about God to anyone.'

That lesson hit home hard, but I never lost my sense of annoyance at his method. I called it irresponsible. He said it was necessary training. As I got to know him better I came to see that something in his past had made him develop the habit of holding his cards very close to his chest. There was a part of him that really liked to spring surprises so as to bring sudden delight into another person's life. There was another part that kept things secret until the last minute in case something should go wrong with his plans and he was left with egg on his face.

I put these thoughts behind me as I accepted a mug of hot sweet tea from Bob and then got busy preparing for our meal. He and Tom had already eaten but kept us entertained with an unbroken string of stories while we filled up. We spent an hour afterwards sitting and yarning fitfully. Occasionally we paused beside deep pools of silence as, almost mesmerised, we sat and watched as orange sparks flew up from the fire. The fire soon died out of them as they rose towards the pendant stars and realised that they could not compete.

It was during one of these silences, as I stared out past Bob's shoulder, that I thought I noticed something out in the bush, at the edge of seeing. It was pitch-black out there, but it seemed for a moment that something moved, some pale blur, a smudge of whiteness in the gloom.

'Did anyone see that?' I asked.

'What was it?' asked Brother Edwin.

'I don't know,' I said somewhat sheepishly. 'I thought I saw something pale move out that way.' I pointed to a patch which had returned to unrelieved gloom.

There had been no sound and obviously none of the others had seen anything. My eyes must have been more tired than I thought. I thought I discerned a knowing look of understanding from Bob, but he said nothing.

'When a man starts to see pale ghosts out there in the dark, it's time he hit the sack,' said Tom. 'You've been driving too long, Brother.'

We all took our cue from that. It was time to sleep.

Edwin and I laid out our swags on either side of the fire, the stony ground both our bed and comfort for the night. I lay for a while gazing out into the immensity of space. The atmosphere was so clear and so untainted by artificial lights that I could discern both the Greater Magellanic Cloud and even the faint blur of its lesser cousin. Looking out from one tiny planet within the Milky Way and seeing two completely separate galaxies gave rise to such a sense of my own smallness and inadequacy that I soon closed my eyes and shut such thoughts out in blessed sleep.

I woke with a cold nose and a sideways look at a threadbare mist still tangled in the treetops. Brother Edwin was up and tending the fire. There was a bit of the boy scout about him. You couldn't help but warm to his enthusiasms even when the contradictions in him drove you to distraction. He clearly loved the outdoors and a whiff of wood smoke. He already had a billy of water boiling. I could hear the throb and bubble of it.

Tom and Bob were well up and preparing to leave, checking their linesman's van and casting an eye over tools and rolls of cable.

'If that's tea you're making I wouldn't say no to some!' I called over to Brother Edwin.

'Tea in bed, is it?' he answered. 'What do you think this is, the Ritz?' Nonetheless, he brought me over a mug and I sat up, warming my hands around its consolation.

After breakfast Tom and Bob left to check the next section of line. We packed up our stuff, washed up and, cradling a last mug of tea, sat down on logs by the remains of the fire to say Morning Prayer.

The reading from the Old Testament for the day was from

the book of Job. The words seemed to have special relevance: 'Man is born to trouble, as the sparks fly upward'.

Old Job knew about crackling fires. The curl of wood smoke was in those words, all the troubles of the world as they caught at the throat, irritated the nose and made the eyes water. Around us the sounds of the bush played as background to the themes of scripture. A flock of wood ducks flew low overhead and the splash of their landing told of a dam nearby.

There was to be one more of Brother Edwin's surprises on this trip. On the way home, after we'd been driving for three-quarters of an hour or so, I felt another of his playful jabs to my already bruised arm.

'Turn right here,' he barked.

'What for?' I asked. A sandy track ran off into the scrub and, on a faded signpost, the letters 'AIRSTRIP' could just be read. 'This track hasn't been used too often,' I added. 'Look how much growth there is between the wheel tracks. Are you sure it goes anywhere?'

'Don't argue,' was all the explanation I got.

After about two miles we drove out onto a cleared area of bush. There were a couple of sheds, one of which was a small hangar. In the distance a windsock hung listlessly from its pole in the still air. Its tattered ends told a story of windier days, and many of them. A man in overalls was working on the engine of a parked Cessna. A dusty airstrip ended in a dancing heat haze in the distance.

As we got out of the car the man came towards us hand outstretched to greet Brother Edwin. They obviously knew each other.

'Gooday, Alan,' said Brother Edwin.

'Thought you were never coming,' replied Alan.

Again I was introduced. Brother Edwin had that silly grin on his face that I had come to recognise as excitement.

'Come and look at this,' he said, and I followed him into the hangar where, amazingly, there stood an old Tiger Moth in immaculate condition.

'Get in, but mind where you put your feet,' said Brother Edwin as he pulled an old leather flying helmet out of his pocket.

'You don't mean you're going to fly this thing?' My incredulity must have been mirrored in the apprehension written all over my face. 'Can you do it? Do you know how?' I asked as something like mortal terror took hold of my legs.

'I keep telling you, don't argue. Just do it,' said Brother Edwin with the broadest of grins across his face.

He climbed into the cockpit and yelled, 'Contact!' to Alan who immediately repeated it then swung the propeller to start the engine.

We were soon bumping our way down the dirt strip and I felt the lift as we left the ground. Brother Edwin was now really in his element. Not only could he do it, he did things with that small plane that I didn't know were possible. We flew back low over the airstrip and then took a wide sweep as we gained height. I could see Alan's homestead and sheep yards some way away from his landing strip. Below us in the far distance a brown, snaking river meandered back to Blaxford and on a distant stretch of road twin plumes of dust showed where a ute had got up enough speed to prance along the crests of the bone-jarring corrugations. The wind was in our faces and I was beginning to enjoy myself when Brother Edwin attracted my attention with a wave of his hand.

'Are you okay?!' he yelled back to me.

'Fine!' I yelled back. If I had known what this was the signal for I might not have been immediately so enthusiastic, for at that Brother Edwin moved the joystick and I became aware of the horizon turning over a full three hundred and sixty degrees. A steady pull backwards on the stick and we were powering up in a steep climb that ended in sudden weightlessness and the cold realisation that we were now hurtling earthward. A perfect loop was what Brother Edwin called it afterwards. At the time the sweat broke out on my forehead and my stomach was taking some time to catch up with the rest of me. I should never have asked him if he could fly this thing, I thought as Brother Edwin looked back at me. He was laughing like a child on a roller-coaster. I suppose he was giving me yet another of his lessons for the day, the one about the closeness of eternity for us all.

We landed with barely a bounce, which is quite an achievement in a Tiger Moth.

'I didn't know you were a pilot,' I said.

'Well, you don't know everything, do you,' he answered. 'Now, I want you to drive this car back to Blaxford and then go out to the airstrip and pick me up.'

'You mean you're going to bring this plane back?' I had no idea what he had in mind and my puzzlement was obvious.

'It's all perfectly simple,' said Brother Edwin. 'I'll tell you all about it when we get back.'

So that was that.

I picked him up at the strip when I got back. He was already there waiting, as I knew he would be. On my way back he had flown low over the road beside me and given me a wave and a grin, then disappeared ahead of me, travelling faster and in a less dusty manner than I was.

That evening after a meal he told me that he had bought the thing and that he intended to use it for some of his parish trips, especially when he was moved to a bigger area up in the north. I was full of questions and could barely keep up with the revelations about this man. He had learned to fly in South Africa and took to it as readily as a child takes to ice-cream. He was obviously happiest when he was in the air. He'd been saving up for a plane of his own for years, long before he joined the brotherhood.

'It makes sense,' he said. 'Look at that time when we couldn't get out to Biscuit Creek because the other creeks on the way were flowing because of rains further north. We could have flown over them and got on with the job.'

'What about expense?' I asked. 'Is the parish going to agree to foot the bill for aviation spirit and maintenance?' I thought of all his talk about, 'Is your journey really necessary?'

'Oh, I've got a few ideas up my sleeve about that,' was all he'd say in reply. He didn't say what they were and it seemed, from the look on his face, prudent at the time not to ask.

I had begun to settle down very well working alongside Brother Edwin. My early fears had gradually been dissipated as I got to know him better. Far from the threatening character that his sheer bulk and occasional gruff voice had led me to believe, he was, in fact, as soft-hearted as a chocolate marshmallow.

He took me with him on a couple of parish visits in the old Tiger Moth. There were things he wanted to check out in its handling and flight. When he was in the air he was always in the best of moods. There was a good physical reason for this. He was not a man to unravel his own story at the merest tug, but one evening as we sat talking on the rectory veranda, he told me part of it.

Some years before, he had been very ill. He was eventually diagnosed as having a tumour on his brain. Things looked desperate for him. He sought spiritual help as well as that of the medical profession. At one of the brotherhood reunions all the brothers had gathered around him in prayer and the bishop had anointed him for healing with holy oil, as it says in the New Testament to do. And the miraculous had happened.

When he next went for his medical check-up the specialist could find no trace of the tumour except some scarring in the brain where the malignancy had been. Thereafter he was pretty well his old self with a profound gratitude to God and an increased sense of being his servant. He was left with an occasional headache which got worse in certain weather conditions. When he was up in the Tiger his head used to clear and he guessed it was something to do with atmospheric pressure. At a few thousand feet above ground he became as merry as Santa Claus.

I found myself thinking that it was a pity that he was

about to move on to another parish, leaving me on my own with this one. Truth to tell I was dreading the time when he would inevitably go elsewhere and I would be left with the awesome responsibility of this wide and dusty parish to cope with as best I could.

One day, a couple of weeks later, the phone rang. 'Is Brother Edwin coming out to us at the weekend?' The question came from Mrs Carruthers way out in the sticks to the north of Blaxford at a place called Wilpunna. I had been there once already with Brother Edwin and I knew it for a centre to which several folk from outlying sheep stations came when they had their occasional church service. Its one asset was that it had a corrugated metal hall where folk could meet, alongside a couple of clay tennis courts.

'He certainly is,' I answered. 'He's right here. I'll put him on.'

Brother Edwin took the phone and his face assumed a look of grave seriousness matched by concern in his voice.

'What's up?' I asked as he came off the phone.

'Oh, she asked if I'd mind picking up a package from the chemist here and if I'd bring it down with me. She has apparently rung the pharmacist already and he says that's okay. Their Nanna's taken a turn for the worse and they need the syringe and her medication.'

'Why the worried look?' I asked. 'Surely that'll be no problem.'

'Well, yes. I can do it all right. But I really wonder whether I ought to go up there as soon as possible. The old lady nearly died a few months back. Perhaps I'd better pick up that prescription tomorrow and fly straight up rather than wait the extra two days. Good job we've got the plane,' he said with a wink.

I didn't doubt his pastoral concern, but I could also see that it was just the situation that suited him. He could now go to the parish council and justify his flying out there instead of taking the car. This was just the sort of opportunity that he was looking for, a chance to justify his use of the Tiger Moth and indulge himself in his passion for flying at the same time.

He asked me if I would pick up the package from the chemist whilst I was out doing the shopping. True enough, when I went round to Peter Limson, the pharmacist, the package was there and ready.

'Make sure she's standing up when they give her the needle,' said Peter, 'and tell them to observe her carefully for the next half hour. If she staggers around too much, hold off from giving her the second dose. This stuff can cause unwanted side effects and they wouldn't want to lose a valuable old girl like that. Inconvenient for them to say the least.'

I duly relayed the message to Brother Edwin as I handed over the package. 'It seemed an odd way of putting things, and even a bit callous,' I told him.

'Oh that's just Peter's way,' he said. 'There isn't much that Peter doesn't know about families around here in a hundred and fifty mile radius. Over the years he's supplied all their pharmaceutical needs and listened to their stories. He knows every family and their circumstances.'

It was Friday and Brother Edwin prepared to leave for

Wilpunna. He phoned Mrs Carruthers and explained that he was coming down straightaway and would stay in the district until Tuesday and visit one or two of the neighbours. He packed up his bag and the little case with the communion vessels and was soon ready to leave.

I took him out to the airstrip and watched as he stowed his gear and stuffed himself into the cockpit, such a big man into such a small space. Then he was off with a roar of the engine and a puff of oily smoke.

I went back into town to do my own preparations. I was taking the service in town on Sunday and then heading off for another service out bush in the afternoon.

On the following Tuesday afternoon we both arrived back at about the same time. That is, I had just walked into the rectory when the phone rang. It was Brother Edwin at the airfield asking me to come out and get him. He seemed to be a bit silent and didn't mention his trip at all which was a bit out of character for him.

It wasn't until the next afternoon that I asked him how things had gone. He looked a bit embarrassed, but then he gave one of his boyish laughs as he told me what had happened. When he arrived down at the Carruthers' place and explained how he'd brought the package as soon as he could because of the old lady's illness, they doubled over with laughter. The old lady came in and joined in the fun. It seemed that Brother Edwin had misheard the original message on the telephone. It was not Nanna that was sick but Nanny, and Nanny happened to be one of their breeding goats whose case was not really urgent at all. At church on Sunday everyone had enjoyed the joke.

I allowed a decent pause while I tried to fight off the look that was forming on my face.

'So, what are you going to tell the Parish council?' I asked.

'Well, that'll be your problem now,' he said with a grin. 'I got a phone call earlier today from the chief brother telling me to head off and take over one of our parishes in the Northern Territory. I'm going in ten day's time, so I shall miss the parish council meeting at the end of the month. I'm sure you'll be able to explain everything adequately.'

I admired his optimism even if I wasn't sure that I agreed with it.

Ten days later I stood on the edge of the Blaxford airstrip and said goodbye to Brother Edwin. As he packed his few belongings into the back seat space and then climbed into the little plane I found a lump in my throat.

'Contact!' he yelled.

'Contact!' I yelled back as I swung the propeller and the engine coughed into life. Edwin couldn't hear me of course, but I called it out anyway. 'Is your journey really necessary?!'

CHAPTER 3

Ferreting Around

'I hope you aren't one of those clergymen with foot-and-mouth disease.'

The speaker was a small, red-faced man who stumped over to me and said it without preamble. I must have looked at him blankly as I tried to size him up and decide whether he was being refreshingly blunt or just plain nasty.

'Won't visit and can't preach,' he explained with a laugh that let the tension out of the air.

It was a couple of months since Brother Edwin had left me as sole incumbent of the parish and the occasion was a sort of potluck parish meal to which all and sundry were invited. I hadn't met the man before, but he turned out to be a bookkeeper for a small local agricultural firm, a nominal Anglican who came to the social events but never to church services. I was soon to learn that such folk often have an edge of aggression to their greeting, laced with a modicum of guilt or yearning about not quite being in the fold wholeheartedly. I could recognise, in his funny remark, the same sort of impulse which makes three year old boys thump others as a ploy to getting to know them.

It was an example of a sense of humour that I was to come

to appreciate as I came gradually to move amongst these folk and visit them in their various homes and rural properties. It was blunt, even slightly aggressive, but it denoted a caring acceptance of a stranger come among them and a desire to test his mettle. In this case my mettle. I could usually give as good as I got and even felt quite at home having come from a large family whose way of relating was to constantly take each other down a peg or two. It was quite different from something I was to meet only a week after I had settled in with a fine proprietorial air.

I was down the street, off to do some visiting of one or two sick parishioners when, as I walked past the stock and station agents with its newly erected front wall, I bumped into, or rather was barged into, by a thin man with a pointed nose who was coming out of the place carrying a roll of fencing wire. He himself was as wiry as the roll he carried and looked as if he'd been designed especially for scurrying down rabbit holes. By the easy way he moved it was obvious that he was fit and limber. In his haste he hit me square in the midriff with the wire and, far from apologising, he let fly at me.

'Bloody parsons.' He spat out the two words and fixed me with a glare of such malevolent venom that I stepped back a pace. I had never met such an intense sense of personal hatred in all my life so far and I wasn't sure what to say or do. I let him go and he climbed into a battered old ute and took off fast without regard for the wear on his tyres. Must have hit his thumb with a hammer this morning, I thought as I went on my way. But the incident had unnerved me. It had seemed so personally directed at me, yet I had never met the man before. How could anyone get so het up about someone he didn't know?

I mentioned the incident to Peter Limson the pharmacist when I next saw him. He was one of the churchwardens who either knew, or knew all about, everyone who ever hid under a log in the whole district.

'Thin man, skin like tanned leather and a pointy nose?' he asked and I nodded.

'That'll be Ferret,' he said. I couldn't help but marvel at the accuracy of the name. 'He's not too bad a young bloke really, but he does have a thing about the clergy. There's something lurking behind that hatred somewhere, Brother. Perhaps you could make the effort to get to know him and sort out his problem.'

I found the expectation that I could work wonders flattering but entirely false.

'Have you any ideas about how I might go about that?' I asked.

'Easy, Brother. Just get into any sport around here and sooner or later you're going to come up against Ferret. You can take it from there,' said Peter.

The confidence of the man was born out of a complete ignorance concerning me and most sports. It wasn't that I didn't have the right genes. My father had been a hockey player of note and had even tucked one or two international matches under his belt. My younger brother was a passable soccer player, but me? Well, I was the one that was different. I simply was useless at all games involving kicking or hitting a ball. In my teens I had been mad keen on cricket, but my enthusiasm was not matched by ability. I would stand at the wicket and swing heartily at anything the bowler could throw down at me. Alas more often than not the bat failed to connect with the ball. I think my father wondered what he had spawned. At rugby and soccer I fared no better, in fact added to my inability to see a ball and connect with it was one further trait and that was plain cowardice. Most sports seemed to me to involve getting hurt in one way or another. It was all supposed to make a young man fit and able.

I looked around my fellow schoolmates and saw that the sportsmen among them seemed to spend a great deal of time sitting on the sidelines with one injury or another and there was usually at least one of them on crutches at any given time. I was all for fitness, 'A healthy mind in a healthy body' as old Juvenal had said and if, as Saint Paul said, our bodies are the temples of the living God, it seemed right to me to keep the body as fit as possible. At college I ran cross-country and rowed but at ball sports I was no good.

I need not have worried about meeting up with Ferret. The local doctor unwittingly took things in hand. He was known simply as 'the Doc' but his real name was Doctor Michael McGee, an Irishman of charm and lunacy.

He rang me up one day and asked me to join a scratch hockey team that he was getting up to play against a town down the line. Somewhere in the dim and distant past, whilst he was a student at Trinity in Dublin, he had been picked to play hockey for Ireland. All my excuses and explanations of inadequacy were swept aside. He countered every excuse with some blarney or other and the following evening saw me down at the oval with the others he had cajoled into his team.

Ferret was there amongst them. Amazingly it turned out that the doctor had once played against my father and his expectations were high concerning my ability. One or two lucky hits seemed to convince him that he had an astute player on his hands. He blithely ignored all the missed shots, the fumbling attempts to reach the ball and the plain farce when one of my feet tripped on the other and I fell over for no apparent reason.

Ferret was under no illusions that he was being asked to play alongside someone who more often than not got in his way. Every time he came within earshot he let me know, with plenty of expletives, just what he thought of my bumbling attempts. 'A bloody octopus under a rock could do better,' pretty well gives the gist of his elevated view of my prowess.

Came the day of the match and we all drove down to show just what our outpost of sport could accomplish. No love was lost between the two towns when it came to sport of any kind. The game turned out to be more like warfare than an occupation for pleasure. I suppose this was to be expected, but hockey provided not only the battlefield but also the weapons. There are rules about how high a stick might be lifted and in what circumstances, but rules tended to go by the board when tempers were inflamed. A hockey stick can inflict significant damage, even when used within the rules, and bruises there were aplenty. I was doubly endangered as I soon found out. Wanting to settle who knows what scores from the past, Ferret managed to give me more than a few taps on the ankle as together we raced for the ball. And he always accompanied it with hissed words of pure venom.

By three-quarters through the game the scores were level on goal count and fairly level on injury count. I was limping badly but managed to hang on somehow until the end of the game. It was just before the referee's final whistle blew that my big chance came. Ferret and I raced towards a loose ball in an attempt to get it before it went over the touchline. I got there first by a whisker and desperately swung with all my might. There came a very satisfying crack and I knew I must have hit the ball. Immediately after, there came another much more solid thump which turned out to be Ferret's shin as a fraction of a second later he ran into my outstretched stick. He went down like a felled tree. The ball, on the other hand, sped away and, cunningly taking a line between a whole melee of opposing players, went slap past their goalkeeper and into the goal for a score. The ref's whistle sounded immediately to mark the end of the game.

It had been the flukiest shot ever and was certainly not a result of any skill on my part. The rest of the team didn't see it that way. I had never received such congratulations before. They mobbed around me and would have carried me off the field had it not been for some strange grunting sounds coming from the felled Ferret. The Doc raced over to him and gave him the once-over. He then declared with professional certainty that he had a broken ankle and organised us to carry him off the field. Naturally I moved in to give a hand, but this seemed to excite Ferret. He gave out a string of colourful language to the effect that even if he were dying he didn't want me anywhere near him. He was quite convinced that I had felled him deliberately. Me, who wouldn't hurt a fly!

We left Ferret in the local hospital to have his ankle seen to and get a couple of days of enforced rest at the Doc's insistence. The mood of the team was still pretty euphoric from the win, but I couldn't get too excited. All I could think about was what Ferret might do to me once he was up on his feet again. He had been antagonistic before. Now goodness knows what he would do. My mood was not lightened when, every now and then, some well-aimed remark would echo my worst ruminations out loud.

'You'd better watch out now, Brother,' said one. 'Ferret can be a terrible man to bear a grudge. I'd keep well away from him for a couple of months.'

I had every intention of avoiding him so didn't need the advice. The story of the incident, however, got out and I was hailed down the street by either one of two responses. Either it was praise for getting the goal that won the match or it was, 'Shame on you for playing dirty and you a man of the cloth too.'

The following Sunday I ran the gauntlet of various joking remarks and someone even rang the bishop to ask whether I was a fit man to be in the clergy. The remarks died down within a fortnight and it was a long time before Ferret appeared on my horizon again. I thought of trying to pay him a visit, but everyone counselled against this. He was still pretty mad and ranted on about me down at the pub, I heard. However, my overactive conscience kept worrying me. Should I not be making every effort to be reconciled with this difficult man? I tossed and turned over several nights of disturbed sleep. Finally I made the resolve to telephone Ferret and see if I could persuade him that I had nothing against him and that the crack on his ankle was purely accidental. I had a bit of an internal battle with myself about whether or not I would bite my tongue and not go on to explain that it was his fault that he had got hurt and that if he had not been so keen to charge into me at every possible opportunity and, in this case, when I clearly was hitting the ball, then he'd still be walking on two good legs.

The next evening I rang his number. He answered in a pleasant voice, one in which he had never spoken to me. Then, as soon as I told him who I was he slammed the phone down with an oath that I just managed to hear. I was a bit fed up that it all left me rather rattled when I was the one who'd done nothing at all. Everyone likes to be liked, but apparently that was the way it was going to be. I remembered the Lord's words that the gospel cuts like a two-edged sword and therefore at least some folk are going to be cut to the quick by its demands.

Later I was to discover that apparently all clergy in any parish cop a bit of a beating, especially from folk they don't even know. It's as if those who stand for goodness and truth somehow seem to draw out the poison of the world's wounds. It is a phenomenon not confined to clergy. Anyone who stands for something will be in line for the brickbats.

So that was that as far as pastoral outreach to Ferret was concerned. There were plenty of other folk to worry about and I was kept busy ministering to their needs. There were always sick folk to visit, house calls on the lapsed and doubting, religious instruction classes at the local school, service and sermon preparation, regular consultations with the organist, confirmation classes, Bible studies and a host of smaller administration jobs within the church. Community involvement saw me chairing the committee that was working towards the building of a town swimming pool, a task which Brother Edwin had volunteered me for before he left, and there were one or two other projects that I had fallen into mainly because I was in town and available. As well as these my regular round of Sunday services took me far and wide. I soon forgot about Ferret and his attitude as I threw myself into doing my job among the folk I'd been called to serve.

It was at the end of November the following year that my sporting talent, or rather lack of it, was called upon again. I left very early one Saturday morning and headed for a little place called Ferryton some ninety miles south-west of Blaxford down the river. It was so named because, at that point, there was a ferry across the river, which could take a vehicle. The ferry was no more than a large, flat-bottomed sort of punt onto which one could carefully drive. The ferry was attached to two cables and a small motor hauled on these to drag the whole contraption across the current. Naturally, because it was the only place to get across, there were a few well-worn tracks converging on it. And, naturally, a pub had been built there, around which a few houses had sprung up over the years.

It was a tiny but lively community and services were usually held there once a month in a creaking hall made of corrugated iron, inside which one froze in the winter and got cooked in the summer. Because the place was situated right by the river it was a green oasis in an otherwise parched landscape. It was the greenest spot in the whole parish. There were gardens kept in bloom with water pumped up from the river. There was also a green sportsground on which was played whatever game was in season. There were even a couple of tennis courts.

Folk would gather from miles around on a Sunday and use the occasion to play, meet, have a barbecue and then some of them would stay on for church in the evening. It was a good arrangement which minimised travelling, which would have been huge if each event were held separately. And it was good for me because I could catch up with all sorts of people whom I could not hope to get to visit within the space of a year. However, this visit was a special one.

There had originally been a little corrugated building put up in the old days for church use. It was known as 'the tin tabernacle', and it still stood there, just! Its frame was so eaten by termites that it was no longer safe. It had been dedicated as Saint Andrews and the congregation still made a bit of a fuss on the nearest weekend to November the thirtieth, his feast day. This year they'd laid on a cricket match on the Saturday and a dance in the evening. There was to be church on the Sunday and then tennis.

I drove into Ferryton in time to get an early cup of tea as folk were still gathering from far and wide. My intention was to catch up with some of the families before settling down to a lazy day watching the cricket match between two local sides. I say local, but in fact they were sides drawn from a huge area. The team that was scheduled to play the Ferryton side came from around Lizard Gully. Most of them had already arrived and a few latecomers drove in while others were padding up. Someone asked me if I'd mind acting as scorer and gave me the scorebook before I could answer. I didn't mind as it would mean that I got to sit in the shade, not in the pavilion but under a large old pepper tree which stood beside it.

The pavilion itself was no more than a small, boxlike weatherboard shed. Beside it stood a rusty but still serviceable rainwater tank filled from run-off at the rear of the roof. In front, in order to drain the gutter along the roof of that side, there was a battered open downpipe looking the worse for wear. Obviously it had taken a knocking over the years from being in the line of fire from various practice balls before the matches. The downpipe stood out from the wall by about four inches. The newly limed boundary line ran up to the pavilion on both sides, and the front wall itself formed the boundary where the pavilion stood.

I was all set for a pleasant day when two things happened which disturbed my complacency. The first was the arrival of a ute which pulled up at the far end of a line of parked cars. With a sinking feeling I recognised it as the one owned by Ferret. Sure enough, resplendent in whites he got out and walked over to the Lizard Gully team. Word had it that he was a good batsmen and the Lizard Gully boys had invited him to make up numbers for their team and open the batting. I shrank back in my chair and hoped he wouldn't recognise me sitting in the shade. Of course, in such a gathering there was no hope of that. He strode past and gave me a withering glance before he went inside and padded up. Lizard Gully had won the toss and opted to bat.

Then the second thing happened. Bill Upton, the

Ferryton captain, came up to me and said, 'Brother, we're in a spot of bother. One of our team hasn't turned up. Would you mind filling in so we can field a team? My wife can keep the scorebook.'

It was the sort of thing that happened all the time in the bush, but it was not welcome news. I gave him all the excuses I could muster. I told him how useless I was at sport. How I couldn't see the ball properly and how I would probably end up losing the match for them. It was all to no avail.

'There simply isn't anyone else we can call on,' the captain said. 'Just do your best and I'll put you at long stop where you're not likely to have much to do. We've got a pretty good wicket-keeper and nothing much gets past him.'

So out I went for a day in the heat of the sun. I wasn't a total disaster at fielding but not far from it. Despite the captain's confidence a few balls came my way and I missed an outside chance of a catch. A few boundaries got past me too and, since it soon became obvious that Ferret had his eye in and was belting the bowlers all over the place, those boundaries were likely to make a difference. Ferret scored sixty not out and the rest of the team racked up another ninety-five which gave them a total of a hundred and fifty five. We all had a cup of tea and a bite to eat and then it was Ferryton's turn.

Things did not start well. The Lizard Gully team had a couple of useful bowlers and Ferret turned out to be an all-rounder who bowled true and he bowled fast. I had to admit to myself that when it came to cricket he had everything that I hadn't. It was obvious that his ankle had healed perfectly from our last encounter. His run-up and bowling action were as smooth and fast as the Cresta run. And his effectiveness was soon shown. In his first over he sent a bullet of a ball down to Bill Upton who was Ferryton's opening batsman. It knocked the centre stump so hard that one of their team had to run and field it. Bill walked off the pitch with the Ferryton score at nothing. It went rapidly downhill from there. Two other batsmen came and went for a total score of twenty.

Things began to steady when Frank Carling came out and took his stance. He moved the score along impressively, but two more batsmen at the other end came and went while he did so. By teatime Ferryton were still way behind and not many men left to go. Bill Upton had put me last on the list and the way things were going it looked as if it wouldn't be long before it was my turn.

After the tea break the tail-enders put up a brave defence while Frank continued to sneak what runs he could. Hopes began to rise that we might make it at least to a draw, but those hopes were soon dashed as another couple of wickets fell. It wasn't too long before it was my turn. Ferryton's last hope! I had only just got the pads on when my moment arrived. Custer's last stand couldn't have looked less promising. Ferryton were still seventeen runs behind. In the whole of my cricketing career I had never made more than nine.

As I took the long walk out to the crease on legs of jelly I hoped that I was displaying more confidence than I felt. Frank met me and told me not to try and hit out at the ball, simply to play defensively and to leave the scoring to him. Ferret was having a word with some of his team-mates and they went off to their positions with grins on their faces. I knew I was in for trouble.

It came straight away without lingering to admire the view. Ferret thundered down to the bowler's crease and let go a vicious bouncer that kicked up dust and then whistled past my face. I could feel the breeze of it as it passed and put my hand to my cheek, firmly believing I'd been struck. It must have passed so near that it gave me the merest graze. If this attack was designed to demolish my confidence still further, then it succeeded. I stood there a shivering heap of misery. It is amazing how annoyingly apt bits of scripture can come into mind at these moments. The Lord's words, 'If someone strikes you on the right cheek, turn to him the other also' came into mine. Roughly translated that means, 'Let him have another go'. He wasn't facing Ferret, I thought. But I had no choice in the matter. In this case there was nothing for it but to face up to Ferret again.

This time the ball was low and came sizzling past my off stump to be taken by the wicket-keeper. I waved an ineffective greeting to it as it sped past. The not very worthy thought came into my head that all I had to do was let Ferret bowl me out and both my agony and his sadistic glee would be over. But I knew that my job was to stay there at all costs so that Frank could perhaps knock up enough runs to get us past the Lizard Gully score.

It was at Ferret's third ball that the miracle happened. The bat actually made contact with the ball. I stuck my bat forward upright and stolid in the best stonewalling kind of obdurate defence. I was not playing for runs, just blocking the ball's progress. The ball did its own work. It clipped the outside edge of my immobile bat and ricocheted off towards the pavilion with such force that it went past all fielders.

'Run!' yelled Frank and, startled into action, I started down the wicket and we ran one and started out for another. And then Frank paused as everyone stopped and watched. The ball had sped off to the boundary where the pavilion stood. At the last minute it hit some small irregularity in the ground and kicked upwards right into the battered downpipe. There it stuck and there it stayed. What everyone was waiting for was the expected umpire's signal for a boundary and four runs. It never came.

'Play on,' was what he said, so Frank and I resumed running. The Lizard Gully team appealed to the umpire in amazement. He told them it wasn't a boundary because the pavilion wall was the boundary line and clearly the ball had not reached it. It had got stuck up the downpipe some four inches short of a boundary.

Frank and I kept running.

'Lost ball,' appealed the Lizard Gully team in desperation.

'Not so,' said the umpire as he shook his head and told them that, since everyone saw the ball go up the pipe, we all knew exactly where it was. To a man the fielders left Frank and me to it as they converged on the downpipe. They tried to shake it and then they hit it and kicked it in an attempt to loosen the ball and put it back into play. It was all to no avail. That ball stayed firmly stuck where it was.

I was getting out of breath running up and down between wickets. We stopped when a great cheer from the Ferryton supporters told us that we had run up eighteen runs, enough to top Lizard Gully's score.

There was much merriment at the barbecue which followed. The Ferryton team and their supporters were naturally overjoyed. Eventually even most of the Lizard Gully team could laugh at the circumstances of their loss.

My own relief was almost palpable. 'That was unusual,' I said to Bill Upton.

He looked at me pensively for a while. 'Unusual? Begging your pardon, Brother, it was a bloody miracle,' he said with a grin.

Ferret did not hang around for any food or drink. He picked up his bat and headed for his ute. As he passed the pavilion he gave vent to his feelings with a last determined swipe at the downpipe. There was a small rattling sound and the ball fell out and trickled to a halt right at his feet. I could see from the expression on his face that miracles weren't exactly his cup of tea.

CHAPTER 4

Picnic at Biscuit Ford

Alf's place was always my first point of call whenever I visited the folk at Biscuit Ford. His knowledge of what was happening in the ordinary lives of all in the district was invaluable. And, let it be said, it didn't harm my reputation as a pastor, who was sensitive to people's needs, to be able to walk in on some remote station and to ask about some matter that Alf had primed me with before my visit.

Alf Green was not what you might call a large man; thin and gangly would be more like it! He looked as if he'd snap in a strong wind. Yet his appearance belied a sort of cunning strength. Like Harry Houdini he'd slid with apparent ease out of more than one situation in which the odds, if you were there to take them, would have seem stacked definitely against him. He was the best man I ever knew at using what little brawn he seemed to have to the best of his ability. All of which fitted him rather well into being a bush policeman. Stuck, as he was, in the small township of Biscuit Ford, which any bushman will tell you was so far beyond the black stump that even the crows couldn't navigate their way back to it, he was, for the most part, free from interference from his supervising sergeant. That supervision was no nearer than four and a half hours drive away over a hundred and thirty miles of assorted gravel, rock, black soil, creeks, clay pans and red sandhills that someone, in a moment of delirium, once referred to as the main Blaxford Road. He relished the daily experience of being thrown into using his own initiative.

There wasn't a mean bone in his body, which some would say was a definite disadvantage to a man of his calling. But by a careful mixture of good humour and native cunning he had earned the respect of the scattered community which he served. In short he was a thoroughly good bloke who kept his ear to the ground and who thereby nipped any trouble in the bud before it had time to burst into flower.

He was famous in the state police force as the man who had found 'Cutter Malloy' after a statewide search involving helicopters, special branch, police dogs and mountains of taxpayer's money. Cutter, as his name implied, was not a nice man to know. He had a habit of performing surgery, of the non-elective kind on people who had crossed him and without the cost of an anaesthetist! In this particular instance he was the prime suspect after the grisly find of a body, done over like the Sunday roast after carving. Alf's particular contribution to the search was in idly looking at the latest copy of the police bulletin one day and finding therein the information that the much-wanted Cutter had the best of alibis, for he was residing in the Brisbane gaol and had been for the past six years. Alf was not thanked when he rang up and pointed this out to the officer in charge of the case.

I was out at Biscuit Ford in the spring. It had rained

somewhere up north and the intermittent Mindoo Creek had flowed a banker for a change. More often than not the Mindoo was simply a depression in the western sands. But occasionally it rained in the inland and in a couple of weeks the creek ran high and the old billabongs alongside it filled up, and even quite large depressions in the land would be turned into glorious lakes, filled with fish. It was a mystery where they came from so quickly after the rains, but they were always there in profusion, luscious yellow-belly and sweet tasting catfish. And there were birds too. The creek was alive with the sound of waterbirds and parrots and zebra finches. Biscuit Ford, for a change, stood true to its name as a ford through which you could splash. The 'Biscuit' part it earned from long ago when an early exploration party reached it, only to find it in its usual state, as dry as a cracker! The town itself was the smallest imaginable. One wide main street with a tin hall and a rather tumbledown store, which doubled as the post office, on one side and the police residence, a boundary rider's cottage, the pub and two other houses on the other. That was it, but it served the community of sheep station families from a surrounding radius of sixty miles or so.

Just outside of town there was, this spring, a beautiful small temporary lake, edged with an area of the greenest grass imaginable. It was the ideal place for a picnic for the Sunday school kids of the district. These were not children who attended a fixed place every Sunday, as in most parishes. These were folk from scattered sheep stations who did their Sunday school lessons in the same way that they did their ordinary school lessons, namely taught by Mum from material supplied by the correspondence school. Each child had three books; one being worked on at the time, one at the correspondence school for marking and comment and one in the mail. It was a good system. Its only inadequacy being that the children learned in unavoidable isolation from each other, so the benefits of mutual interaction were denied them. What was needed was some event to bring them together for a change.

I was at the police house with Alf and his wife Julie.

'What do you reckon to holding a picnic for the Sunday school families?' I asked.

'Good idea,' said Alf.

'We could barbecue some fresh fish, for a change,' chipped in Julie.

'We could hold a fishing competition,' added Alf.

'We'd need to order a mountain of bread for all the families,' said Julie.

'Loaves and fishes,' I said. 'No problem. It's been done before.'

So that's how the well-remembered picnic and fishing day had its beginning. A day was fixed and Julie got on the phone to all the mums to organise the tucker. Alf drew up the rules for the fishing and other activities.

Came the day and it was a glorious one. The only fly in the ointment was that both Alf and Geoff, the boundary rider, were not there for the beginning. Word had got round that a couple of unsavoury-looking characters had been seen driving at night on the back tracks, mostly away from the main road. There had been some distant strange and muffled thumping sounds heard from time to time. So,

Alf and Geoff took the ute, into which they piled Geoff's motorbike, and set off down the creek from where the most recent activity had been reported, to see what was going on. Alf's nose told him that something smelled fishy, and he was right as it turned out.

Meanwhile the picnic got into full swing. There was some preliminary food and drink to keep the raging pangs of childhood hunger at bay. After that, various things had to be done. Some of the parents set to and dug a longish shallow trench into which they piled plenty of twigs and leaves and fallen timber. This was set alight so that a good hot bed of embers would be available when needed later on. Then the whole lot was covered with heavy gauge mesh fencing, the idea being that there would be plenty of available barbecue space for all the fish that would be caught by the competition participants. Mothers and assorted helpers buttered bread and made coleslaw and salads. I was busy arranging various games and activities which involved the youngest to the oldest. And the fishing competition got under way.

The contestants ranged from the rank amateur to the keenest aficionados. Amongst the latter was Miss Vercoe. Old man Vercoe had died a few years before leaving his property in the capable hands of his daughter. She was fortyish and a bit severe, but she ran a good place and had the respect of the locals. What she didn't know about sheep wasn't worth knowing. She also had a passion for fishing. There wasn't a lot of local opportunity, except in farm dams, but every year she went to the coast for a break and spent the most part of it fishing. There was no problem at all in hooking her in for this local competition. When asked, she was brisk in her acceptance and was even seen to smile at the prospect.

When the others took their various places spaced out along the edges of the inland lake, she wandered farther afield, downstream a bit, and took up station at a place where the creek flowed cool and deep at the point where it left the lake. It was a nice quiet spot, away from the chatter of the less experienced anglers. And it was beautiful too. On the far side the bush came in close to the water where the gum trees bent over their own reflections. Miss Vercoe baited her hook with a nice fat witchetty grub and settled down to some serious fishing and let the peace of the place seep into her as, for a while, she forgot about the falling wool prices and rising shearer's wages. This was as near to paradise as she could imagine.

Downstream Alf and Geoff, travelling near the creek on a bush track, came suddenly upon a battered truck, parked behind a bit of a sandhill. As they stopped and got out to investigate there came from not far away the unmistakable *crump* of gelignite exploding in water. A muddy fountain, rising briefly, just beyond the trees indicated the source of the explosion. Then came silence.

Alf and Geoff took off at a run towards the creek and found what they expected. There on the bank was one man whilst wading in the water was another clad in shorts and T-shirt, busily gathering up more fish than you could imagine in one waterhole. They were floating belly up, either dead or stunned by the explosion. It was a very efficient method of fishing, but it wasn't legal.

As soon as they realised they were not alone, and especially as they took in Alf's uniform, both men took off in opposite directions. The one on the bank headed into the bush, making for the truck, as Alf supposed. The other splashed his way across the water to the western bank where he thought he'd have a better chance of escape. Geoff ran for the ute and grabbed his motorbike. He had the benefit of local knowledge and, as he headed north upstream, he knew of the place where the water ran shallow over a rocky shelf and where he could cross the stream and go after the bloke who was running upstream on the far side. This he did and was soon hot on the heels of the culprit. He could see him dodging through the trees and bushes about three hundred yards ahead. Then, suddenly, he saw the man go down, tripped by a snaking tree root, and he watched with fascination at what happened next.

The man, as it happened, had fallen slap bang right on top of a large bull ant's nest. They, naturally, resenting the intrusion into their ordered daily routine, instantly poured up out of their holes and all over the intruder, in biting and offensive mood. As Geoff watched, the man was seen frantically tearing off his clothes and simultaneously diving into the creek in the effort to relieve himself of his tormentors. There came a scream as he hit the water, for he had, by chance, dived precisely opposite the spot where Miss Vercoe was having her moment of peace. But the scream did not come from Miss Vercoe.

At the sound, heads came up in instant attention from all over the picnic site. It came with remarkable intensity from a man who, as he dived, got a very sensitive part of his anatomy hooked on the end of Miss Vercoe's line. But it was a second scream, more piercing than the first, which caused immediate abandonment of the egg and spoon race and had everyone running to see what was happening. That scream came when Miss Vercoe, with instant response to hooking something at last, began to reel it in. Then, with remarkable aplomb, considering she now had an audience of dozens of open-mouthed parents and children, she managed to land her catch. As the poor man struggled up the bank, clutching his torn flesh in agony, she sternly told him to stand still as, with a practised hand, she felt for and got the hook out of him. Then, always prepared for any emergency, she reached into her fishing bag for her first aid kit, adeptly peeled a band-aid from its packet and neatly stuck it round the wound to the cheers of the onlookers.

Someone wrapped a spare tablecloth around the shivering victim. Someone else retrieved his wet clothes from the creek and they were soon steaming dry next to the fire trench. Geoff, who by now had recrossed the river on his motorbike, took charge of his prisoner by tying him to a tree and giving him a hot mug of tea. The children drifted back to their games and the other fisherman threw in their lines again, not hoping to catch much after the waters had been so disturbed. Beside which, had they known it, there wasn't really much to catch, since the illegal fishermen had blown that hole the day before.

Downriver Alf too was having success. He doubled back to the hidden truck in time to see the other man rev the engine, let in the clutch too fast and bog the vehicle to the axles in soft sand. The man had just enough time to hop out of the truck and escape upriver on his side before Alf could catch him. A similar chase took place as had happened on the other side of the river. Alf got in the ute and the man ran upstream, dodging in and out of the trees, which made pursuit difficult. Alf knew he had him, for he was making for the picnic site. His entry to that placid and innocent scene was not quite as eventful as that of his mate had been, but he nonetheless caused a minor stir as he staggered into the arena with Alf in hot pursuit.

The man was stopped by one of the fathers, who happened to be returning from answering a call of nature. As he stepped from behind a tree he was hit by the villain, who ran slap into him, rebounded, lost his balance and sat down backwards rather suddenly, as luck would have it, right onto the mesh which covered the fire trench. The wire sagged dangerously but kept him from immediate immolation on the red-hot embers. However, he did get branded on the hot wire and he sprang up with a yell, not as piercing as the one as his mate had managed but creditable nonetheless. He wore the checkwork brand on his rump for a long time afterwards. Alf hopped out of his ute and collared him. Then, thrusting his police revolver into the hands of Julie, his wife, and, with a sidelong wink to Geoff, said to her, 'Here, love, keep your eyes on this one for me while Geoff and I go back and recover their truck. If he looks like moving, shoot him.'

Julie looked uneasy as she gingerly waved the gun about. The freshly collared villain looked plain terrified as he pondered the gun in her uncertain hands. He didn't feel like moving a muscle but lay on the ground, face down, until someone fetched some burn cream from Miss Vercoe's first-aid kit.

Alf and Geoff borrowed a four-wheeled drive from one of the families there and headed back to collect the evidence.

Whilst the excitement died down a second time, the mothers and caterers began to get worried about food. There was plenty of bread and cakes and the like, but Miss Vercoe's human catch was the only thing that had so far been landed.

'What a pity. I don't think we're going to have too much to barbecue. I was looking forward to some nice fresh fish,' Julie said to me with a worried look.

'Loaves and fishes, remember! I think there'll be enough,' I replied with more assurance than I felt.

Well, the day went on without further event for the next hour or so until a honking horn and the grinding of gears made it evident that Alf and Geoff were back, having towed the truck out of its sand bog. What is more, there was great relief and joy when it was opened and Alf discovered so much dead fish that there was more than enough for the day. So much was there, in fact, that every family took enough leftovers home to stock their freezers.

'Wasn't that evidence that you ought to have impounded?' I asked Alf later that evening as we sat on his veranda enjoying that nice feeling of a day that had turned out all right in the end.

'We'll keep a bagful in the freezer in case the magistrate wants to see some,' he said, 'but I don't think he'd want it. Would you be grateful if I turned up at your place with a ton of rotting fish? We may as well use it. No one else will!'

'You were right, Brother,' said Julie. 'The Lord did provide in the end.'

'Yes,' I said thoughtfully, 'though sometimes I wish his ways were not quite so mysterious. He does have a tendency to leave you waiting until the last minute ... and then to overdo it sometimes.'

I was later to learn from Alf that the flesh wounds to the two rogues had soon healed up, thanks no doubt to swift treatment, but it was a long time before they ventured out of town and into the bush again. It was much longer than that before that particular picnic was forgotten. In fact, I'm told that folk around there still talk about it to their children.

And years later, word has it that even Miss Vercoe can be seen, on occasion, to crack a wry smile when she baits her hook with a nice fat grub.

CHAPTER 5

Spades and Blades

I first met Colin Morris when I went to visit Mrs Ezekiel one day. He was up on her roof which had been stripped back to its skeleton of supporting timbers.

'You look as if you've taken on quite a job.' I hailed him safely from ground level.

'Too right, Brother!' he yelled back. 'This place has got a good dose of white ants, even into the roof timbers. It'll take me a few weeks before I'm finished here, more if too many folk die in the meantime.'

I must have looked puzzled, for he came down his ladder and introduced himself to me.

'Colin Morris,' he said, 'but everyone calls me Nails. That's on account of the fact that I'm not only the town carpenter but I also double as the undertaker. So, we'll be meeting each other from time to time, professionally, as you might put it.'

'Nails?' I repeated.

'As in, another nail in your coffin.'

I nodded in understanding. I never knew such a place as this for nicknames. Everyone seemed to earn one. I wondered what they called me behind my back. There have been brothers in this town ever since the brotherhood was formed at the turn of the twentieth century. Most folk simply called us 'Brother', or usually shortened to 'Bruv'.

Nails was an arresting sight. I never saw anyone with such long arms. I thought of a gibbon I once saw in the zoo. His arms were not only long, they were also different from each other. His left arm was pretty normal, muscular and tanned from much exposure to the weather. It was his right arm that startled. It was even longer than the left and it was thin, and pale as a bedsheet. It ended in an unusually long hand which he never fully straightened out; a gibbon with an eagle's talon. He saw me looking.

'I was born with some kind of condition,' he explained. 'Not much pigment in the right arm and then a growth spurt did the rest.' He put out his right hand to shake mine. His grip was like a vice and I winced.

Mrs Ezekiel came out when she heard me shout up to Nails. She was not one to be upstaged by a mere carpenter and certainly not by one of the undertaking kind. She soon had me shepherded inside and away from the common gaze. And she got down to the business of her request for me to come and see her.

Now, don't get me wrong. Mrs Ezekiel was a good woman. Whatever she took on, she did well. She was a natural organiser which is a mixed blessing in any parish. Trouble was that she looked out at everyone else's normal fumbling efforts and got frustrated to the point of anger if she saw they were making a dog's breakfast of any job. I pitied Nails in his position. She was the sort of person who would be out checking on progress every five minutes. No wonder he'd started on the roof. It was as far away as he could manage to get. Mrs Ezekiel had that effect on people.

What she wanted to give me was a quick run-down as to who, in her opinion, I should give priority on my list of parish visiting. She certainly had her finger on the pulse of the place, mostly for the wrong reasons, but her information was always useful.

This morning she wanted to tell me about the Blade girls, as she called them. These turned out to be anything but girls. They were sisters, both in their sixties. They had married the twin brothers Alf and Ted Blade who had been prominent graziers in the district. Both brothers were long since dead and their widowed wives had pooled their resources and now lived together out on one of the Blade properties.

According to Mrs Ezekiel, these two simply ought to be visited because their father had been a prominent political figure in the old days, a member of the state government no less, and he'd been knighted! As such they apparently had some standing in the local community. They also deserved a visit because they were solidly faithful in attendance at the little bush church, which sat on the corner of their property.

Alarm bells began to ring when I heard this. I had come across such arrangements before. In the past some kindly farmer or grazier would donate a plot of ground to the church, even put up a building at his own expense, so that folk within an area did not have to make the long journey into town to get to worship. It often worked well in the beginning. Then, after the original donor died and another generation took over, the rot would set in. The sons, or more usually their wives, would get to treat the place as their own private chapel. With that attitude went the extension of that idea. They got to thinking that they owned the priest too, so that, if he was not careful, each successive incumbent would be treated as a private chaplain and hauled over the coals if he didn't see himself in the same way. Apparently the Blade widows were of that mind. I could see that Mrs Ezekiel rather approved of the attitude herself. She admired strong women, who stood up for themselves, as she put it. I got the picture that the sisters had acquired a fitting name when they married. They were sharp as knives and prepared to live up to their name if anyone crossed them. In the end the description told me more about Mrs Ezekiel than the two sisters.

As I left Mrs Ezekiel's place that morning I looked up at Nails to say goodbye. He was next to the chimney and he cupped his ear in a gesture that told me had heard every word of our conversation, which came up the flue. He gave me a conspiratorial wink. I decided that he was okay and certainly no fool.

True to my word to Mrs Ezekiel I managed to find time during the next week to go and see the widows Blade. I was not sure what to expect. I had a sort of mental picture of two old tartars and probably well to the right of Genghis Khan in their political outlook. As I drove the sixty miles out to their place I had a little time to mentally prepare myself to meet what I imagined would be these two formidable women.

Over the years since then, I have learned that my

imagination can cause me a lot of undue worry. It is best not to worry too much in advance about what, or who, one might meet. Things rarely turn out as you imagine them.

When I got there I found charm itself personified. The two sisters were not as tall, not as ferocious, not as demanding, not as anything that I had let myself imagine. They met me as I opened the gate into their enclosed garden. Both were dressed sensibly for a pair of working women. It was obvious that they played a hands-on role in the running of their property.

'Thank you for phoning before you came out,' said one. 'I'm Alice and this is my sister Emmeline.'

'Hello,' I said, 'Brother Mark! But then you know that.'

'Do come inside,' said Emmeline, 'and call me Emmy. Everyone does. I hope you drink coffee. We brewed some in anticipation of your arriving about now.'

Inside, the old bush house was cool and smelled of antique wood and polish. It also carried a fair whiff of wealth. The coffee was good, very hot and served not in mugs but in some very fine porcelain cups. The sisters pumped me for information about myself. I'm not sure what they were expecting, but I apparently measured up. We got on well together. These were cultivated women who read widely, kept up with the news and the stock market and yet expressed great concern for local folk who were having a harder time on the land than they themselves were.

We passed a pleasant twenty minutes or so of bread and butter conversation. Then, out of the blue, I heard Alice say, 'Of course we were both whores, you know, until we married our husbands.'

All things considered I took that sudden revelation rather well, I thought. Emmy had just poured me a fresh cup of coffee. It was very hot. I gulped in an involuntary swig in response to Alice's words and coughed violently as the scalding brew hit me. The resulting pantomime saw me jump up, spill some liquid on the carpet (Axminster) and guide a shaking cup and saucer almost successfully back onto the coffee table. It seemed to cover the moment's surprise adequately.

I put on my most understanding look and said, 'It must have meant a huge change of lifestyle then, when you got married and came out here.'

'Oh, it was,' said Alice. 'We came from the city, you know. Before we married of course we used to see so many people. Well, in our line of work that was natural. When we got here it took us quite a while to adjust to there being so few folk around for most of the time. I know that I longed for the old life for a long time. I still have such good memories of those times.'

'So, how did you come to meet up with your husbands?' I asked. These two had certainly got my interest and my full attention.

'They picked us up on the Manly ferry,' said Emmy with her eyes shining at the memory. 'We were making our way over to meet up with a couple of clients for the afternoon and these two big, strong, handsome men started making conversation. Before we knew it we had agreed to meet them and go to a show that evening. They quite swept us off our feet.'

'And have you any regrets?' I asked them. They seemed

to revel in the fact of their past. It puzzled me. To say the least it was not what I expected from such apparent pillars of the Christian community.

'Regrets? No, none of those,' said Alice. 'We got to love the country here, and the lifestyle over the years. There was one time soon after we came that we did look at whether we would start in business in Blaxford, but it would never have really paid. There are so few people and those who needed our services just wouldn't have made the effort of driving into town worthwhile.'

'It wasn't because your husbands were not in agreement, then?' I said.

'Oh, not at all. They were quite understanding but agreed with us that it would have been simply not worth it financially.'

I sat there rather bemused. I had never yet met such openness about what most people would have considered a dark skeleton in the cupboard of their past life. These two presented me with something of a challenge. They seemed to revel in what they had been. As incumbent of this parish I was charged with their soul's health. I knew that as a priest it was my job somehow to bring this particular pair of God's children into an awareness of how their former lifestyle was not according to what God wanted for them. But the word 'repentance' didn't seem to be in their vocabulary. Quite frankly I was stuck. I wasn't sure what to say next. Put it down to inexperience. In that pleasant drawing room, surrounded by the books and objects that spoke of a cultured awareness of fine things, I just could not see my way forward with these two. Besides which, the conversation veered off into different territory and I missed the moment. I decided it was best to get to know them a little better before any more direct confrontation. I would take my newfound knowledge away with me for the present. I would think about it. I would pray for them and about what they had so freely told me and then I would come back to the subject when opportunity next presented itself.

It has always been my practice, ever since ordination, not to leave a home without at least praying for God's blessing on all who dwelt there. I stood up to go and asked them if I might pray for them and their families.

'Oh, please do,' they said together.

'It is so nice to meet a clergyman who knows what he is about,' said Emmy.

That reply stung me a bit. It was a barb to one who so obviously didn't know what he was doing. I put the thought behind me and got on with the business in hand. Standing there in the doorway of their house I prayed for God's blessing on them. I prayed that his will might be known amongst and within them. I prayed that all former sin be dealt with and then forgiven. I covered everything as best I could, just in case there were other skeletons yet to be revealed.

And then I left. I felt uncomfortable. They were delightful women and I had enjoyed their company immensely, but I felt, nonetheless, a sense of deep failure. Surely I should have been able to do more than offer some generalised prayer. Surely I was supposed to succeed in bringing sinners to repentance. These two had beaten me for the moment. Then, as I drove home doubt set in. The Lord's words, 'Let he who is without sin cast the first stone,' rang in my ears. Was I being too hasty in judgement concerning these two?

I didn't see them again for some time. The parish was huge and it took me all my time to get around its thousands of square miles of country. The little church attended by the Blades only met for worship once a month.

It was not long, however, before I met up with Nails Morris again. Our paths were to cross professionally several times in the ensuing weeks. He had the reputation of being a hard man, but as I gradually came to know him, I realised that his apparently hard exterior was really a front to try and hide his emotions underneath. He coped by his apparently offhand manner. He would visit folk in the local bush hospital and pop his head round the door of some small ward as he gaily sang out to a patient, 'It won't be long before I'll have you.' He made what seemed like joking remarks about the deceased. But I could see that this was his method of distancing himself from the pain of it all. It was after the burial of a child one day that I caught him standing hidden behind the hearse. He was quietly wiping his eyes, away from the gaze of others. He was a real softie at heart.

One day he was called upon to drive down to Warrok, a town about a hundred and thirty miles down the line, to get the body of a former Blaxford resident who had died there. He took with him an old fellow called Milton who sometimes helped him.

Not long after leaving town they came across a man who was trying to hitch a lift. They stopped and discovered that it was none other than Paddy O'Halloran.

Now, Paddy was one of society's wrecks who had washed

up in Blaxford like so many others who had come to the end of the line. He lived in a tin humpy down by the river and seemed to subsist on potatoes and methylated spirits. When they drew up alongside him it was obvious that Paddy had drink taken, as he would have said. In fact he was barely able to stand up. He said something about getting to Warrok to visit a mate. Milton was all for leaving him there as the only two seats in the hearse were taken up by Nails and himself. But Nails pointed to the empty coffin in the back and said that they could lay him in that and give him a sleep on the way there. So, they hefted him into the back and proceeded on their way, to the sound of Paddy snoring.

Some time later, as Nails gleefully related to me, a great noise came from the coffin. They stopped to see what was wrong. Apparently Paddy had woken up suddenly and taken a look at where he was. As they opened the back of the hearse Paddy sprang out and took off down the road, away from the hearse. 'Mind you, Brother,' Nails confided to me later, 'he was stone cold sober when he left us.'

Several funerals came and went. Parish life kept me busy and time was stretching out since I had last seen the Blade sisters. In the meantime, as I drove from place to place, I would occasionally worry at the problem of how to face them with what I felt. It just did not seem right that two apparently fine Christian women should so delight in their shady past. I had no problem with the fact that they had a past. All of us do. All of us live part of our lives in ways that we come to regret. These two sisters were fine women, but the necessary stage of Christian repentance seemed missing in them. My own conscience pricked me, for I knew that I was duty bound to try and do something about it. How to approach it was my problem.

And then it was too late. One day I got a phone call from Emmy telling me that her sister Alice had just died from a heart attack. I felt awful. Not only was I sad for Emmy, but I had let Alice down. I should have made time to see to her soul's health, and now she was dead. Of course I went straightaway to see Emmy.

The funeral was mostly arranged by a nephew of Alice. He flew over from Perth for the event. He asked if I would mind if he gave a small eulogy, outlining Alice's life. I readily agreed. Obviously he knew her and her life much better than I did. As we made arrangements for the funeral I naturally asked if there was a favourite Bible reading that Alice had liked.

'Oh, of course, I should have mentioned it,' said Emmy. 'She especially liked that story from Saint John's gospel, chapter eight, I think. It's the one about Jesus and the woman caught in adultery. She always said that it showed the great love and understanding that the Lord had for those whom society rejected.'

This bit of news did not make me feel any better. Great, I thought, first she was a whore, now she wants to remind us all of it at her funeral. What on earth was I going to say at the service, especially preaching on that bit of scripture? It would be true to say that I approached that particular funeral with more trepidation than any other I've done.

On the day itself I met with all of the family just before the service. The nephew, who was giving the personal eulogy, very kindly gave me a copy of his address just as we went into the church. He explained that this was just in case he got overcome with emotion and couldn't proceed. I agreed to take over and read it should that happen.

When it came to his turn to speak, however, he was fine. He spoke in a loud, clear and compassionate voice and I found myself following his words on the paper copy that he had given me. He finished the preliminaries and then he turned the page and spoke of Alice's early life.

'As you all know,' he said, 'my dear aunt was the daughter of Sir Gareth and Lady Mary Hoare. He was a member of parliament and a cabinet minister. She was very proud of her maiden name. In her early working life she and her sister Emmy ran a real estate business and sold seaside houses at the top end of the market. There's many a fine home on the beach at Manly that passed through their hands. In fact it was on a trip over to Manly on the ferry that she and Emmy met their former husbands.'

I could hardly believe what I was hearing and audibly breathed a sigh of relief. When the time came I preached with new understanding about the woman taken in adultery and how she must have felt misunderstood. I have never felt more chastened at a funeral in my life.

The service in church ended and we then made our way to the parish hall for refreshments provided by Mrs Ezekiel. We did not go to the cemetery because Alice had expressed a wish to be cremated. Now, in cities and large towns this presented no problem. In this case, however, the nearest crematorium was at Lawton, several hours drive away. Some close family members and I were to drive down and take the committal later that afternoon. I wondered how Nails's old hearse would take the journey and sidled over to him to ask.

'She'll be right, Bruv,' he assured me. 'It goes along okay in top gear. It's only in the lower ones that she plays up a bit.'

I did not feel very reassured but needn't have worried. The whole trip and the committal went off without any problem.

It was three weeks later that the final drama was enacted. And I do mean drama. The little urn containing Alice's ashes had arrived back and several family and friends and neighbours were to gather at the local cemetery and deposit the ashes in their final place of rest. Nails insisted that he drive us out. His job, he said, was not complete until those ashes were disposed of properly.

The local cemetery was situated not far out of town opposite the golf club. It was a flat, black soil patch which cracked in the heat of every summer and flooded whenever the river broke its banks which was often enough to cause problems. In the past several funerals had had to be put off until the cemetery dried out.

It was the local custom to park the cars of the mourners just outside the cemetery and only the hearse went in with the mourners walking in procession behind. We followed Nails and the hearse at an erratic pace. The hearse had seen more years than most of the folk in attendance. It ground its way out of town in a series of bounces, like a drunken wallaby. Its clutch slipped and its second gear was shot. Those on foot either dawdled along in the haze that came from its exhaust or were forced to run like emus when Nails changed up to third.

The Blades were different from most others in that someone had built in time past a family mausoleum on the only slight hillock in the cemetery. It was a square, ugly brick affair into which coffins were originally placed on shelves. There was no opening into this brick box. When it was necessary Nails would knock in a small square of brickwork built into a special frame at the back and then brick it in again after the funeral. It had been ten years since it was last opened.

Nails and I had previously agreed on the best way to proceed. He had already been out and made the opening through which he would get into the mausoleum. He had also taken out two bricks on the other side, the side that would face the mourners and me during the service. Before the committal he was to quietly enter the brick chamber and then at the right time he would be standing inside ready to receive the little urn of ashes as I placed them inside through the two brick opening. This, we thought, was the proper and decorous thing to do.

The mourners never noticed that Nails was missing and, give him his due, there was not a sound from him as he waited inside the mausoleum. We proceeded with the service, which was simple and short. However, when the time came, Nails got a little overenthusiastic. I said the words of final committal and moved to place the ashes reverently inside. As I did this an arm shot out of the opening, a pale, long arm with a talon on the end that positively grabbed the urn out of my hands and pulled it inside the brickwork. It looked for all the world as if some demon from hell was dragging poor Alice's remains down into the darkness. Some of the mourners gasped and one lady fainted. It was a service that was to go down in the Blade's family history.

Surprisingly Emmy was not upset. She saw the funny side of it and reminded everyone that Alice had had such a sense of humour that she was probably looking down laughing her head off. She greeted Nails with hoots of laughter when the poor man finally appeared somewhat shamefaced out of the back of the family tomb.

I invited everyone back to the rectory for a cuppa after the service. I had a couple of young and earnest evangelical theological students staying with me at the time. They were up from the city on a sort of learning placement. Emmy, God bless her, soon took them under her wing and got to chatting with them as they stood around drinking tea. As I passed by I distinctly heard Emmy say, 'Of course I was a Hoare before I was married. Those were such good days, very fulfilling.'

I caught her eye as I passed and she gave me a surreptitious wink. Then the penny dropped that this was a game that she and her sister were accustomed to playing on any unsuspecting stranger. I gave her a wink back and remained silent. After all, it was good training for the two young men. Let them flounder with it as I had done. I'm sure that Alice looked down and smiled. Perhaps the good Lord did too.

CHAPTER 6

Going For a Song

Every now and then I would pop in to the jeweller's shop. It was right at the end of the main street and was the domain of one C Gunter Koppel. C Gunter, as he was known by everyone in town, was more of a clock mender than a jeweller, but the two went together as one business because clock mending itself did not provide a living wage. He was a new Australian and had originally come from Vienna and his rather thick Austrian accent seemed to go rather well with the interior of his shop.

One Tuesday morning when the winter sunshine washed along one side of the street, I walked resolutely past the bakery's tempting odours and on to the end, until I stood outside of C Gunter's shop. It had a narrow shopfront with a rather small window. The window display, if you could call it that, consisted of watches, clocks and various items of jewellery apparently thrown in at random. Artistic display was not one of C Gunter's strong points.

Inside, the shop was fairly dark, except for the bright light on the bench where the clock mender was at work. He peered through thick lenses and looked like the gnome in the garden next door. The narrowness of the shop meant that there was little room between the counter and the side wall. It was a dangerous place to stand. The wall behind the waiting customer was covered with exotic timepieces. Especially dangerous was a group of Swiss cuckoo clocks. These had been hung close together where they lurked waiting for the unsuspecting customer who might come in and stand waiting. I once made the mistake of paying a visit at noon whereupon, from behind me, a dozen well-carved cuckoos almost pecked me to death.

I always enjoyed my visits to C Gunter. He had something interesting to say on most current issues and his stories of his past life were of the kind that held the listener entranced. He was so grateful to have found a new life in his adopting country and was concerned not simply to be a receiver but a giver to the community that had welcomed him into its midst.

On this particular Tuesday morning there was a specific reason for my visit. Word was filtering round the town watering holes that C Gunter had plans of staging an opera. I knew that he had more than a passing interest in music and I had heard him play the piano at various local concerts. He was a pretty competent pianist, but an opera? I wanted to check out whether the stories were true.

After a short time of chitchat about current happenings around town I asked him about his plans. His face glowed like a nightlight and with an intensity that should have warned me that this was a man possessed of a long-held ambition.

'Yes,' he said. 'I have always the music of Bizet liked.

We have, I think, the talents in town to stage his opera *Carmen*.'

To say the least I was a bit bowled over by his confidence. In my few years in town I had never encountered too many singers, certainly not ones with voices that could take on an operatic role. Oh, the local folk sang with gusto all right. It was not enthusiasm that was lacking but tone.

My mind raced immediately to Mrs Ezekiel. Every Sunday she raised her voice, and oh how she raised it, in praise of God. She could be heard from a block away. Her voice flew high over all others. It was loud. It was piercing and, above all, it was off-key. She also was a woman of great social commitment to the community. Whatever was on in town she usually had a finger in it. On getting to know her one was inclined to remember the butcher who, one day, 'inadvertently' chopped off the fingers of one of his customers. No matter what steps were taken, to keep meeting times and places only in the hands of those who were directly concerned, Mrs Ezekiel invariably turned up like a blowfly at a barbecue.

Please, please, I found myself silently praying, don't let Mrs Ezekiel hear of C Gunter's plans. Out loud I found myself asking, 'But what would you do for an orchestra? An opera needs an orchestra.' Even as I said it I knew, with a fatalism born of years of studying the faces of the slightly mad, what C Gunter Koppel had in mind.

'Not at all,' he answered. 'I myself the orchestra will be. The whole opera can be staged with piano accompaniment only. To train some singers is all we have to do, with a little bit of voice production, yes, and some small acting skills.'

The boldness, the sheer confident assurance of the man almost made me take a step backwards. I remembered the cuckoos just in time.

'What about a leading lady?' I said. 'The role of Carmen is one that taxes a professional, yet alone an amateur. I doubt whether there's anyone in the whole town and district who could take it on.'

His face grew almost incandescent with pleasure as he told me, 'A niece I have who lives in Vienna. She is a good singer and I have heard from her that she wishes to visit her old uncle. She is arriving here in three week's time. She has jet-black hair. She will make a perfect Carmen. Such a treat we are in for.'

I was still trying to get my imagination round the whole idea and I found myself mouthing the usual pleasantries. 'Well, whatever comes about, I hope that Miss Koppel will enjoy her visit,' I said.

'Oh, her name is not Koppel,' he answered. 'She is the daughter of my married sister. Her name is Stitz. This is a famous name in Austria. Her father is in the government. But, of course, we all call her by her first name, such a pretty name it is. She is called Annaleise.

As the weeks went by C Gunter was as good as his word. I had shared my thoughts about Mrs Ezekiel with him and he craftily went to see her first to enlist her help with the refreshments for something he was thinking of running. Mrs Ezekiel, who was as susceptible to flattery as most folk, jumped at the chance. It was only later that she heard that the 'something he was running' was to be an opera, but by then it was too late for her to be involved on stage. Then there came advertisements for those interested in taking stage parts. A motley crew turned up for the audition, but although several promising voices and acting talents were chosen, there was no one who stood out for the lead roles.

A date had been fixed for the public performance. It was to be a Saturday evening. The only problem I had with that was that it was the very weekend that the bishop was coming. Every now and then the bishop decided that it was time to descend on a parish in what he called a pastoral visit. He had consulted his diary and this was the date that suited him. But then, he was a great music lover and he knew a thing or two about opera. I decided that it wouldn't hurt him to be exposed to what a small community could do in that line, for better or for worse. If it turned out to be for worse, then he'd at least realise what I was up against. What's more, since the event was to include refreshments, it would mean one less meal and one less opportunity for him to meet all the people who wanted to shake his hand at some contrived event that I would have to organise.

I met C Gunter one day as he closed his shop for the evening. He confessed to me that his plans were being held up because he had, so far, been unable to find a male singer to take on the part of Escamillo.

'Perhaps you'd better pray,' I said to him.

'Maybe you are right,' he answered. 'Everything else I have tried.'

We were walking past the Royal Hotel at the time when suddenly we heard from within the bar a voice raised in rather inebriated song. C Gunter stopped in his tracks. 'That is the voice that could do it,' he said.

'Are you sure?' I said with some doubt. 'If so it's the quickest answer to prayer I've yet seen.'

C Gunter was a man of action. He pushed open the bar door and I followed him in. Standing, or rather swaying, at the bar giving full voice to all and sundry was Pepper O'Neill. Now, Pepper was a man I had encountered often. He lived quite some way out of town and earned his living doing a variety of jobs – part shearer, part fencer, part drover, part general dogsbody. He stayed out of town for weeks at a time until necessity drove him in to do some shopping and catch up on old friends. His last stop was always the pub, where he invariably got tanked to the eyeballs. To put it mildly he was not the most reliable of men.

Once or twice before, I had played host to Pepper as he sobered up overnight in my spare room. It was better than letting him drive his ute home on a dirt road with the usual hazards of bends, culverts and kangaroos. Between us now C Gunter and I persuaded him to leave the pub and stay in town for the night. C Gunter wasn't averse to hitting a man when he was down. He put it to Pepper, there and then, that he could really do something for the community if he agreed to be in his opera. Pepper, who was just about still coherent, gave out what seemed to be some affirmative noise which C Gunter, rather optimistically I thought, took for a rather mumbled assent.

In the morning, as always, it was a rueful Pepper who sat in my kitchen drinking coffee.

'Was I too bad last night?' he asked me.

'No worse than usual,' I said.

'It's very good of you to keep putting up with me like this,' he drawled in his slow bush voice.

'Maybe, maybe not,' I said. 'But this time there could be a bit of a price.'

'What d'yer mean?' he asked warily.

So, I explained to him about the opera and how he had agreed to take the part of Escamillo. I must say that he took it on the chin, which he rubbed thoughtfully.

'S'pose I could give it a go,' he said. 'Can't be worse than shearing daggy sheep.'

And he was true to his word, in the short term at least. He began well and seemed to enjoy the rehearsals, but then he began to miss the odd one, even when he was known to be in town. Sometimes he could be ferreted out of the pub before he got too worse for wear. But his attendance grew more and more ragged. C Gunter and I put our heads together to try and figure out a way to entice him into town more often. There just was not another voice around like his. If Pepper went, then the whole enterprise was down the gurgler. To be honest, half of me hoped he would go.

In the end, we need not have worried. Something happened that really got his interest and ensured that he was there at rehearsals, and before time too. That something was the arrival of C Gunter's niece. As soon as she stepped off the train word flew round town about her. To put it mildly, she was easy on the eye. In fact she was gorgeous. Someone in town was heard to remark, 'What that girl hasn't got isn't worth having.' She had dark hair as her uncle had said, but she had so much more – and in every department. She was not too tall and her figure was what young men dream about and older ones remember for a long time. She had a charming smile and all the lads in town fell in love with her. Pepper O'Neill was no exception. In fact Pepper fell the hardest of all.

Annaleise was soon accepted into the social fabric of the town. Everyone, it seemed, liked her. She had an easy grace that would listen to what folk said and she looked you in the eye in a way that made you believe that she thought that you were the only person in the world worth talking to.

It is usually a mark of how well a person is accepted into a community when they acquire a nickname. For some reason the lads around town began to call her Gloria and soon everyone took it up. I imagined that it was because of her hair, which was her crowning glory and, it had to be admitted, she also had a glorious voice. She soon had the rest of the proposed cast eating out of her hand. What is more, she raised the expectations of all those involved with the production of the opera. If she could do it so well, then they would try their hardest not to let her down. No one wanted to be compared unfavourably with her.

And so the rehearsals proceeded. There were the usual setbacks. C Gunter hammered so hard on the old piano in the town hall that he broke two strings and a blind piano tuner had to be fetched from down the line to fix it. Mrs Ezekiel chucked a wobbly about some minor matter of organisation, but she always did that no matter what she took on, so nobody took much notice. Half the cast caught colds but recovered by the time the opera was due to be staged.

At last the great night arrived. The event had been well publicised and folk from even way out of town came in to stay the night and enjoy a bit of culture. The town hall was packed with an expectant mix of men, women and children. The bishop and I had seats at the front and settled back into as much ease as the town hall stacking chairs could give.

C Gunter appeared, dressed in a green velvet jacket and yellow tie. He looked more like a gnome than ever. He sat at the piano and began to play. This soon brought a hush to the audience as they waited for the curtain to open.

All went well until it came time for Escamillo to appear. There came a pause, a very long pause, as we waited. The pause grew longer and the audience, sensing that something must be amiss, grew a little restive. Escamillo did not appear. The pub was next door to the town hall and my mind began to imagine a likely scenario. I slipped out of my seat and made my way backstage to see what was up.

Then came salvation. Out of the clear night air there sounded over the town the unmistakeable wail of the fire siren. Half the cast belonged to the town volunteer fire brigade and a good many of the audience. There was a general stampede towards the exit doors. The opera was abandoned as the firemen raced to the fire station followed by carloads of eager spectators. A fire always attracted a good crowd and even an opera had rightly to be abandoned until everyone knew just whose place was alight.

The only thing to do, to cover the gap, was to serve what was left of the audience with a cup of tea and some refreshments. To give Mrs Ezekiel her due, she always did provide enough for the event and something extra just in case. I talked to what was left of the cast and asked what had happened to Pepper. It turned out that when called upon to give an actual performance, his nerve had failed. Only then had he suddenly realised the enormity of what he had subjected himself to, the loneliness of the actor in front of his audience. His exact words as he left were, 'I'm not going out there by myself and sitting there like a shag on a rock.'

I followed my hunch and went next door to the pub. Sure enough, there was Pepper, still in his stage clothes, dressed as Escamillo, sinking one of several beers which were lined up on the bar. Apparently the comments from the rest of his drinking mates were as nothing compared to what he felt like in front of a legitimate audience. I took him by the arm and almost force-marched him out of the door and back into the hall. The diversion of the fire left us ample time to get some black coffee down his throat and to read the riot act to him.

Eventually everyone returned from the fire. It had only been a small grass fire behind the saleyards. Seats were filled again and we got on with the show.

Pepper, visibly shaking from a combination of native fear and the effects of the dressing down I'd given him, walked onto the stage blinking like a bandicoot emerging from a log. He made a slightly false start but settled down and thereafter he was fine. He even seemed to be enjoying himself as he got his teeth into the role.

After that the performance went pretty well without a hitch, and it has to be said that it wasn't too bad at all, all things considered. The audience cheered and the cast felt as only performers can when greeted by such insistent applause. People mingled as they enjoyed a second round of food and refreshment.

The bishop was in his element, meeting people and dispensing a smile here and a cheery wave there. He was clearly impressed by the talent of the leading lady. I caught sight of her out of the corner of my eye and made my way towards her through the crowd.

'Come and meet the bishop,' I said. And I managed to steer her to where he was standing. She had grown up in a very devout family and a bishop to her was a person to whom great deference should be paid. She was still in her stage costume and wore an off the shoulder gypsy dress that left one wondering what kept it up. She gave the bishop a little curtsy which revealed more cleavage than was healthy for any bishop's peace of mind and made me forget what I intended to say.

'Bishop, may I introduce Gloria Sti—' I stepped back from the precipice in the nick of time. Faced with the profundity of that magnificent bosom, I knew in that instant with an awful certainty just why the lads had started to call her Gloria. I did a quick mental retake and manage to stammer, 'May I introduce our glorious leading lady?'

Behind me Pepper O'Neill almost choked and spilled his beer.

The bishop shook her hand and was soon deep in conversation, congratulating her on her performance. He looked like a mariner about to be shipwrecked. It didn't last long. Mrs Ezekiel, not to be outdone, soon commandeered the poor man and steered him away into safer waters.

'Of course it was very nice, Bishop, but don't you think

the singing could have been a bit beefier?' she said in ringing tones. 'If I hadn't been so tied up with the refreshments I'm sure I could have added something to it all.'

The bishop, who knew her of old and had heard her sing, gave her a disarming smile then turned his head towards me and rolled his eyes heavenwards. I took him by the arm and guided him through the throng, back to the rectory and a glass of his favourite nightcap which I just happened to have in the cupboard. Tomorrow was Sunday and he was going to need all the sustenance available to face up to the singing of our choir, Mrs Ezekiel included.

Later in the week I ran into C Gunter in the bank. He was still overcome with the success of *Carmen*.

'My niece I have put on the train this morning,' he told me. 'She returns to Vienna but will come back again next year. I think, now that we have introduced the people here to opera, that we will do it again next year, yes? Maybe we could aim for some Wagner?'

I thought of the prospect of Pepper O'Neill in *Lohengrin*. 'Let's wait and see,' I said. After all, there might be another fire, a bigger one that took all night to quell, or Pepper could be away droving. There was plenty of time to work on a strategy. Forewarned is forearmed, they say.

CHAPTER 7

The Water Driller

It was getting dark, at that point of twilight when the light of the darkening sky just about equalled the intensity of the car headlights. I was driving home after a day visiting a couple of families out on the southern extremity of the parish, just over a hundred miles out of town. The track wasn't in bad condition for one that was not used a lot, not too corrugated, so I was keeping up a fair speed. I had the window wound down, for it was pleasantly cool after a hot and dusty day. The sky had that wonderful nacreous look that is the product of sunset glow through dust in the atmosphere. Against its lustrous background, like figures inset into a Japanese screen, there appeared the characteristic wavering 'V' formation of ibis flying west. Not long afterwards a few high-flying pelicans went the same way. Whenever I saw the waterbirds flying west like this, when we were in the middle of a drought, I wondered how the birds knew that it was going to rain. How did they know where water would be found, and when, and that the great cracked saltpans in the west would soon be lakes teeming with life?

On the ground, at the blurred edges of the day, things were hard to see. It would have been wise to stop for a while and wait until the night had set in when vision was clearer down the headlight's tunnel, but I knew that I had an early start the next day and I didn't want to be too late getting home and to bed. And then it happened. A blur of movement at the periphery of my vision resolved itself with awful certainty into a kangaroo in midair and dropping right into the middle of my path. He hit the car on the downward part of his jump and he hit it just on top of the radiator. There was the sound of escaping steam from the engine as the roo rolled on the ground and then, amazingly, picked himself up and hopped somewhat drunkenly away. It was a big old-man red and must have been around six feet high. My first thought was, thank heavens he's okay. There is nothing worse than hitting an animal and seeing it drag itself off with a broken leg and have to go hunting it in the dark in order to put it out of its misery.

My car did not fare so well. The roo had pushed the radiator back and down. The fan had then cut a neat circle into the fine mesh of small pipes that made up the radiator itself. The vehicle was undriveable and I was stranded on a back track in the approaching dark and miles from anywhere. I stood beside the wrecked vehicle listening to the faint hiss and tinkle of cooling metal and considered my options. I thought of walking to the nearest property, but I wasn't too sure how many miles away that would be. 'Lord,' I prayed into the still night air, 'what do I do now?' It was a half-hearted sort of prayer. I was already dragging my sleeping bag out from the back seat. I would sleep on it and see what turned up in the morning.

I don't know what I expected a rescuing angel to sound

like. I was just settling for a night on hard ground when I heard mine. The noise was distant. It came as a sort of low rumble from far away. Then it deepened and grew imperceptibly louder. The night was so still that sounds out there would carry for miles and I listened to that sound for ten minutes as it came nearer and nearer. And then came vision, the distant pinprick of headlights gradually getting brighter. Miracle of miracle there did seem to be another vehicle on this track.

I waited until I figured the driver would see and then switched on the car lights. He was coming up behind me, so I put the gear lever into reverse so that the reversing lights would come on. Then I sat there switching the lights on and off so that they would, I thought, be more noticeable.

Eventually, with a hiss of air brakes, the monster pulled to a juddering stop. And it was a monster, a great big, yellow-painted contraption, all hydraulic hoses and bits protruding from every angle. It belonged, as the signage on the front door said, to one Jack Larkin, water driller.

As I was later to discover, Jack was a most unlikely angel. At some time surely someone had removed the extra letters 'r' and 'i' from the middle of his surname. He got down from the driver's cabin and took in the situation with a glance

'You've chosen a God-forsaken spot to break down, haven't you?' he said with a grin as wide as the road as another figure was climbing down out of the passenger side of his rig. 'I'm Jack and this is my offsider Trevor.'

The introductions were made in that slow drawl that is often found out in the bush, a slow way of speech that is sometimes mistaken for stupidity by city dwellers. These men were not stupid. In no time at all they had dragged out a towing chain and soon I was wedged between them in the rig's cabin and my car was being towed securely and effortlessly behind the rig.

I introduced myself. 'I'm Brother Mark, and this is my parish.'

'So, it's maybe not such a God-forsaken place, then,' said Jack. Trevor grinned. These two had an easy rapport that transcended words.

We sat in companionable silence for long stretches at a time as the big engine drummed and the rig ate up the dark miles. I sensed that Jack was not the kind of person that would take too many questions at a time. He needed the silence to brood on goodness knows what imaginations were going through his mind at the time. But every now and then the cogs stopped whirring and out would come whatever it was that had been travelling along the production line for the past ten minutes.

'Just been doing a job down in the south-west corner,' he said. 'Hasn't rained there for about a year. Everyone wants the water driller when there's a drought.'

And so the hours passed until we reached town. Bits of information about each other dropped into the long silences until it felt that I had known this man and his offsider for years. As we rolled into town I asked, 'Where are you staying? Have you got some place to go?'

'Oh, we'll park the rig somewhere quiet and drag out our swags,' said Jack.

'Better than that,' I said, 'I've got spare beds at the rectory and a decent hot shower. You're welcome to stay with me.'

And that is what happened. We rolled up to the forecourt of Simmos, the only garage in town, and parked my car for him to discover in the morning. He was used to repairing my vehicles. The unmade roads I travelled all year soon shook every nut and bolt loose and meant that repair bills were a constant item. Then we drove the rig over the street and parked it off the road beside the rectory where we had a late meal and a shower before hitting the sack.

After that, Jack and Trevor always stayed with me whenever they came through town. Jack was an avid reader and also an inveterate storyteller.

One day, about six months after I first met him, he and Trevor rolled into town after a visit to Sydney. He told me what had happened there, and I've no reason to disbelieve him, even if he sounded a bit tongue-in-cheek as he said it. It seems that Jack had got a bit of a name for himself in drilling circles. There was some sort of convention or gathering at which water drillers and earth scientists and geologists met every now and then in order to share ideas and information and look at core samples and generally keep up to date with what was being thought about and discovered. The drillers of course had valuable, on the spot experience as to what was actually down below the surface, which wasn't always what the geologists said they ought to be finding. Jack had been asked to give a talk on what he'd learned over the years. He'd spoken innumerable times to local rotary clubs and other groups interested in the earth sciences and had been to Melbourne to similar meetings there, but he had never met and spoken to the Sydney group.

Trevor had always gone with him and knew Jack's spiel by

heart. This time, it appeared that Trevor had tackled Jack about his forthcoming talk. Trevor reckoned that, since he could give the talk as well as Jack could, he should be given a chance, for a change, to pocket the speaker's fee. Jack told him that he was talking out of his bum, but the notion sank in and began to appeal to the larrikin side of Jack's nature and he called Trevor's bluff. So, they ended up having a small wager on whether Trevor could carry it off and agreed that they would change places for the event. Trevor would appear as Jack and Jack would sit in the background as his offsider.

And things had gone well. Trevor had spoken with apparent authority and even humour and received quite an ovation at the end. Then the chairman did the dirty on him and called for questions from the audience. Again Trevor acquitted himself well. He'd picked up enough knowledge from Jack to answer most of what was thrown at him by way of clarifying questions. He was going well until a smartly dressed and well-spoken man got up and everyone fell silent. This was Professor Lambton, professor of geology at the university. He asked a real curly one based on the latest scientific findings of a team from his university. It was all about hydrostatic pressure and strata settlement as a result of pumping underground water from aquifers and had Trevor really beat. But he rose to the occasions, like a true bushman.

'I thank the learned professor for his interest and his question,' he said, 'but if you'll forgive me for saying it, that is a question that any driller's assistant would have considered. And to prove it,' he went on, 'I'll ask my assistant and offsider

Trevor to come up here and give you his answer.' Then he sat down and left it all to Jack from there. They were both still laughing about it as they recounted it to me.

'But could you really answer the professor's question?' I asked.

'Well, as luck would have it I happened to read something about it in a magazine one day and it looked interesting, so I'd followed it up at the Mitchell Library before the meeting. I think I gave the Prof more than he was expecting,' he said.

Now, I happened to have a leading lay member of our diocesan synod staying with me at the time. He worked for a minerals exploration company and was their chief geologist. I could see that he and Jack did not quite hit it off. Jack's story seemed to him to imply that all professional geologists were objects of fun and he went to bed with his feathers quite ruffled.

In the morning he took off in his four-wheel drive and headed north-west to do some survey work. He'd be back in a couple of days, he said. The way he said it left us in no doubt that he hoped Jack and Trevor wouldn't still be there. He needn't have worried. Those two were about to leave to go out in the opposite direction and start to drill for water at Ron Borne's new place.

Ron and his family had lived for years further out on an ancient ironstone ridge which gave neither sustenance nor hope to anyone. The family had struggled for years to make a living and, when a timely bequest came their way, they decided to buy a property to the south and east of the town and which was kinder to animals and those who bred them.

It lay between rocky hills and even had a creek running through it during really wet winters. The creek had not run for several years and Ron needed a more reliable source of water. It was a lovely day and, since I had not had a day off for ages, I decided to go out to Ron's place and have a look at it and see whether he wanted his new home blessing. I had been asked to bless the old one, for Ron thought that such a procedure might cause the Lord to smile more benignly on the family fortunes. I wasn't sure that this was the best motive, but I went anyway. We can all do with as much blessing in this life as we can get. I also wanted to see how Ron reacted to Jack.

We arrived at Ron Borne's place about midmorning. The thunderclouds loomed blackly in the west, but it turned out to be drought weather thunder, all sound and light and about six heavy drops of rain.

Ron was a man in his mid fifties. He was tall and had been really eye-catchingly handsome in his youth, so the local female population kept telling me. He showed the marks of long hours spent out in the sun, with wrinkled skin, and was as brown as a pixie. It was his full head of unruly hair which caught your fascinated attention as soon as you saw him. An explosion in a mattress factory comes to mind. He was ever the gentleman, being generous to a fault, especially with his time when he saw that someone needed help, but he wore his Christian faith round his neck on a tight string of certainties. I have seen such men go completely to pieces when the clasp of that necklace broke. Those who were more sensitive and hesitant by nature fell by the wayside or limped behind him as the walking wounded. All of his children, except Kevin, the youngest, left home early and licked their wounds at a safe distance. Kevin stayed on and helped his father run the place. He was Ron's shadow and deferred to his father in every decision. He seemed to have no initiative himself at all.

Over time, as I got to know the kind of person that Ron was, I realised that he was the product of fervent faith and poor education, a mixture that often leads to trouble. He quoted the Bible ferociously and read it every day, which is more than can be said for most. But for him there was only one version that cut the mustard and that was the old King James version. Any other translation was anathema to him. He seemed to think that God himself had spoken in Elizabethan English and that was the end of the matter.

When Jack and Trevor stepped down from the rig he greeted them effusively enough. 'Ron Borne,' he said, holding out his hand. 'Borne by name and born again by the grace of God.'

Jack, I could see, gave a wan smile under the shadow of his hat. He had been brought up by strict Roman Catholic parents and knew all about such certainties from another perspective.

'Follow me,' said Ron. 'I'll show you where you're going to drill.'

This rather startled Jack. Usually his clients wanted him to walk or drive over the place and tell them where, in his professional opinion, was the most likely place to find water, and how far down it would be.

Jack said, 'You seem sure that you've got water.'

'Of course,' answered Ron. 'I prayed about it and went

from paddock to paddock asking the Lord to lead me to the spot.'

'And did he tell you?' There was real interest in the tone he used.

'I'm sure I know the spot to drill,' said Ron, I thought a little defensively.

'You won't be needing my discovery skills, then?' said Jack with a bit of a twinkle in his eye.

'I presume that you're talking about water divining.' I knew that steely edge that had crept into Ron's voice.

'Some people call it that,' said Jack, and I knew what he was in for.

'No matter how desperate, I'd never use the devil's tricks.' The words were said with that quiet determination that meant that one of Ron's string of certainties was being assailed. 'The Bible tells us quite clearly, "There shall not be found among you anyone that maketh his son or his daughter to pass through the fire, or that useth divination". Deuteronomy, chapter eighteen and verse ten.'

Jack wasn't a man to show much emotion, but I thought I detected a slight stiffening of the jawline at that.

He was on a hiding to nowhere if he pursued an argument about it. I had been here before with Ron. I had had an interest in dowsing for many years. I had a friend, a fellow priest, who had the gift himself. The trouble with literalists like Ron was that they took a word at face value when we all know that in any language one word can often mean two or more different things. My favourite example is the word 'cleave'. It can mean to split apart, but also it means the exact opposite, to hold together. Not for Ron and his like, such subtleties. The word 'divination' meant one thing to him and it was wrong.

I'd argued with him, to the point of exhaustion, that the Bibles we have are translations from the original Hebrew and Greek and that when you translate from another language you often can't pick up the full meaning of a word. 'Divination' was one of them. In the ancient world, and still in parts of the modern one, attempts were made to divine the future course of events by peering at animal's entrails, or throwing chicken bones to see how they landed, or a whole lot of other activities which we would call superstition. What the good book is condemning out of hand is trying to tell the future by such means.

Ron just couldn't, or wouldn't, see that water dowsing was not divination in the fortune-telling sense. It was simply a gift that some folk had, of being able to discern and know through their bodies when water was near, and even how far away it was. I personally had no problems with people using that gift. When my priestly friend demonstrated to me, with a bit of bent wire, that he could tell where there was water, I was as suspicious as the next man that some sort of trickery was at play. Then he got me to hold the wire. It did not move ... until he put his hands under my elbows. As soon as he did that, the thing went berserk in my hands. I couldn't stop it.

Afterwards I reflected that if animals can detect the presence of unseen water and even make their tracks to follow the course of an underground stream, then surely it is possible that some humans have retained that ability.

Jack had more sense than to get into an argument with a

client. If the man wanted him to drill in a chosen spot then that's what he would do.

'There are two ways we can agree upon for payment,' explained Jack. 'We can put a test bore down for a fixed amount and if we find water, all well and good. However, after we reach a hundred and twenty feet down, then you pay me so much a foot until either we strike a good flow or you want to give up.'

'And the other way?' asked Ron.

'You pay me so much a foot from the beginning. If we come onto good water before a hundred and twenty feet then it's cheaper that way.'

'Then so much a foot it is,' said Ron without hesitation. 'My leading from the Lord is that he has provided good water not too far down.'

'Well, let's get started,' said Jack as he and Trevor climbed back into the cab of the rig.

Ron and Kevin got into their ute and we all followed them to the chosen spot for the bore. I watched the setting up process with interest. I had never seen a borehole being drilled and when all was ready it amazed me at how fast they proceeded. The drill bit went down the first forty feet in no time and then they hit rock, which slowed things a bit, but even then it was surprisingly fast to the uninitiated. In three hours they were down to nearly a hundred feet and there was not the slightest wetness in what was coming up the drill shaft. At a hundred and twenty feet Jack stopped drilling and walked over to Ron.

'How far do you want me to go?' he asked.

Ron did a quick calculation, dividing what he could

afford to spend on the drilling by the rate per foot, and told Jack to keep going for another sixty feet at most. He looked a worried man. He'd expected a result by now and he went back and sat in the ute. I guessed he was praying.

By the end of the afternoon the borehole was down more than the stipulated hundred and eighty feet. Ron had twice been consulted and had extended his original limit both times. The deeper the drill went without result, the longer became all of our faces. I knew Ron was sailing close to the wind financially. He'd paid more for the new place than he originally expected and he was in danger of cleaning himself out with this venture if he went down much further. His face took on a terrible grey look.

By the time we all sat down in Edna Borne's kitchen for an evening meal, gloom was written on every face.

'Will you just look at yourselves,' said Edna, who always tried to look on the bright side. 'Things could be worse. It's not the end of the world.'

'Close to,' said Kevin at the end of the table.

It was not the happiest of meals and its conclusion was worse. Conversation had been a bit muted and it was stopped altogether when Ron gave a little moan and slipped suddenly off his chair onto the floor, where he lay immobile. Edna rushed to help him and Kevin sprang up and phoned the doctor, who in turn rang the air ambulance. Within hours Ron was down in one of the city hospitals being treated for a stroke.

During the many ensuing weeks that Ron was absent making a slow recovery it was natural that many things got put on hold. Edna went to stay with her sister in the city so that she could be near Ron. Jack and Trevor had two more jobs to do within fifty miles or so. They moved on to these until a decision could be made about what to do about Ron's job. But it was Kevin who turned up trumps as he met the new situation. With his father out of the picture he took over the running of the place and surprised everyone, himself included I suspect. He ran things with amazing decisiveness, even flair. He had ideas, good ideas, which he began to implement. He was not as narrowly fixed as his father, less full of certainty and willing to give ear to anyone who might have a different viewpoint. He certainly did not lack a Christian faith, but his was a more exploratory belief. He was more like a person on a pilgrimage than one who knew he had arrived.

It was Kevin who got back into touch with Jack about the bore. He met him along the road one day as Jack was moving his rig and they got to talking about the unfinished job. Jack, who had more than a streak of generosity and compassion, well hidden I might say beneath a rough exterior, came out with an offer to come back to the Borne place.

'Look, I believe there is water under your place, but not in the spot your dad insisted upon,' he said to Kevin. 'I'd be willing to foot the bill in putting down a trial borehole, but in a place of my choosing.'

With his father so ill and the place almost broke Kevin jumped at the chance. Besides which, he'd heard me express my views on dowsing to his father and happened to agree with them.

It had been over six weeks since Jack and Trevor had stayed with me and the geologist was back again. I didn't take to him. He seemed to think that because he was on the diocesan synod every parish rectory was available to him for free board and lodging, despite the fact that his firm paid him an accommodation and food allowance for the times that he was away from home. Amongst the clergy, most of whom shared my view of him, he came to be known simply as 'The G'.

This time The G's fancy four-wheel drive had broken down and it was going to take Simmo at least three weeks to get a part from the foreign manufacturer. There wasn't a hire car to be had in town. The G was stuck and he didn't like it. He looked at all the options and decided that the best thing was for me to drive him down the main road until we hit the railway track and he could get on a train and make his way home. I told him I would do it but so that I didn't waste too much time and petrol I'd like to do some visiting on the way down. That would mean leaving in the afternoon, visiting one or two places and staying the night at the Borne's place before driving on the next day. He wasn't too happy about it but reluctantly agreed. He didn't want to be stuck with me for the next three weeks. The sentiment was mutual.

We headed off in the afternoon after I'd rung Kevin to inquire about his father's condition and ask if we might stay the night. I told him not to worry about food as I would bring the meal. Mrs Ezekiel had been round and brought a prepared casserole in a pot. She always knew everything at least three hours before it happened and when she learned that The G was with me she insisted on feeding us. In her mind anyone who was a member of the Diocesan Synod's

Standing Committee was the next thing to the good Lord himself and should be looked after properly. Kevin said he'd be only too glad but explained that he'd got an early start the next day as Jack was coming back in the morning to do some further drilling. This could lead to some sparks, I thought, but kept the information and my thoughts to myself. I didn't want The G deciding that he might stay longer after all.

We drove into the Borne place in early evening and got down to warming up the meal I'd brought. We were halfway through eating it when I heard the rescuing angel. The sound of Jack's rig was unmistakeable. Jack and Trevor came in and the air between The G and Jack fairly bristled.

'There's a paddock on the edge of your place down south near the dividing road that I wouldn't mind running the wire over,' said Jack to Kevin.

The G chimed in and cut across the conversation, rather rudely, I thought. 'You shouldn't let yourself be taken in by this baloney about water divining,' he said. 'There's absolutely no scientific basis for it and in my view you'll be wasting your money.'

A dangerous little smile began to play around Jack's lips. By now I'd got to know him well enough to know the signs. He was up to some mischief that appealed to his sense of humour.

'You can think what you like,' he said. 'Every man's entitled to his own opinion. But if you're so sure about your professional judgement you wouldn't mind a little bet on the result then would you?'

At this The G nearly choked. He dithered and fumed

inwardly, but in the end the temptation to prove Jack was a fraud proved too strong to resist. 'All right,' he said, 'you're on. How much shall we say?'

Jack appeared to be deep in thought. Then he said, very hesitantly, as if not too sure that what he was about to say was wise, 'Okay, if you're really sure about it, why don't we agree that if I'm totally right in my predictions then you pay for the cost of the drilling. If you're the one that's right, then I pay. Will that suit you?'

The G looked as if he'd had the wind knocked out of him and I half expected him to back down. The stakes were a bit high. But he took note of the rest of us all looking expectantly at him and I could see that he was too proud a man to lose face.

'You're on,' he said with deep and unchristian malevolence. I could see why he enjoyed meetings of the synod.

'Hang on a minute,' I interjected, 'what about catching that train?'

'I'll catch a later one,' he said and he stumped off early to bed.

After breakfast in the morning The G was all for rushing ahead with the project as soon as possible. He was fairly humming at the thought of putting Jack down over this. After all his geological training and experience he knew in himself in the cold light of a fresh day that he would be proved right. Jack, on the other hand, took his time. He finished his breakfast and offered to do the washing up. He sauntered over to the rig and began to check it over with methodical slowness. Anyone could see that he was winding The G up to fever pitch, anyone that is except The G himself.

Eventually he took a bit of bent wire out of the toolbox and he and Trevor climbed into the rig. We followed them and drove off to the far paddock which Jack wanted to walk over with the wire.

I knew Jack was good. I didn't know how good. He walked back and forth with slow deliberation. The wire twitched in his hand once or twice. Each time that happened he stopped and changed direction for a while and moved until the twitching ceased. In this slow, methodical way he gradually reduced his area of search until, all of a sudden, the wire seemed to leap almost out of his hands.

'This is the spot,' he said almost so quietly that we hardly heard him breathe it.

'Rubbish,' said The G. 'You've about as much chance of finding water under here than I have of levitation.'

'We'll see,' said Jack. 'In fact I'm prepared to tell you exactly what we shall find as we drill down.'

'Impossible!' exclaimed The G.

Jack took no notice of the interruption. He continued smoothly with an astonishingly detailed summation of what he expected to find. 'First we'll drill through forty-five feet of regolith – that's this sandy top layer. Then we'll hit limestone and drill through that for sixteen feet when we'll hit a layer of coal, no more than a couple of feet thick.'

'Absolute rubbish!' The G spat the words out of his mouth with such certainty that he could have been Ron's twin. 'I don't think you've a snowball's chance in hell of finding coal around here. No one's ever found coal within two hundred miles of here.'

Jack was unfazed. He continued smoothly. 'After that

there'll be sandstone for another twenty feet and then we'll get into some water, but not much worth bothering about. We'll drill straight on through another band of rock for another thirty-five feet and that's where we'll find good water. The flow should be about two thousand gallons an hour.'

The G almost went berserk. 'Are you trying to convince me that by simply feeling that wire in your hands you can give us an accurate assessment like that? Nobody could do that. It's impossible. What did I tell you? The man's a fool!' He looked around wildly at us as if looking for confirmation. He didn't get it.

'I'll stick by what I know,' said Jack. 'A bet's a bet and it's going to be a pleasure to take your money.'

He got back into the rig and he and Trevor began to position it over the spot he had chosen. It took a while to set things up to Jack's professional satisfaction and it was late morning by the time that the actual drilling began. There was a sort of metal collar around the spot where the drill rods went through. It had a hole in the side and, as the drilling proceeded, material coming up the inside of the rods was gradually blown out. We could immediately see what was being drilled through at any time.

Jack was right about the first part. At exactly forty-five feet the note of the drill changed as it began to bite into rock. Right on cue after a further sixteen feet the sound of the drill changed again and up came a different sort of material. 'That's the coal,' said Jack, and sure enough the black stuff began to come out of the drill hole. And so it went on. Everything that Jack had said would be found was there and at the depth he'd predicted, until finally they hit good, clear, pure water.

The G stood there with eyes wide open. Saint Paul on the Damascus Road couldn't have looked more stunned at the revelation. With the wind knocked completely out of his sails he seemed to lose something almost physical. He looked like a suddenly deflated balloon. To his credit, though he may have been proud and full of himself, he was nonetheless also honest. He took out his chequebook and wrote out the full cost of the bore and silently handed it over to Jack. As I drove him off to meet his train he kept shaking his head.

'I wouldn't have thought it possible,' he muttered over and over again. He was a much quieter and more reserved man whenever I met him thereafter.

Several hours later on my way back home I called in to see Kevin. Jack and Trevor had packed up the rig and were preparing to leave.

'I reckon you ought to have this,' said Jack as he endorsed the cheque which The G had given him and handed it to Kevin.

'But we still owe you for the first bore,' said Kevin. 'If I take this you go away with nothing.'

'The look on that bloke's face as he paid up is payment enough for me this time. Besides which you're going to need all the help you can get to put this place on its feet as well as looking after a sick dad. Take it! You can repay me by doing a good turn for someone else some day.'

Before he drove off I said to him, 'Jack, that was amazing. I didn't know that you could be so accurate with your dowsing.'

Jack grinned and said, 'Well, part of it was dowsing, but to be honest part of it was native cunning.'

We were looking from the house down a long slope of land and could see where the new bore was in the distance.

'I always keep a record of what we find whenever we drill,' he said. 'Do you see that stand of box trees beyond where we've just been drilling? There's a small rise behind them and behind that rise, no more than seven hundred yards from where we were this morning, is a bore I put down eight or nine years ago for old Doug Salmon on the next property. I simply detailed off what we found when we sank that bore. I knew it would be about the same, it being so close.' He grinned as he put the rig into gear and drove off. 'See you around,' he said as he waved goodbye.

As for Ron Borne, he recovered fairly well in time. He was never as well as before and his concentration wasn't up to much. He mellowed as people mostly do after a severe illness. He saw how well Kevin was running the place and was content to let him continue while he played second fiddle. I often wondered what he thought of Kevin's decision about the bore and how Jack chose the place to drill. It was a couple of years later before I asked Kevin about it.

'Oh, he was really pleased about the water. But as to how we chose where to drill, I never told him and he never asked.'

CHAPTER 8

The Last of the Yanta Blacks

I hadn't been in Blaxford for long before the feeling began to grow strong in me that I was treading on someone else's territory. It was a feeling that grew stronger as the first couple of years went by. It wasn't so much the name of the town, which was in dispute. Some folk said it was because this was the place where the original folk who lived here crossed the river, while others said it was named after one of the early white explorers. The Aboriginal peoples who had walked this area for tens of thousands of years were not well represented in the community, yet everywhere I went I found evidence of where they'd been. It was amazing the number of sheep properties that had a collection of stone axes, grinding stones and stone knives for skinning animals. These collections were often simply a pile of stones under a bush in the homestead garden. They had been idly thrown there over the years as the family gradually found them out in the paddocks.

I was visiting the Monks' place some one hundred and thirty miles north-west of Blaxford one day when I was taken out into one of the paddocks by Jenny Monk who had a passionate interest in local history and the native people who had originally lived in the area. The paddock was large, perhaps five miles square. Since the stocking rate for this dry country was only one sheep to every ten acres, and since anyone needed at least four and a half thousand sheep in order to make a living, the smallest property was forty-five thousand acres. Some of them were as big as three hundred thousand acres. There was plenty of room to get lost and plenty of ground for finding things. Jenny had come across an area of blackened ground which was impregnated with fat. A little scraping around the area had produced various artefacts .She concluded that this had been an Aboriginal fireplace and got very excited about the possibility of it being thousands of years old.

'Hang on a minute,' I said. 'Your ancestors only settled this place halfway through the nineteenth century. These things may be less than two hundred years old, not thousands.'

She stopped and thought awhile. 'I'd never really thought about them being so close to us in time,' she said, 'or that they were still using these stone tools so recently. They must have used the same basic tools for thousands of years.'

'That's right,' I said. 'People speak of these things as if it was all centuries ago, but to the few black folk still around here its recent history, and painful history at that.'

Some months before, I had been visiting Waterloo Station, a sheep property some hundred miles south of where the Monks lived. The name always amused me. When people settled the district and came to name their holdings it was amazing what they came up with. Many of the names were obviously simply the place name of where the family had come from in whatever land they had their origin. Others, such as Waterloo Station, were common and well-known names that went together in a different context. There was also a Euston Station in the parish despite the fact that both were hundreds of miles away from the nearest railway line.

Waterloo took in some different country from that which was found in most of the parish. Here the flat plains suddenly gave way to an eruption of rocky hills that had a beauty all their own. Huge, honey-coloured boulders reared up into fantastic shapes against a cobalt sky. In between these rocky outcrops there were valleys of tumbled stone with twisted old bush trees growing up through them. It was not easy going picking one's way on foot.

I had been taken into this place by the owner of Waterloo, a man in his late seventies, again with a vital interest in the people who had moved through this land over the centuries. His name was Gilbert Watson and he had lived on the place all his life. He knew every tree and bush and he was intent on showing me something special.

I picked my way carefully between the stones, but he was as nimble as a cricket. He suddenly veered off to the left and jumped down into a little hollow.

'Come and look at this, Brother,' he said over his shoulder.

I jumped down beside him and there in a natural fissure in the rocks was the reflection of the sky. The hole was small, but there was permanent water down there. All around us the bush was dry as a cracker, but here in this one small spot was life. Little zebra finches fluttered around. They knew where to get a drink.

'The Aborigines knew this place,' said Gilbert. 'They'd come through here on a regular migration because of the water. They were no fools. A white man could die within feet of here and never know there was life-saving water so close. You have to be in the habit of looking for the signs which are there. That flock of finches is just one of them. The black fellows obviously used to stay awhile around here.'

'How do you know that?' I asked.

'Because of this,' he said and led me up and away further through the narrow gorge as it narrowed still further. 'Look up there.'

I looked and saw a dark opening in a small, rocky cliff.

'Here, I'll give you a hand up,' he said and, as I took his hand and his sinewy arm, he hauled me up beside him to a little rock platform in front of a shallow cave. The place was a virtual art gallery of paintings done in natural ochre. There were hands stencilled by people who had mixed the colour with water in their mouths and then blown it out, like a sort of spray gun, over hands stretched out over the rock. There were images of goannas and emus and kangaroos, the animals that they hunted for food.

'That waterhole down there reminds me of a verse in psalm 84,' I said.

'I know it,' said Gilbert. 'It's one of my favourites, the one about going through the vale of misery and using it for a well.'

'That's the one,' I said. 'That's the old translation. It means not so much misery as dryness. Someone has rendered it as "Who going through the valley of dryness finds there a spring of water".' Seems to fit this place, doesn't it?'

Both Jenny Monk and Gilbert Watson had a deep respect for the land. They viewed its ownership as a sacred trust upon them and were passionate about treating their part of it in the best way they possibly could. In a way they were close to the folk who had gone before them for so many centuries. It was a case of the land owning them rather than them owning the land. In a word, it was sacred. These two were unusual in this. Most other white folk looked after their land but treated it as a possession for them to do with what they wanted. Being amongst the stone hills and valleys with Gilbert was to sense something of his belief and was certainly to get a sense of thousands of black and naked feet that had trodden this ground before us.

In town there were a few Aboriginal families which had assimilated into Western white culture. The odd one or two held down jobs as storemen or council workers and lived in Western style houses. Most, however, lived on the edge of town to the north. They lived in tin humpies banged together with old corrugated iron and other bits and pieces. There was no electric power, no sewered toilets and no fresh water on tap. They were a dispirited people. That just about everyone seemed to treat this as a normal state of affairs made me angry inside. It was all so obviously unjust.

I had the same feeling about the folk who lived in a collection of shacks and tin huts to the south of the town. This is where the misfits among the white men had ended up. These were the drunks and others who for one reason or another simply did not fit in with everyone else.

Blaxford was at the end of the railway line that stretched inland from the coast. It seemed that some people just ran away until they got to the end of the line. The town had a disproportionate number of such folk. So, at opposite ends of the town there were groups of people who had had the stuffing knocked out of them. One lot were black, the other white. And from both came individuals who knocked on the rectory door and asked me for a handout on a regular basis.

I paid a few visits to the folk in the humpies at both ends of the town. I always came away feeling frustrated, for in both cases I was confronted by a culture which, quite frankly, I did not understand. From each of the two I got different stories. From the outsiders who were white I came away with stories of broken marriages, betrayal, various life traumas induced by the last war and plenty of drinking to try and escape life's pains. People lived singly and to themselves. In the black community there was just that: community. The Aboriginal people, although disinherited and often turning to drink, were nonetheless still a people who lived as if they belonged together. Despite being the object of discrimination and great injustice they knew and accepted one another and shared whatever they had, even though it wasn't very much.

One of my favourite characters was a man I came to know simply as Steve. I first met him not long after I first arrived in town. It was while I was watching a film one balmy summer's night at the town open-air cinema. A figure, as dark as the night around us, slipped into the seat beside me and punched my arm in a friendly kind of way.

'You an me's friends, eh, Brother?' The voice was strong and confident, not a hint of deference or pleading.

'Is that so?' I said. 'What's your name?'

'I'm Steve,' he said and then went on, 'Look, Brother, I've lost me rosary beads an' I was wondering whether you'd give me a quid to buy a new set.'

I was not taken in by that one, and I had a sneaking suspicion that I wasn't meant to be. It was a sort of test for a new brother. So, I said, 'If I had it on me I'd almost be persuaded to give you a quid just for the story, Steve, but you know that you have to come up with a better one than that.'

He was not at all put out. He slid into the dark again with a cheery, 'See you around again, Brother,' and I was left to enjoy the film.

Some months later I was out in the church grounds doing a bit of tidying up. The cockatoos had been active in the tops of the silky oaks and there were twigs and leaves scattered everywhere. The birds seemed to like to play at pruning and would nip off the growing tips from the ends of the branches seemingly just for the fun of it. I watched as Steve approached. He stooped down and left his shopping hidden under the bushes in front of the rectory then he walked boldly up to the front door and knocked. I nipped in the back door and through the house and opened the door at which Steve was waiting.

'Oh, Gooday, Brother,' he said. 'I wonder whether you could help me out a bit. I've got no money to go and do a bit of shopping for some tucker.'

'Would that be the kind of shopping you've already done and carefully hidden under those bushes?' I said.

A broad grin erupted across his understanding face. 'Ah,

well, we try it on, eh, Brother!' Again he was not put out. This was part of a well-practised game that he played on any gullible white fellow. In part it amused me that this man had learned to play the game so well, that he had become so adept at surviving the complete takeover of his country by men from another culture. But in truth, it also left me with a deep well of anger that had forced this fine man to trade in his native dignity for a bottle of cheap wine and a plug of tobacco. I didn't understand the mechanism behind all of this. I was simply aware that at some level a deep injustice had been done, and continued to be done, to the original people of the land.

I made several attempts at understanding by paying more visits to the place where Steve lived with his extended family of aunts and cousins. To my eyes it seemed to be a place of more squalor than dignity with countless children and dogs playing together in the dust. Runny noses and eye infections seemed to be the norm.

My attempts at conversation were frustrating. I soon came to realise that there was a secret, almost shy, attempt to give me the answers to my questions, which they thought I wanted to hear. I couldn't even scratch the surface of their culture. However, one thing was crystal clear. This was that Steve seemed to hold the respect of his people as a sort of leader. They deferred to him. No matter what sort of a clown he made of himself in the white folk's eyes, he was not seen as such by his own people.

It was hard to see Rousseau's noble savage in any of these folk, but in Steve there was evidence of what the best of them might have been. As I probed deeper and talked to the locals it became clear that the Aboriginal folk in the settlement and surrounds of the town were not the original inhabitants of this particular piece of country. They had moved up the river only in comparatively recent times and had gradually displaced the local tribe. In fact all of the original people had died out, so I was told by Gilbert Watson.

I asked Steve one day about his people taking over from the original folk.

'Too right, Brother,' he said. 'Too many of them blackfellas around here when my people come. We 'ad to fight 'em.'

That was all he said. It amused me that he should describe another tribe as blackfellas when he himself was as shiny black as a ripe plum, but it spoke of some residual feeling still present, an awareness that he belonged to a particular people. He was a man with a foot in both cultures both black and white. He had learned to survive. I sensed that he might be less at home with black men from another people than he was with white folk.

He had occasional work as a shearer and certainly got on easily with his fellow shearers, when he was with them, that is! He caused the shearing contractor no end of bother because he had a disconcerting habit of ending up in the police lockup just when the team were all set to go out to start at some distant shearing shed. Usually it was because he'd been on the grog the night before and had been taken in to sleep it off. But occasionally his native habit of sharing his belongings led him to believe that other folk might think that way too about theirs.

On one occasion I met Nipper, his contractor, down the street carrying a cake.

'Look at me, Brother,' he said. 'I'm off to the police again to try and get Steve released. We're due to go out today and I really need him. I'm a man short as it is.'

'And why the cake?' I asked.

He looked a bit embarrassed. 'It's the wife's idea,' he said. 'It's Steve's birthday and she insisted I take him a cake. I ask you?'

'You could always bribe the policeman with it instead,' I suggested.

'It might even come to that, Brother,' he replied with a grin. 'It might just come to that.'

Some months later I got a sudden call from the hospital. Gilbert Watson had been taken ill and wanted to see me. I dropped everything and went. I found him looking very frail and obviously seriously ill.

'Glad you could come, Brother.' His voice was much weaker than that of the old Gilbert I had got to know. 'I think it sensible to assume that I'm near the end of my pilgrimage in this world. I've lived a good long life and it's time to tie up the ends of a few things before I go.'

As always I admired his forthrightness. There never was any evasion of the issue for Gilbert. He went straight to the point.

'Have you got something particularly on your mind?' I asked. 'You know as well as I do that the Lord promises his forgiveness to those who turn to him.'

'Yes, I do, Brother, and there's something that I've held onto for twenty-five years that I want you to know about.'

'Go on, then,' I said.

'Well, Brother, back in 1940 there was an old Aboriginal

man. He used to wander around the whole of this country. He always claimed he was the last of his people – the last of the Yanta blacks, he called himself. We simply knew him as Old Man Tuckerbag. He still had the old ways about him despite all that had happened to his people. I'd often come across him as he wandered over our place. I remember they took him into hospital here when he was getting pretty frail and I came in to see him. He sat on the veranda all day chanting his old songs and keeping time by tapping on his tobacco tin with a stone. To hear him was to have the hairs on the back of your neck stand on end. There was something ancient, even timeless about the sound of him.

In the end he simply walked out of the hospital here and returned to his nomadic life. I think he wanted to die out there and free and not closed within the white man's four walls. A few weeks later I was out riding our boundary fence when I came upon him, or rather what was left of him. He had obviously got his wish and died out under the open sky. It was just on the edge of those rocky outcrops which I showed you, not far from that waterhole.'

'What did you do?' I asked.

'I did the right thing,' he said. 'I got in touch with the policeman at Blaxford – there was only one of them in those wartime years – and I reported the death. The policeman was a nice old sensible sergeant named Bert Cummins. He had to use up some of his precious petrol ration to make the trip out to us. I put him on one of our horses and we rode out to where the old fellow's body was. Bert Cummins took a considered look at the body and said that it was obvious that he'd simply died of old age. Then he explained what would have to happen. The death would have to be reported to the coroner, the coroner would have to travel all the way out from mid state somewhere; there wasn't one in Blaxford. He would look at the body and then there would have to be an inquest to pronounce on the cause of death and then the remains would have to be transported to the nearest cemetery and buried. All in all it would mean involving a great many people over several weeks. He stayed quiet for a moment and then he turned to me and said, 'Look here, Gilbert. There's a war on and we both know that we haven't the spare manpower for all of that. And we certainly don't have petrol to spare either. This is a poor old Abo who has died of old age in the place where he spent his life. There's nothing sinister here; no crime has been committed. What say we go back to your place, get a couple of shovels and give the old man a decent burial right where he is? You're a Christian man. You can say a couple of prayers over him and nobody else but us needs know anything about it. As you say he was the last of his people, so there aren't any relatives to try and find.'

'So, that's what we did, Brother. Bert Cummins died long ago, so only I know where the old man is buried. What's still on my conscience though is the fact that it wasn't quite legal. His death was never ever reported to anyone. And it would have been nice to have given him a proper funeral, if you know what I mean, something in keeping with his own culture.'

'Sounds to me as though you did the only decent and practical thing in the circumstances,' I said. 'There are maybe some secrets that should die with a man. Besides which, you have made your confession to God through me and you know that what is told in such a confession can never be told to anyone else by the priest concerned. It's God you have to answer to, not the authorities. So, lighten your heart. I'm going to place my hand upon your head and declare God's forgiveness to you, as I'm bidden by my calling to do.'

And there and then I did just that. It was as solemn a moment as if it had occurred within the walls of any church building. It wasn't only Gilbert who had tears in his eyes in the considerable silence that followed. I sat beside him, praying inwardly until he was ready to speak again.

'There's something I want you to do for me,' he said eventually.

'Fire away,' I said. 'Anything that's possible.'

'Well, when I go I want to be buried on my own place. I've lived there all my life and I understand that old black man. Like him it makes sense to me to be laid to rest in the land that has nurtured me all these years. I want to be buried right next to where I buried him.'

'I can understand that, Gilbert,' I said, 'but that could be difficult. There are all sorts of rules and regulations about where a body can be buried now. The land has to be legally set apart as a burial place. It's a time-consuming process and quite frankly, old friend, I doubt whether we have that sort of time available.'

'I've done it all already,' he said. 'Some years ago I made inquiries about what it would take to arrange for such a burial out on our place. You're right about it being a lengthy process, but I eventually managed to get a plot delineated for the purpose. It's all on paper and describes the burial plot in detail. Naturally I included the old man's grave within it. So, it's all arranged, Brother. One thing more. I'd like you to come out and do the service when I do fall off the twig.'

'If I'm still here, it would be an honour,' I told him.

'And, as for the secret dying with me,' he said, 'it might be a better idea to explain it all at the funeral and make an occasion of just why I've chosen to be buried where I have and alongside that old man.'

As things turned out Gilbert recovered enough to be able to be sent home to enjoy his remaining days in the place he wanted to be. There was time enough for me to visit him and talk some more, time too to talk to his nephew John and his wife Sue. They had been running the place during Gilbert's declining years and would have to make the arrangements when Gilbert died.

One day we wrapped the old man up in some rugs and padded him with cushions as we put him in his car for a careful and slow drive out to the spot he had chosen for his last long rest. He pointed out four large stones which marked the corners of the burial plot.

'See that spot there which is a little bit depressed from the surrounding ground? That's where the old fellow is buried, Old Man Tuckerbag, the last of the Yanta blacks,' he said. 'Perhaps you could put a memorial stone at his head with those words on it.'

And that's just what we did in the end.

Gilbert lasted just another two weeks. He died peacefully sitting out on a sunny day on the veranda. The funeral was a memorable one. Folk came from all over the district, for Gilbert had been part of the landscape ever since most of them were born. Even Nipper's shearing team, which had just started at the next property, took the day off to attend. Along with them came Steve, dressed in an old jacket. I was glad to see him. It seemed somehow right that at least one black man should be there when we were going to bury Gilbert. After all the committal prayers of the burial service would be read over both men who were laid to rest there, even though the one death was separated from the other by nearly thirty years. Since God is eternal that little time difference wasn't going to worry him, I guess.

We held the first part of the service at the homestead. Gilbert's niece played for the singing on an old upright piano which had been dragged out onto the veranda. The congregation was gathered in the garden. They would never have all fitted into the house. For the committal part of the service Gilbert's coffin was placed on the back of an old dray and we all piled into a fleet of vehicles to go out to the hill country where the old man of the Yantas was buried. Now that Gilbert had died I was free to explain to everyone what had happened and how it was Gilbert's dying wish to be buried alongside the old black man. I told them that the committal would be for both of them and so tie off the ends which Gilbert had felt needed doing.

When everyone had got there and arranged themselves around the grave it was time for me to speak about them both, then to commit both men to the land, that same land which had given meaning to their lives and which each had loved, that land which now would cradle what remained of their mortal bodies. I used as a text that verse from psalm 84 about going through the valley of dryness. Gilbert had always found a wellspring of hope in any of his often hard circumstances and it fitted in with the old black man's wandering through these parts.

It was a solemn moment and after I had finished speaking there was an expectant silence, as if something more needed to be done. I asked Steve to step forward and say something on behalf of Old Man Tuckerbag, that last black man of the Yanta people, long interred besides Gilbert's fresh grave.

'I not speak, Brother,' he said. 'I sing him.'

'Okay,' I said, 'that'll be fine.'

'And I not sing him his people's song. I have to sing him my people's song.'

With that he kicked off his shoes. He was not wearing socks and his horny toes felt for a better purchase on the earth. Then he moved a little bit to the right, then a little bit to the left, a small rhythmic movement. As he did so he took out of his pocket two carved round sticks which he cracked together in time with his rhythmic movement. The sticks made a surprisingly loud, hollow sort of crack. And then he began to sing, or rather to chant, in a far-off dreamy sort of way. It was as Gilbert had described it. The hairs on the back of my neck prickled and I think we were all transported into a time beyond time. No one spoke, no one even moved. Somehow it was appropriate. More than that it was inevitable and transcendent.

Gradually Steve's body became still. His song ended, the rhythm sticks put back into his pocket and there was a profound silence broken only by the continuing tick of insects in the dry grasses.

'He's proper dead now,' said Steve and, picking up his shoes, he stepped back into the crowd.

I doubt whether there is a person who was there who didn't remember that funeral to his dying day. I looked at Steve and, in the lengthening shadows of that place, I realised that he had achieved something in the eyes of all who were present which he had never done before, despite all his clowning and playing at games and trying to put one over the locals. In front of those two graves, with the late afternoon sun playing on the backdrop of the wild tumble of those sentinel yellow rocks, he had stood magnificently, just for a while, as a man of dignity on the land that claimed him.

CHAPTER 9

Saving Larry's Bacon

I had decided to take a few easy hours after a late breakfast having completed a four-day round of visiting in the western reaches of the parish. I had got in late the night before, or rather in the early hours of the morning. I dragged a chair outside under the shade of one of the big old silky oaks on the church side of the rectory and had just settled down with a good book when, wouldn't you know it, the telephone rang. I took the book indoors with me – somehow I knew that I wouldn't be getting back to it – and picked up the phone. It was Ada Pearce, one of the parish RE teachers.

The law of the land declared that state schools were secular institutions and, therefore, the regular teaching staff was not permitted to give any religious instruction or education. The law, however, made allowance for such instruction by saying that local churches could appoint and train their own folk to teach religious education and that these were permitted to enter schools and teach one session per week.

'Brother! I wonder would you have a minute to come and see me? I'm a bit flustered and need a bit of advice.'

'Put the kettle on,' I said. 'I'll be straight round.'

I drove the couple of miles out to north Blaxford where she lived, wondering whatever was the matter. Ada Pearce was not the panicky type and she kept her life pretty much to herself. I had never known her to ask for advice before. She was a small woman in stature but not in determination. Stubborn is not quite the right word to describe her. It was more that she was aware of how small she appeared to be and was not going to let bigger people intimidate her. She stood her ground. Whenever anyone challenged her views on anything she would give as good as she got, often more, but the emotional effort took it out of her and she always looked like a wrung out dishcloth after the effort. She was kindly but certainly was not to be trifled with.

As I drove into the front gate of her place I entered a cool haven of soft purple shadows, lit with splashes of bright primary colours where the sun managed to punch its way through the foliage of her many trees. It took a second for my eyes to adjust after the glare of the black soil country that surrounded the town on three sides. The other side was bounded by the river, which flowed cool, deep and greenish between steep banks lined with fine old red gums.

Ada had been a widow for these last ten years and had stayed in the house that she and her husband had moved into when he took early retirement because of illness. The house was built of rammed earth and the thick mud walls kept the inside as cool as a meat safe. It had three acres of garden round it, mostly given over to fruit trees. Guinea fowl gabbled noisily in the grasses and through the flowerbeds; little old ladies in grey spotted dresses.

Ada heard me arrive and came out onto the veranda

to meet me. She stood in deep shade, but I could see immediately that something had ruffled her feathers.

'Oh, thank you for coming, Brother. I wouldn't have called you, but I need to talk to someone I can trust and who won't gossip.'

She opened the screen door and led the way to her kitchen at the back of the house, where she sat me down at her scrubbed deal table. As she busied herself making a pot of tea I looked out of the back window and sat bolt upright at what I saw. Before me was a scene of utter devastation. Instead of the neat piece of lawn and a patch of vegetables, which I knew so well, there appeared to be the beginnings of major roadworks. Plants had been flattened, the lawn partially dug up, shrubs leaned drunkenly and the clothesline lay on the ground, its garland of washing trodden into the mud.

'Whatever has happened to your garden, Ada?'

'Larry's pigs,' she said.

'Oh dear,' I said. Inwardly I thought, here we go again.

Larry Williams was a florid-faced, round ball of a man with an extra bulge for a belly. To describe him as a redneck would be to understate things. His views on everything from politics to business were of the black and white kind and more negative than positive about most things that folk saw as progressive, a difficult man to deal with. And deal he did, in anything from stock feed to second-hand refrigerators. Larry was Ada's neighbour in the sense that he owned several acres adjoining one of her side fences. He didn't actually live there which was at least one small blessing for Ada. He lived in an old rambling house in town which once had had a nice garden but now was surrounded by anything that could survive the summer heat, a wild jungle of everything dry, stiff and spiky that forced its way between a tumble of old stoves, car parts and slowly rusting bric-a-brac. In the block next to Ada he kept the pride and joy and consuming interest of his life, his pigs.

'When did they get in?' I asked.

'Yesterday,' said Ada as she placed two mugs of tea on the table and a plate of home cooked biscuits. 'I've been at him to fix that fence for months. But you know what he's like, Brother. He just says, "Yeah, yeah" in that condescending way he has and you know for a fact that he doesn't intend to do anything about it.'

I had a mental picture of Ada as a little bantam hen sounding off at Larry as a great big turkey cock. Relationships with women were not one of Larry's strong points. He seemed to treat most of them as a necessary evil. There was some deep hurt there from the past, which I had not got to the bottom of. Larry was not a man to wear his heart on his sleeve and talk about such things. The word around the traps was that his wife had died years ago. He did, however, have a daughter Noeline upon whom he doted. Nothing was too much for her.

'Where are the pigs now?' I asked Ada.

'I managed to chase them back through the hole in the fence,' she said, 'but you know what pigs are like. They dig down beside the fence and get their snouts under the wire and push up until they've got a hole big enough to romp through. I've patched the fence up as best I can, but the little blighters will soon push their way back in. I really don't know what more I can do.'

'Let me think about it,' I said, mainly because I hadn't the faintest idea what else to say at the time. To my dismay I heard her answer.

'Oh, would you?' she said as if I had lifted the burden from her. Well, I was there to lift burdens, but I wasn't too sure that I was supposed simply to transfer them to myself.

I said my goodbyes and left. She looked after my retreating figure and, as I glanced back, I caught a glimpse of another Ada, a rather tired figure who was content to let someone else take over for a change.

I mulled the problem over for several days. I knew a little bit about pigs. In my teens I had regularly got a job in the holidays for a few weeks with an old hill farmer in Devon. He had a rather run-down mixed farm, but he was wise in the ways of animals. He showed me one little trick that I thought just might come in handy in Ada's situation. A plan was beginning to shape itself in my mind, but I needed to check out one or two things before I even mentioned it to Ada. In any case, there was a big question as to whether she would approve of it.

In the middle of it all I happened to meet Larry down the street one day, or rather, I saw him on the other side. He seemed to be agitated. He moved his hand minimally as if it was jerked on the end of a puppeteer's string. Then he nodded his head. Clearly he was trying to attract my attention, hoping nobody else would notice. I smiled, encouragingly I hoped.

He came diagonally across the road with his eyes fixed on something about two hundred yards along the street as if he were set to going there without delay and not coming over to see me. Every now and then he did a sort of sideways scuttle so that he would end up where I was standing. He looked like a crab doing the tango. At the last minute he turned his head towards me and said, 'Oh, hello, Brother,' as if he'd just noticed me there. That he wanted to speak to me at all was unusual. Larry was a man who gave the impression that he thought he might catch something nasty if he got too close to anyone connected with the local church, me definitely included. This time, however, he wanted a favour.

'Ah, Brother,' he began, rather diffidently for Larry. 'Could I have a word?'

His eyes were searching desperately for some kind of place to which we could retreat so that as few folk as possible might see us talking. Just along the street were the shire offices, in front of which stood an area of ground with a couple of seats in the shade of some large cottonwoods which rattled in the breeze. With a sinking feeling I led him to a bench which was in deep shade and asked him what I could do for him. I imagined it was going to be something about Ada and the pigs. But I was wrong.

'It's my Noeline,' he said. 'She's been and got herself into ... well, she's taken up with young Dolan from out Biscuit Creek way.'

I noticed the quick change of tack. 'He's a nice young fellow,' I said. 'She could do a lot worse.'

'I know that, Brother. The thing is, what do we do about arranging a wedding for them?'

'Tell them to come and see me. I'm sure we can arrange things from there. Only, make sure they come and give me at least a month's notice. The law requires that. And they'll need their birth certificates too. They are both of marrying age, aren't they?'

'No problem there, Bruv.'

'That sounds fine,' I said. 'Oh, there is one other thing, while I'm talking to you. It's about Ada Pearce. She's going bananas trying to keep your pigs out of her garden. Do you think you could go out there and mend that broken fence today? Otherwise you might lose your precious pigs, and you wouldn't want that, would you?'

'Yeah, yeah,' said Larry in a disinterested voice. 'I'll get onto it sometime.'

'I'd say the sooner the better, wouldn't you?'

'I'll get round to it, Bruv,' he said. And I knew that infuriated feeling that Ada had in trying to deal with a man like Larry.

Within the week the young couple turned up on my doorstep and we got down to preparations for their marriage. We fixed on a date about five weeks away. In due time the practical arrangements for the reception were all in hand. There was only one place in town that was really adequate to the occasion and that was the shire hall in the main street. Noeline came and asked, on behalf of her father, if the Church Ladies' Guild would do the catering. There was no problem there. They were known for their catering at just about every wedding in town.

'Oh, and Father says he's got a nice little pig that he's fattening up for the day,' said Noeline.

'That'll be fine,' I said. At the same time wondering how Larry and Ada would get on over this one.

By coincidence, later that same day I got another agitated call from Ada. Larry's pigs were at it again and she was having the devil of a job trying to commandeer one of them and steering it back to the other side of the fence.

'Have you got a large bucket or an empty garbage bin?' I asked her. She replied that she had. The bins had been emptied only that day.

'Good,' I said. 'And what about that shed in your back garden? Can it be locked and will it hold a pig?' She said that it did and it would. 'I'll come right out,' I said and put the phone down.

When I got out to her place Ada was in a right old state. A rather remarkable looking youngish pig was having the time of its life in among her garden beds. The pig had an unusual pattern on its face. There was a broad band of black right across its eyes. It looked for all the world as though it was wearing sunglasses.

'It's always that same one that's the most trouble,' said Ada. 'I've chased the others back through the fence, but this one is impossible.'

'Nice little pig,' I said by way of comment. 'I ran into Larry the other day down the street and I mentioned the fence to him. I asked him if he could get around to mending the fence right away as it was causing damage to your garden and that you were upset. He said he'd get around to it.'

'Fat chance,' said Ada with some heat. 'Look, Brother, this has been going on for too long. Whatever can we do about it?'

I noticed the inclusive 'we' and, knowing what I had in mind, felt rather like a conspirator in some dark plot. Which I suppose I was.

'Let's get this pig into your shed and safely locked away and then I'll tell you what I've got in mind,' I said.

'Yes, but how?' asked Ada.

'Hand me that little bin you've got there and I'll show you a little trick I learned long ago in Devon.' I took hold of the bin and continued, 'You see, pigs don't like their heads to be in the dark and will always back away to try and get out. You simply corner the pig like this.' We had got the offending animal cornered at an angle in the fence by this time. 'Then you give it a helmet, like this,' I said as I lunged towards the animal and pushed the bin into its face until its head was completely covered. The pig acted right on cue and began to try and back out of it. 'Then all you do is steer it backwards until you get it where you want it. Just hold that shed door open for me and shut it tight as soon as the pig is inside.'

Ada did as I'd asked and in no time at all the pig with the sunglasses was safely locked up.

'What now?' asked Ada.

'I was coming to that,' I said. 'Don't you have a cousin who lives out Rocky Creek way, who keeps a few pigs himself?'

'Yes,' said Ada rather doubtfully.

'Well, Rocky Creek is a good fifty miles out of town,' I said. 'It's probably as good a place as any to hold a pig until Larry gets round to mending that fence.'

'You mean, hold the pig as ransom,' said Ada, catching on at last and beginning to laugh at the prospect.

'Exactly!' I said. 'Tell Larry you've waited long enough and he can have his pig back when he's finished mending the fence. He won't like it. Larry likes to be in charge of things and to be bested by a woman will hurt his pride. I think it won't be long before the fence is fixed. I'll take the pig out to your cousins once you've phoned and fixed things up with him. He will be prepared to do it, won't he? He seems to me like a man who would like to put one over on Larry. Wasn't there some dispute between him and Larry about a second-hand fridge Larry sold him which promptly broke down?'

'Oh he'll do it all right. There's no love lost there,' said Ada confidently. 'But have you got a trailer with a cage on it that you can transport the pig in?' asked Ada.

'I think I know where I can borrow one,' I said with a grin.

Later that day I rang Larry and asked him how the wedding preparations were going. We chatted about them for a little while and then I asked him, 'Larry, don't you have a small trailer with a cage on it for moving odd bits and pieces around?'

'Sure do,' said Larry, 'Very useful it's been too. Why do you ask?'

'Well, I was wondering whether you'd lend it to me until tomorrow. I've got a couple of urgent jobs to do. One thing is that I've a fair bit of rubbish to take out to the tip, and you know how the stuff blows off a trailer and makes a mess all along the tip road if you're not careful. I was thinking maybe if I could put it in your cage I could get it all to the tip in one piece.' I was confident that he'd agree. Larry wasn't going to do anything to get me offside until after his daughter was well and truly married.

'Good thinking, Bruv,' said Larry. 'Sure, you can borrow it. It's parked out the back of my place. Just come around and hitch it up any time.'

I went round and fetched the trailer and then made a great show of loading my rubbish into it and taking it to the tip, including stopping twice on the way out to speak to people about parish matters. So, everyone knew I'd borrowed Larry's trailer for the rubbish. It was after dark that I took the trailer out to Ada's, loaded up the pig and then drove to Rocky Creek with it. Larry's trailer was back in his yard next morning.

What happened next I gradually learned from both Ada and Larry. Each of them phoned me at intervals. Ada rang to give me a progress report and Larry rang to try and get me to go out and make Ada see sense. Larry had eventually been out and discovered one of his pigs was missing, a pig which could be easily recognised by the markings on its face. He got into a shouting match with Ada over their dividing fence. Larry accused Ada of stealing his pig. Ada had told him that of course pigs would go missing if the fence was broken. They had a few such exchanges over the ensuing couple of days.

Larry was getting madder and madder about his lost pig. He was sure that Ada knew more than she was letting on. But Larry was in a difficult position. He was aware that Ada was in charge of the catering team of the Ladies' Guild and he didn't want to upset plans for the wedding. If he upset Ada too much then she might pull out of the arrangements for the reception. This being a small town there wasn't much else in the way of finding another caterer, not without getting some professional in from outside and far away, a thing that would cost him very dearly indeed. So, Larry fumed and spluttered.

'Serves him right,' said Ada with steel in her voice.

Through it all I had to tread as delicately as Agag of old.

Larry appeared at my front door on the fourth day of the pig's disappearance.

'That woman has got my pig. I'm sure of it,' he fumed.

'Do you think so? Where on earth would she keep it?' I said.

'She as much as told me yesterday,' said Larry. 'She said that the pig would probably come back when the fence was mended. Then today she was much more definite. She told me, "You mend the fence and the pig comes back!" I wouldn't mind so much if it was any of the others, but I was fattening that particular one up for the wedding reception.'

'In that case wouldn't the simplest thing be to go out and replace that fence with something better able to keep your pigs in?' I asked. 'You're going to have to do it sooner or later surely.'

'No woman is going to get the better of me,' stormed Larry. 'I'm sorry, Brother, but you are going to have to do something about that woman. She's one of your flock.

'Ah, if only it worked like that,' I said in sweet innocence. 'Besides which, she's as good as promised you'll get your pig back. I don't see that you've got a real problem.'

'The problem is time, Brother. The wedding's fast

approaching and I need that animal to feed us. If it's not back beforehand, your Ladies' Guild had better come up with some good tucker to replace it.'

And there matters stood. Each one of them refused to budge. I had to admit that I had underestimated Larry's resolve. I thought that once the pig disappeared he'd fix the fence. I hadn't reckoned on the extent of his stubborn pride. Ada, however, was quite calm and resolved about it all.

'Let the man sweat it out,' she said one day. 'It will show him that he can't bully his way into everything he wants. I can be just as stubborn as he is.'

In the end things worked themselves out, as things mostly do in time.

The day of the wedding drew near and all was ready. The service itself went off without a hitch and the guests all repaired to the shire hall for the reception. The ladies of the guild took themselves off to the kitchen, which meant that there was no awkward meeting of Ada and Larry whilst the guests mingled and chatted over their drinks.

When everyone was called to sit down for the meal I could see that the father of the bride was a bit on edge. I must admit that I was too. I had been assured by Ada that the catering was all in hand and there was no need to worry about it, but I couldn't help but wonder what she was going to serve up in place of the missing pig.

When it came time for the main course I was surprised to see Ada herself emerge confidently from the kitchen with a large covered platter in her hands. She marched right up the middle of the hall between the tables of guests until she got to the high table at which sat the bride and groom and their parents and various other close relatives. She set her offering down right in front of Larry and, as she removed the cover with a flourish she said, 'I told you you'd get your pig back.' There on the dish in all its glory was the head of the pig, still wearing its sunglasses, the traditional apple in its open mouth and nested down on a bed of finely roasted potatoes.

Larry's face was a picture of mixed emotions. I thought he was going to explode. The veins stood out on his forehead and his features writhed in torment as anger and relief fought each other for expression. I discovered that I was holding my breath and couldn't help but wipe the sweat from my forehead.

Then the unexpected happened. Larry let out a great bellow of laughter. A couple of drinks must have mellowed him and his relief was self-evident. 'I never thought I'd see the day when a woman got the better of me,' he said. And there and then he stood up and offered his hand to Ada. 'I'll fix that fence tomorrow for sure,' he said. 'You've certainly put me in my place.'

After that things went really well. Many of the guests had got wind of the dispute between Ada and Larry and had also been holding their breath a bit until that moment. The sudden release of tension was like a cloud lifted and I doubt whether I shall ever see a wedding reception that ended on such buoyant optimism and good will all round.

I've often wondered whether I was justified in being the author of that little event. Some problems need drastic action to get a resolution. But I also learned that the resolution of one problem can easily give rise to another.

Larry was as good as his word. He turned up at Ada's place the very next day with new star posts and ringlock and put in a brand new fence that was pig proof down to eighteen inches underground.

A week or two later I called out to see Ada again on a couple of guild matters. She came to the door and I could see straightaway that she was distressed about something, agitated in a way that I'd rarely seen in her.

'For heaven's sake, Ada. You look as flummoxed as a headless chicken. Whatever's the matter?' I asked.

'It's Larry,' she said. Exasperation was ringing through her voice.

'What's he done now? Surely things have been patched up between you and him.'

'Rather too well, I'm afraid. He took the pig thing in good part in the end, didn't he, Brother, but there's the trouble. He's been going round town telling everyone he meets what a great woman that Ada Pearce is and that he never thought there'd come a time when he so respected a woman for the strength of her convictions. He's taken to calling out here every day with offers of help to dig my garden and fix the hinges on the door. He even brings me little gifts of things he thinks might be useful to me. He's quite a different man. But, Brother, he's more trouble, now that he's being so nice, than he ever was when he was nasty. What on earth am I going to do?'

Her face had coloured up rather nicely as she related all this to me, so I guessed that there might be more behind her bluster than she intended, or even yet knew in herself.

'Treat him politely but firmly is all that I can offer. Of

course,' I said with a grin, 'if a miracle happened and he turned up in church one Sunday then we'll know you've made a conquest, won't we?'

'Oh, Brother,' she said, blushing more deeply. 'Of course we know that's not going to happen.'

But, blow me down, three weeks later it did.

After church Ada drew me aside and whispered, 'Call it "pig evangelism", Brother.'

CHAPTER 10

Blood is Thicker Than Water

'Someone's holding up that water.'

Two weather-beaten folded arms rested on the dining table and moved slightly as he said it.

'Some so-and-so is definitely holding up that water.'

Pat O'Brien gave his considered opinion in a voice thick with an accent learned in County Wexford. He had the red hair, now fading to sand at the edges, of a true Celt.

'So you've already said,' returned his wife Clare in tones of pure practical outback upbringing. She was motherly, busy and took no nonsense from Pat. What he lacked, she had; they were two sides of the same coin. He was inclined to fly off the handle at anything that he judged to be unjust. Mind you, judgement, more often than not, did not have time to be brought into play. A man of visceral reaction was Pat.

'What do you think, Brother?' he asked me.

'Could be, I suppose,' I answered, not wanting to commit myself too wholeheartedly to one of Pat's little explosions, nor wanting to become the meat in this domestic sandwich.

I'd only arrived that afternoon and was now sitting feeling stuffed to the gills after one of Clare's magnificent dinners. Roast lamb with mint sauce and baked potatoes.

I had rung before I set out to visit them and came bearing gifts, mostly fresh milk and vegetables. Such an offering always got a visit off on the right footing. The land was too dry and the water too precious for most people to grow their own vegies and they relied on what the mailman could fit on his truck or other visitors might think of bringing.

It had been a dusty journey out. Four hours of driving on dirt roads that, for the most part, were corrugated from too long a use and shook not only the car but every bone in my body. The vehicle sounded more like a fully laden scrap metal truck than the sleek, comfortable car portrayed in the adverts when I bought it. It was long past time for the shire grader to be active in these parts.

I remembered the first time I had called on them. During that drive out and as I topped a small rise, one of a series of red sandhills, I saw two figures in the distance through the mirage-like heat haze. When I got nearer they turned out to be two men on horseback riding towards the road. I stopped where I thought their direction of travel would intersect with mine and waited for them to reach me.

'Hotter than hell in the waterbag, ain't it?' said a voice from under a wide-brimmed hat.

'Hotter than hell,' repeated his companion.

'Sure is,' I said and meant it. The sun beat down like molten metal and even the birds were still.

'What are you two doing out so far on a day like this?' I asked.

'Could say the same to you, mate,' was the reply. 'We're boundary riders checking on the fences for Tulloch.'

'Checking the fences,' echoed the other.

I nodded in understanding. Tulloch Station was one of the largest in the district. At three hundred and fifty thousand acres it provided plenty of scope for patrolling fences and fixing them.

'And I'm Brother Mark, the resident bush brother in Blaxford,' I said.

'Bloody hell, a parson!' exclaimed the one. 'You wouldn't have anything to drink in your car, would you, Brother? Me throat's as dry as a stranded whale.'

'Bloody parson, dry as a whale,' came the response.

'I've got some water,' I said. 'Other than that all I've got is a couple of cans in the esky.'

'ALL he's got is a couple of cans?' said the first with incredulity.

'All he's got,' said the other.

'I'm afraid it's not very cold. I put it in the esky when I set out, but it's sure to have warmed up in this heat.'

'Don't worry about that, Brother. It'll go down a real treat.'

'Real treat.'

And down it went as we sat in the shade of a small tree – no more than a large bush, really – the horses tethered to the fence for a while.

'How far am I from Pat O'Brien's place?' I asked.

'You'll find his mailbox on the left about twenty miles down the road. Turn left along the track in and after a couple of miles you'll cross the river and the house is not much further on. You can't miss it. Give him my regards when you get there.'

'When you get there,' came the reply which somehow by this time I was expecting.

'Who shall I say it's from?' I asked.

'Just tell him Cracker sends his best, and this here is Alan,' he said, pointing to his companion.

'Alan,' he said. 'That's me real name. Everyone calls me Parrot. Dunno why.'

We each resumed our journeys. It was hot and uncomfortable in the car, but I did not envy them their task and more hours under the sun before their day was finished.

I found the O'Brien's mailbox okay and drove down their track. After a while I crossed a small depression in the sand and then I drove on and on for miles. Eventually I came to realise that I must have missed the house, so I turned around and headed back the way I had come. When I did see the house it was obvious from the direction I was now travelling. Coming in the original way it was hidden behind a small rise and a good stand of trees obviously planted to give shade to a house. When Pat and Clare came out to greet me and I told them of my encounter and the directions I had received, they had a good old laugh.

'One thing puzzles me,' I said. 'Cracker said that I would cross the river before I got to you. I didn't see any river.'

'Ah, well, if you were looking for actual water you wouldn't have, Brother,' said Pat. ' The Parrangee River only flows when it rains up north and there hasn't been any for months, so of course it's dry at present. It's just a depression in the ground, but you must have driven through it.'

And that was the background to Pat's remark at the table

when I visited nearly a year later. There had been really torrential rain hundreds of miles away, up in Queensland some three weeks ago, in the area that fed into the river. Allowing for the water's slow progress through the thirsty landscape it was now well overdue at the O'Brien's place.

'We all really need that fresh water,' continued Pat, 'and some rotten greedy so-and-so is holding onto it.'

'How could he do that?' I asked in my innocence.

'Somebody has dammed the bloody stream,' fumed Pat. His face had turned a colour which was redder than his hair. The artist in me wondered what colours you might mix in order to get such a lively hue. 'And then diverted it into his own storage dams. You've seen how shallow the river's course is, Brother. It wouldn't take long to scrape up a temporary dam with a tractor and blade.'

'I see,' I said. 'But is it really likely? Everyone knows that all the folk downstream need their share. Who'd be so mean as to stop it?'

'We shall see, won't we?' said Pat with some conviction. I caught the look on Clare's face and it was a look of trouble.

'I know you, Pat O'Brien. You've got on that stubborn look of yours. If you're thinking of going looking upstream for the culprit, then think again,' she said. She shot me a look as if to say that I should back her up. Then with one hand she flicked back a wayward strand of hair which was daring to stray over her eyes, turned to the Aga and grabbed the kettle with the other. Like her, it was coming nicely to the boil. As she filled the teapot a silence, gravid with all the things that humans are unable to say at such times, hung in the air. Like Noah's dove of old it had nowhere to settle.

It simply hovered in hope. It seemed that it could not settle because it couldn't do so in peace. We simply sat and drank our tea.

There are moments when something ought to be said, but for the life of us we can't think of anything helpful. I sat and prayed an inward prayer telling God that I was grateful to be so trusted as to be brought even to share this couple's awkward moments, but did he have to make it so uncomfortable. 'Fix it, Lord,' was never going to be a theologically sophisticated prayer, but its effect was startling. All three of us jumped as the telephone rang. As with every miracle great or small the secret was not in the event itself but in the timing.

Pat got up and went to answer it. It was a neighbour whose young wife was having some problem with her baby and would Clare be able to tell her what to do? That got Pat and Clare talking again and she went to the phone and promised to go over and do what she could. She left, saying that she'd be gone for a couple of hours and would Pat see to this and to that and remember to shut the chooks up for the night.

As she went out of the door the air seemed to have cleared, filtered by the normal practical things that have to be done. I uttered a quiet 'thank you' and went out to help Pat with the chooks.

In the morning we all got up early. The day had dawned with a change in the wind. It had moved round to the east overnight and the oppressive heat of the northerly had gone. I thought I would never get used to the change of diet which travelling in the bush entailed. As we sat down to breakfast Clare asked, 'One egg or two with your chops, Brother?'

'Oh, one will be fine,' I answered as one who had been brought up in the austerities of wartime Britain. Mentally I had made the adjustment to the necessities of what was and what was not available out here a hundred and fifty miles out of town. The chops, of course, came from the sheep they raised and the eggs from the chooks they kept. Fancy cereals in packets were not even an option. Besides, as countless bush folk kept telling me, you need something substantial under your belt if you're going to do a hard day's work. My mind had adjusted to the idea, but my stomach didn't change habits so fast. I always got up from such breakfasts feeling like David loaded down with Saul's armour.

'What's your program for the day, Brother?' asked Pat in what I thought was a tone of rather forced nonchalance. He seemed to want something of me but wasn't prepared to say it outright.

'I haven't got any fixed plans,' I said, which was true. 'I don't have to be back in Blaxford until the weekend. I like to give myself a few days every now and then when I'm free to visit a few folk or do whatever the good Lord puts in my way.'

'Ah, I was hoping that was the case.' I could see that Pat had something in mind for me to do. 'Only Clare and I were talking things out late last night and I was saying to her that it would be a good thing if we could find out who is holding on to that water. Maybe he could be persuaded to let the rest of us get a share of it. That's only fair, isn't it, Brother?'

I could feel myself being lured into Pat's trap, so I answered with an indeterminate 'um!'

'So, Clare said that she was worried about me charging

in like a bull at a gate and making things worse and, if I did go, wouldn't it be better if I were to take somebody along who could talk to the culprit in a calm and reasonable way? And, well, we both thought that you might go.' The last bit was said in a rush and I was reminded of all the times when I was young and trying to persuade my parents that it would be to the good of the whole world if I were allowed to stay out late just this once.

'Well, what exactly would be involved, and for how long?' I asked. I had visions of trekking for endless uncomfortable days on a journey I did not want to take, to a place where I would not be welcome.

'I thought we might leave later today, after we've got a few things together. We could each take a horse and lead another to carry our swags and stuff. You can ride, can't you?'

I thought back to the few occasions on which a horse and I had come into contact. So I was very careful to explain, 'It's years since I've been on a horse and, even then, it was a very quiet one. I'm not what you might call a natural on horseback.'

'That's no problem,' said Pat heartily. 'I'll put you on Snooze there. She's a quiet little pony but dogged. She'll walk all day.'

Something must have registered on my face that gave Pat the impression that I still didn't think that this was the best of ideas.

'Come on, Bruv, you'll enjoy it. What could be better than some easy days off in the bush? We'll sleep under the stars for a couple of nights and then get a comfortable bed at Mick's place. You remember him?'

I remembered Michael all right. He was Pat's twin brother. He had bought his present place only a few years before after moving from where he was farming down south somewhere. Word had it that there had been some trouble of the violent sort and he was lucky that he hadn't ended up in gaol. He was even more mercurial than Pat, red of face and full of bluster, a fine fellow when he was in good humour but a terror when having drink taken, as Pat put it in the Irish way.

So, that was how I came to be swaying rather uncertainly in the saddle as we ambled up the dry river bed on a late spring evening. I found that there was something mesmerising about travelling through the bush on horseback. In a car everything seen through the windscreen is one stage removed from reality, a bit like looking at an endlessly rolling film of the scenery but without the proper soundtrack. Here in the stillness of the evening every background sound seemed to be magnified, the creak of leather, the muffled sound of hoofs on river sand, that special shuffling of birds hidden behind foliage as they settle themselves for the coming night. We'd been going for about three hours and all I could think of was a bed soft and comfortable. Little rivers of fire seemed to be flowing up my back and down my thighs.

'We'll make camp round this next bend,' said Pat. 'It's a nice spot. Camped there once a long time ago, green grass beside a deep pool. Might even still be a skerrick of water in the waterhole despite the long dry.'

Wishful thinking! When we got there the grassy sward turned out to be a fairly level stretch of hard sand and the deep pool was as dry as the Sahara.

We dismounted and I attempted a walk about on starched leg muscles. My body did everything to complain except actually creak when I wandered around picking up firewood. Pat was obviously more used to this kind of thing. He was soon organised, horses seen to, utensils out and tucker for the evening's meal laid out methodically. He gave me a small shovel.

'Dig in the sand at the bottom of the lowest point of that river bed there,' he said.

I looked at him doubtfully as he pocketed some cartridges and picked up his shotgun.

'Water,' he explained. 'You'll probably find some not too far down. Even in a long dry the stuff often flows down under the sand. I'll get us a couple of bunnies for a stew.'

I did as I was told and after ten minutes or so I was down into damp sand. A few more shovels full and I was deep enough for water to start seeping slowly into the hole. I began to ladle it into the billy with a tin mug. There wasn't much of it and it took a while, but we soon had the water boiling on a hot fire and then two steaming mugs of tea which went down well. I discovered that between sips I could iron my thighs with the hot mug and eased the pains a bit.

The neigh of a horse out of the gathering dusk was the first indication that we'd got visitors.

'Heard the shotgun and came over to see who it was,' said Cracker.

'Who it was,' repeated Parrot.

'Can't have trespassers on the great Tulloch Station,' said Cracker with a grin.

'Great Tulloch,' came the response.

'You should worry,' said Pat. 'I hear the boss is taking a break up on the Gold Coast. Left you two in charge, has he?'

'That's right. We're our own men for the next fortnight.'

'Men,' said Parrot.

Pat invited them to join us for a mug of tea. Then he explained what we were doing.

'Great idea!' said Cracker. 'I'd prefer something long and cold out of a can if you've got one.'

'Got one,' said his shadow.

'No tinnies, I'm afraid,' explained Pat. 'Not much room for too many stores on the horses.'

'Too bad! Tell you what though, we can four-wheel drive up the river bed sometime and bring you some. One good turn, eh, Brother?'

'Nice thought,' said Pat, 'but you'd be mad to try. You're bound to get sand-bogged in the soft stuff. Why do you think we chose to use horses?'

'No, she'll be right, mate. I know this country. Anyone'd think we haven't got a clue.'

'We haven't got a clue,' said Parrot.

I caught Pat's eye. He was standing behind Cracker and nodded vigorously at this. He was having trouble holding in his laughter. So was I. Then they left us to it. We unrolled our swags and slept the sleep of the just while the darkness held up the canopy of stars above us.

It was on the morning of the third day that we came across it. Pat let out a bellow that would wake the dead.

'My own brother, my bloody brother! Wait till I get at him.'

Across the width of the river there had been bulldozed a low dam of fresh earth. An old D9 tractor stood as a yellow sentinel at one end of it, the paint streaked with the deeper rust marks of a machine that had spent its life outside in all weathers. Black grease edged with a crust of red dirt oozed from various points. Its huge blade was still shiny from recent use.

We rode the horses up to the top of the river bank then dismounted and tethered them to a long, low branch of an old red gum. Then we strolled over to the D9 and on to the top of the earth wall. It was not a massive structure but just high enough to hold back the water and let it spill sideways over into a natural depression to the right-hand side behind the dam. Enough water had been diverted to form an enormous lake alive with the sound of waterbirds. An explosion of black ducks burst into the air as we came to the water's edge. A flotilla of pelicans was doing manoeuvres not far out. There was the refreshing sound of flowing water as it still tumbled into the rising lake.

Pat knew the area well. A series of gilgais through the trees usually marked the course where the river had originally flowed. Now, with the extra inflow, there was this lake which was both wide and long, much wider than an average billabong. Looked at objectively it was a marvellous sight, its shoreline fringed with reeds and the light reflecting silver as it caught the breeze-ruffled surface.

'Lovely sight,' I said in all innocence of what the remark might do to Pat's feelings.

'My own brother,' was all he could utter again and again.

'What are you going to do?' I asked him when he'd cooled down a bit.

'I'm going to blow that dam and release the water,' he said with some conviction. 'There's a couple of sticks of explosive in one of those saddlebags. I brought them along just in case direct action was needed.'

'So, you're taking the diplomatic course first, then,' I said. 'Is that why you brought me along?'

'Diplomacy nothing. There's only one thing my brother will understand and that's *fait accompli*. We'll blow it first and talk afterwards.'

He walked back to the edge of the dam and slithered down to the bottom on the dry side. 'Let's have a look for a good spot to place the charge,' he was thinking aloud. Pat knew what he was doing. Some years ago he'd worked for the Roads Department where he'd done a course in the use of explosives. As he moved back to unload his gear from off the packhorse he called up to me, 'This might take me a while. You can go off and look at the ducks, then if anyone asks, you didn't know what I was doing, right?'

'You're putting me in a very compromising position,' I said with some heat. 'Couldn't we do what I'm supposed to be here for and go and talk to him about it?'

'Enjoy your birdwatching,' grunted Pat.

I left him to it, not feeling very happy about it. I'd got my binoculars with me and was soon immersed in the wildfowl that were in abundance on and around the lake. Half a dozen pink-eared ducks swam into view and grabbed my attention. Ducks in pyjamas, I thought as they showed the black and white zebra stripes on their flanks, the telltale small smudge of pink on the side of their heads just a fleeting impression. As I lifted the glasses in order to see what was flying in the middle distance I caught sight of something else. Away to the left there was a plume of dust, a car travelling on a dusty track. I walked back to the dam.

'Someone's coming,' I said. 'Saw his raised dust over there.'

Pat was halfway through his task. At the news he straightened up, walked briskly over to the ponies and unslung his shotgun.

'My brother'll be mad as a cut snake when he sees what we're up to. Best be ready for him.'

'You're not thinking of shooting him?' I asked, appalled.

'Believe me, I'm tempted, Brother, but a bit of a scare was more what I had in mind. I might need to hold him off for a bit until we can get this little job done.'

'We? Don't include me in your family vendetta,' I said. 'I'm here for the diplomacy, remember?'

It wasn't long before Mick arrived and pulled up at the opposite end of the dam from where we were. He was driving a battered old ute that bore strong testimony to a bush mechanic's skill. It was clad in an assortment of metal panels of various colours obviously cannibalised from several other vehicles. Mick got out, a dead ringer for Pat.

'What the bloody hell do youse think yer up to?' was his less than friendly greeting as he took in the situation and the half completed explosives job. 'And what are you doing here, Brother, caught red-handed. You ought to be ashamed, and you a man of the cloth.'

'Don't look at me,' I countered. 'I only came along for the ride, and to see justice done.'

'What kind of justice would that be?' said Mick

'The ancient kind that says thou shalt not steal thy neighbour's water. Come on, Mick. There are folk downstream who are depending on the flow of this river. You wouldn't like it if someone upstream from you had dammed the river, would you?'

'More fool them that they didn't,' he said. 'A man should use his initiative. I can pump out of this lake for months. If the good Lord sent it shouldn't I pay him the compliment of using it?'

'Not at the expense of others, and you know that. Now, how about we all sit down and talk this over like fair-minded men?'

'Fair-minded, is it? Ask my brother Pat there if it was fair-minded when he stole his wife Clare from me, and me having courted her for the past two years.'

We stood facing one another across the river. We were beside the D9 and Mick was backed up against his ute, out of which he now took his shotgun. 'Great,' I murmured. 'Gunfight at the great Parrangee dam! And with family grudges from the past thrown in.' I sent up another silent prayer for help. It was beyond me what I could do, what I would have to do, if these two weren't to do each other serious injury.

There were long silences as the two eyed each other warily. Occasional sallies of bravado were hurled across the intervening space between them.

'I'm going down to remove that explosive and you'd do best to get on your horses and ride off home,' said Mick.

'You take one step towards it and I'll blow your windscreen out for starters,' replied Pat. 'I mean it.'

'You've no right to come onto my place and cause damage,' retaliated Mick.

'And you've no right to help ruin decent folk.' He pointed downriver. 'There are people down there whose stock are dying for want of water. Have a heart, man. You've now got plenty in store. You should let the river run its course again.'

'Look,' said Mick. 'I'll tell you what I'll do. It'll take up to another week for this lake to fill. How about I give it another three days and then break the dam. There's still plenty of flow in the river. That's a fair compromise, isn't it?'

'Another three days, another several thousand dead sheep,' said Pat.

There followed a long silence. It was eerily silent in fact. There wasn't a breath of wind and the bush had grown strangely quiet. Even the birds seemed to be holding their breath. I looked up to see what the cause was, some predatory hawk passing over maybe. What I saw was something we hadn't seen for months. Away to the north clouds were forming, not little wisps of cirrus but great big piles of mountainous white vapour. This looked like the quiet before the storm in more senses than one.

It was the merest rustle, the tiniest whisper of sound that made me look down. They say that peripheral vision will identify movement when forward looking sight can't detect it, some ability from our ancient hunting past perhaps. I thought I saw a leaf move down there at the base of the new dam. I looked down more intently, trying to discern what it was. Then the dead leaf moved again, no doubt about it this time. Behind it, from a hole in the ground there emerged one small green frog. It was thin and looked fairly dehydrated. It had obviously been buried for a while as it had waited out the dry, as frogs do. It took a couple of tentative hops, then a couple more until it had travelled a few feet from where it emerged.

'This looks promising,' I said. 'That frog knows more than we do.'

'This is no time for nature study,' grunted Pat without taking his eye off his brother.

I looked down again at the frog, or rather at the hole from which it had emerged. That little hole now framed a very bright eye which sat above a mouth out of which a forked tongue was flicking. The snake slid out of the hole towards the frog. The frog had obviously sensed the snake's presence, for it suddenly hopped away, the snake in hot pursuit. As its tail left the hole there came a slight darkening of the earth around it. Then, very slowly, one drop of muddy water formed, then another and another until the surface tension broke and they spilled out of the hole and down in the wake of the snake.

After that there was no stopping it. Drop followed drop until there was a continuous trickle. The trickle grew larger and so did the hole. Within seconds the flow became as thick as a man's arm, then as thick as a thigh with the water now pouring through.

The two brothers looked down and what was written on each face would take chapters to describe. We all jumped back instinctively as the dam broke and the impounded waters above charged through. In no time at all the river level fell and water no longer spilled over into the lake. Of the former dam there was neither sight nor evidence. Instead for as far as we could see downstream there now stretched a ribbon of fast flowing muddy water. Somewhere in its depths two sticks of sodden and now useless explosive were eddying along into oblivion.

There was a long silence as Pat and Mick continued to stare at each other across the life-giving stream. Then the amazing thing happened. Simultaneously they began to laugh; couldn't stop themselves. All animosity had apparently gone in an instant, washed away with the water.

'Ah well,' said Mick, choking back great sobs of mirth, 'it was worth a try anyway.'

'Never saw anything like your face when that dam blew,' wheezed Pat, doubling over with glee.

'You'd both better come up to the house and have a bit of lunch,' said Mick after a while. 'That river may be flowing, but I doubt it's too deep to wade your horses through.'

I shook my head in disbelief. I would never understand the Irish.

'*Fait accompli*,' said Pat. 'Everybody understands *fait accompli*.'

As we rode off and followed behind Mick in the ute the first huge drops of thundery rain began to fall on the parched land.

Later, on our way home, we came upon Cracker and Alan, not too far downriver. They were standing on the bank looking disconsolately at the four-wheel. It was bogged, high and relatively dry on a sandbank. More than that, it was half buried, right up to the doorhandles in mud and silt. Alan had a shovel in his hand but hadn't started to use it yet.

'We got bogged in soft sand,' said Cracker, 'then the water came and swept us along for a good hundred yards. Ended up like this, broadside to the water and full of mud. Lucky the thing didn't roll over.'

'Roll over,' said Alan.

'It's going to take you forever with that one shovel,' said Pat. 'Brother Mark's got ours. I'm sure he won't mind giving you a hand.'

'Thanks very much,' I said as we both started to dig. We took it in turns for the next hot hour.

'What happened to the tinnies?' I asked. 'I could sure use one now.'

'Too bad, Bruv, they got washed off the back when the river came down. They're probably buried under ten ton of sand somewhere.'

'This is going to take forever,' said Cracker.

There was no response and we all looked up at Alan, startled by his silence. Then a broad grin creased his face.

'We need Mick's D9,' he said in wonderment at the novelty of an original remark.

It was so obvious, even a parrot could have thought of it.

'D9,' he said as an afterthought.

CHAPTER 11

Give Us This Day ...

If you can learn to read you can get an education! It's an old adage but still true. Nothing replaces the printed word for sheer availability of information, not even computers.

As I toured around the vast area of my bush parish, I constantly came across folk who, through rebellion or circumstance, had left school early and gone out into the workaday world with barely the basics necessary for the understanding of things. Yet time and again, I sat down under the shade of some tree or veranda with a shearer or jackaroo, a station cook or boundary rider and was asked to discuss matters of which I knew little and the other knew much, for they were readers. Reading itself, of course, is not enough. There is something in the human mind that does not accept all that it takes in at face value. Knowledge pushes out and tests the boundaries. Is it true? How does it fit in with what I have learned about other things? In a word, personal knowledge needs to rub shoulders with other people's experience. If it does not, then there is a sort of inward growing of convictions that may well be twisted. Old Francis Bacon had it right in his essay 'Of Studies' in 1625: 'Reading maketh a full man; conference a ready man; and writing an exact man'.

These thoughts, or something like them, filled my head whenever I went out to buy a loaf of bread, for our town baker was a great reader. His name was Miller, which is a profession one step back from baking. One can imagine the family progression from one to the other. Like nearly all Millers he originally attracted the name of 'Dusty'. He arrived in town as the new baker and so everyone called him 'Crusty' instead.

Crusty was a small and fidgety man. He worried at things like a Jack Russell terrier with an old sock. Once he caught the sniff of an interesting fact or idea he began to quiver. He would thrust his muzzle into it until he found something he could clamp on to. Then he would drag it free from all attachments and worry it to death, or until he felt he'd got out of it all that it would yield.

In the still small hours of the morning, whilst others were asleep, he would get up and fire up his ovens. As he mixed and kneaded dough with his hands his mind was doing the same with what he had ferreted out of the latest book he was reading. The trouble was that the questions he eventually framed seemed to have little to do with the facts that had started off the worrying process. So it was with some apprehension that I entered his shop. I was almost always at the receiving end of some obscure question, the answer to which involved a sort of paper chase back through all the mental gymnastics to what had started him off. Buying a loaf from Crusty could be a very time-consuming business.

One Monday, when the air was still and the dust of summer had more or less settled, I pushed at the screen door of the bakery and found him sunk in gloom.

'What's the point?' he said.

'Why so gloomy?' I countered.

'Well, I've been thinking,' he replied. 'There's no future in being a country baker. The big bakeries in the major cities are taking over more and more. Already they are sending bread out to many bush towns and every supermarket sells the same brands. It won't be long before even remote towns like ours are getting regular supplies freighted out to them. What will become of small independent bakeries then? I've no son, no one coming up to take it on when I'm gone, and even if I had, he'd be hard pressed to make a living. I sometimes wonder whether it's worth carrying on.'

I had encountered Crusty in this kind of mood before. It was no use applying sweet reason to him whilst he was in it. This was more about how he felt about himself than about the rationality of his situation. Stalling him was the only thing to do and tackle the issues at a later time. An invitation to him to come round to the rectory in a couple of evening's time did the trick and I was off with my loaf in record time. Not that I was unsympathetic. His dilemma about the worth of what we do was one that hits most of us sooner or later.

Wednesday came and with it a ring on the doorbell and Crusty all of a quiver. Whenever Crusty came round he trembled with anticipation. He'd walk straight into my study and peruse my bookshelves as soon as he'd decently said 'hello'. This time, however, I got in first.

'Sit down, Crusty, and let's talk about something at the heart of my life and of yours.' Obediently Crusty sat! He looked as expectant as the dog on the 'His Master's Voice' records.

'I've been thinking,' I said, 'of what you were saying a couple of days ago about being a baker. It ties in with some reading I've been doing about the Lord's Prayer. The interesting thing about the Lord's Prayer is that it's the one thing everybody knows about Christianity, even if they're not believers. And those of us who do believe know it by heart, say it regularly and would, presumably, agree with what it says. Yet when you really consider it there are some phrases in it that are hard to pin down with absolute meaning. For example, what does the phrase 'lead us not into temptation' really mean? Presumably the good Lord wouldn't deliberately do so. And right at the heart of the prayer is a phrase which is of interest to you as well as to me.'

'What do you mean?' said Crusty.

'Give us this day our daily bread,' I said. 'You seem to me to be in the one profession above all others that is given worth by the good Lord himself. Right at the heart of his teaching is the importance of daily bread. That must give a respectable place in the scheme of things to all who are in the business of providing it. In fact,' I warmed to my theme, 'He called himself the Bread of Life and was even born in a town, Bethlehem, which means the house of bread.'

That took the wind out of poor Crusty's sails for a moment, but only for a moment! His eyes lit up as he mentally clamped onto the idea. 'Never thought of it like that,' he said. Then, with his shake noticeably increasing, 'It's a privilege really, isn't it? Anyone from grower to miller to baker to distributor of bread is part of the way that God answers that prayer. I don't know what to say. I'm all overwhelmed.'

We sat in comfortable silence for a while as the significance of the thing sank deeper into him. And then I put my foot in it. When enough has been said for the occasion the only wise thing to do is shut up. But I didn't. In fact I raised a further doubt. There were times afterwards when I bit my lip and hoped that all would turn out well for Crusty. What I said next was to send him eventually on the longest journey of his life.

Into that comfortable silence I said, 'Even so, there have been questions raised as to the exact meaning of those words. It seems so obvious at first glance, but it raises some questions. Is it a request quite literally for bread, or does it imply provision of a wider kind? Is it perhaps a prayer that all our needs may always be met? And what does the word "daily" mean? Are we simply to ask for food for one day only at a time and live in faith for long-term provision? Biblical scholars have been trying for years to tease out what the Lord might have been getting at. The problem is that all the New Testament books were written in the common language of the time and that was a kind of patois Greek. Even the Roman occupiers of Palestine had to speak the language. It's a bit like English in many parts of the world now. It's often the one common language in many places where there are multiple local languages. Trouble is that people use their own version of it in which a word may have a slightly different meaning from its use in England. With the original New Testament writings it's a case of translators reading as much as they can of classical Greek at the time and other contemporary inscriptions and documents in the local version of it. Then they have to come to the best decision as they can, from the context of the word, about the best translation of it. What we read in our English translations of the Bible is just that, a translation.'

'I know all that stuff about the good book being a translation from the original tongues. It's in the beginning pages of my Kings James Bible,' said Crusty. 'However, surely there can't be too much difficulty about a simple phrase like "Give us this day our daily bread". It's pretty self-evident, isn't it?'

I had to admit to myself that once you start reshaping a man's fervent but simple faith then you'd better have something better to replace it. Part of my responsibility here was to help bring fresh understanding without destroying something valuable to him. So, I heard myself saying, 'Ah, if only it were. The problem is that the word in Greek that is translated as "daily", isn't found anywhere else, either in classical Greek or in the kind used in the New Testament. There is simply no other written record of that word. In Greek the word is *epiousion*. The construction of the word shows that it's got something to do with regular provision, but "daily" is really as close a guess as its possible to make without reference to any other known use of the original word.'

'I still don't see the problem,' said Crusty. 'People come into my shop every day and buy fresh bread. It's what they need to keep them going for the next twenty-four hours.'

'From your perspective as a town baker, that's simple

enough,' I said. 'But Jesus was looking at things from a much bigger viewpoint. He was laying down the rules for regular prayer for his followers. More than that, He was laying down the rules for living. Was He simply suggesting that they rely day by day on God's provision, and were not to plan beyond that, an exercise in daily trust? Or was He telling us to pray for tomorrow's bread today, a piece of heavenly loaf whilst we are still here on earth? The questions have come thick and fast to the biblical scholars. Some suggest that it's simply a prayer of trust about all of God's provision. Others say that it could be a specific prayer for particular need at a particular time. Without any touchstone, any reference to common usage at the time of Jesus, it's hard to grab hold of any particular meaning with certainty.'

'Well, thanks a million,' said Crusty. 'Here I was with a new found certainty about the worth of what I am doing, and now you tell me that no one knows what the good Lord meant.'

'Yes,' I said ruefully, 'trust me not to keep my big mouth shut. But, surely, whatever the precise meaning of the words used, it is clear that daily bread of some sort had a priority in the mind of the Lord. You're still in the one profession above all that was given real worth by Him. What you do is important. More than that it's vital.'

'Well, I could have been a carpenter,' said Crusty. 'That was pretty important to Him too. But, you're right, Brother, what I do is important. Still, it would be good to find out what exactly He had in mind by that word "daily".' There was a long pause while I could just about hear the cogs turning in Crusty's brain. Then, with a new found gleam in his eye that I had learned to beware of, he said artlessly, 'And how would you go about finding that out? Where would you start?'

Despite the apparently offhand way that Crusty asked the question, I knew that some sort of fire had been ignited in him. That telltale gleam in his eye was evidence enough on its own. But it was an increase in his terrier-like tremor that really gave the game away.

I got up from my seat and went over to my bookshelves and searched a while until I found a book I had in mind. I took it down and handed it over to him. 'Perhaps it might help you to read this,' I said. 'It gives brief details of what's at the heart of this question of meaning in The Lord's Prayer.'

He took the book from me and opened it immediately. I knew that he would be immersed in it as soon as he got home. He was that kind of person.

We had a beer together and talked some more, but I could see he was itching to follow up on the questions I had dumped into his lap. He took his leave and I had an early night for a change.

About a fortnight later when I was in his shop, he said, 'I'm going away.'

'Where? And for how long?' I asked, rather astonished at this sudden turn of events.

'I'm going on a trip for a couple of months,' he said.

I'd never known Crusty so much as take a step out of town, so I was naturally inquisitive. 'What's brought this on?' I said. 'And what will we do for bread whilst you're gone?'

'Don't worry about the bread,' he said. 'I've got a cousin who was a baker. He's retired long since, but he's agreed to come and stand in for me while I'm gone. He's a bit forgetful, but he's a good baker. He'll see you right in that respect.'

I noted the qualification, 'in that respect' and the words 'a bit forgetful'. I wondered whether there was more about his cousin than Crusty was telling. 'So, where's this trip to?' I asked. 'A couple of months is a long time.'

'It's because of that book you lent me,' he said and somehow I felt accused, pinned at the heart of something uncontrollable that I'd started. 'I read about all the attempts to make sense of that word "daily" and of how archaeologists had dug up various bits and pieces which had half the word on clay tablets, or a similar word. It got me fascinated. I haven't had a holiday for years and I thought I'd go and have a look at some of those ancient places in the Middle East. It came to me that instead of wandering aimlessly around various tourist spots, I could hang my journey on a purpose. I'm going to go to some of those archaeological sites and see what I can find out.'

I must admit that Crusty had surprised me. He was as good as his word and, before a month was out he had departed on his journey.

His cousin Ken duly arrived and settled in. He was, as Crusty had said, a bit on the aged side but was amazingly agile for his age. His forgetfulness soon became apparent. He would get so involved in talking to folk that he forgot to take their money. They would ask for a dozen bread rolls and he would come up with six small white loaves. The townsfolk soon got the hang of him and became rather protective. An honesty system prevailed so that the poor man did get paid for his efforts. Out in the bush it was another story.

Some of the bread was ordered in by folk who lived up to a hundred miles out of town. It got sent out to them twice a week on the mail run. But his forgetfulness soon took another form. People began to find strange objects in their bread. The Wilsons, way out west on the banks of the Butterburr Creek, found the keys to the bakery in a wholegrain loaf. If they had put the loaf in the freezer with the others it might have been weeks before they were recovered. As it was they didn't come back until the next mail truck. Then there was the incident with our church organist, Miss Ridley.

Miss Ridley was a small, bird-like woman. Her delight was in the smallness of things. Her house was adorned with tiny pieces of china and small statues of animals made in pewter. You could always tell when it was Miss Ridley walking in the distance because, from time to time, she would stop and stoop down to examine some tiny flower beside the footpath or a particularly shaped pebble. She was a faithful soul who was there without fail every Sunday and took her duties very seriously. She would draw up a list of all the hymns to be sung over a period of the next three months. This was a labour of love that took hours and hours to complete. It involved her in reading all the set Bible readings to be used at each service in Sunday worship and then matching up the most appropriate hymns. It meant that she had to know the hymns like the back of her hand and carefully select ones that echoed what folk would hear being read from the scriptures on that occasion. I have often had to do it myself and, believe me, it was no small task.

After she had chosen all the music to be used she would note them down in her neat little handwriting in one of those small loose leaf notebooks. Naturally she used the smallest one made. So there were pages of the stuff. Each little bit of paper held six or eight numbers.

It so happened that she had a wad of these pages, her completed work for the next three months, in her hand when she called into the bakery one day on her way to practise on the church organ. The pages were held together by a paperclip, stretched to the limit of its tolerance. She ordered a loaf for herself while she chirped merrily to Ken. And got a little flustered when he forgot to take her money. Neither she nor Ken noticed the slight puff of wind that came into the shop as another customer opened the door. Nobody noticed the precious pages blown off the counter and onto a bench lower than and off in a corner behind the counter. She went on her way oblivious of her loss. It wasn't until the next day that she remembered that she had meant to deliver the list to me, but by that time the damage had been done.

The lost pages, minus their paperclip, had eventually ended up all over the bakery. Ken, when he came to clean the place up, simply picked each one up, screwed it into a ball and placed them near where he was working, intending to put them in the garbage bin. It is still a mystery how some of them got incorporated into a batch of dough. The long and short of it was that the bread that day came out like fortune cookies, each with its own scrap of paper hidden inside. These tiny scraps, with their lists of numbers, were distributed far and wide. The Coombs family out on Robin Bore Station read theirs and took them to be the numbers in a colour-coded catalogue of bridal wear. They'd been arguing for days about what the bridesmaids should wear at an upcoming family wedding. When they compared numbers, the colours looked so right that all argument ceased forthwith.

Old Alan Keevers, a gambler on the horses from way back, read them as a list of likely winners for Randwick races that day. He immediately rang his bookmaker and made a small fortune on the results.

Young Elizabeth Dovers mistook her page as the list of recommended revision pages from her school science textbook and got top marks in the ensuing exam.

Even Pepper O'Neill got a piece. He was out fencing in the never-never and had smoked his last roll-your-own with not a scrap of ciggy paper to make another. Salvation for him came at smoko when he cut into the loaf he'd bludged off the mailman.

As the days went by, all sorts of such stories came to me. Each one told of some blessing or other that the recipient had received. 'Give us this day our daily bread' was a prayer that seemed to be more than adequately answered in a dozen separate cases.

Miss Ridley was of course in great distress. She had worked hard at the music list for the greatest celebration of the Christian year. We were in the middle of Holy Week and the precious list of all the carefully chosen Easter music had been lost.

I invited her into the rectory and sat down with her to make a fresh list. It would not be too difficult, for the Easter hymns are the best known after Christmas carols. I put the kettle on and took hold of one of Ken's fresh loaves, intending to make us a couple of sandwiches to sustain us as we went to our task. As I cut into the bread I found yet another scrap of paper. On it was written the list of Easter hymns in Miss Ridley's spidery writing. It seemed that God had smiled as he taught us that nothing gets really lost in the kingdom of heaven. It all gave me cause for deep thinking on the subject.

I wondered how Crusty was getting on with his own particular brand of research. Since he went away on his journey of discovery I had received from him a selection of colourful postcards that marked the course of his journey. There were cards from remote locations in Turkey, several from Syria and Israel as Crusty took in the more famous sites of biblical occurrences. One gave news of an archaeological site where a tablet had been found containing the first half of the 'daily' word, *epiousion*, but nothing more to suggest its meaning. Another came from the place where Jesus had performed the miracle of feeding the five thousand. Clearly Crusty had been very moved at this place and his handwriting resembled his voice when the trembling took hold of him. And then there arrived a card from Cairo.

I received it just before the time when Crusty was due back home. I could almost feel him shaking as he wrote it. It seemed that he had made a last detour to the site of an archaeological dig in North Africa. The site being uncovered had been a Roman fortress in New Testament times. And there they uncovered some wooden tablets with writing on them. They had been perfectly preserved in the desiccated earth of that area and the writing was in the Greek patois that was in use all around the Mediterranean at that time. Written, for all to see, in the only known example of the use of the word outside of the Lord's Prayer, was the word *epiousios*. The tablets turned out to be a list made by the Roman army quartermaster. It was a list of requirements for the next expedition.

Crusty came home a very tired but happy man. He had soaked himself in the atmosphere of places that had deep meaning for him. As we sat one evening out on my back veranda he told me of his excitement at his last discovery. 'Give us this day our daily bread' was a prayer to be supplied with enough food and resources to perform the next expedition in the Lord's service.

'It means give us enough to do the next bit of the job,' said Crusty. 'I can relate to that. Somehow that prayer gives me confidence simply to keep putting one foot after the other. I've learned through my journeying to take one day at a time and leave the rest for the longer term in God's hands. He knows what He is doing.'

We were interrupted by a visit from Miss Ridley. She came around the house and found us sipping cold beers as we took in the beauty of the evening. I had rarely seen Crusty so relaxed, so at peace with himself.

'I do hope you don't mind my intruding, Brother,' she said, 'only my nephew is staying with me at present. He's come up for a day or two from the city. He hates the city and is looking for work out in the bush. Trouble is he has no training. He says he'd really like to be a baker. I wonder, Crusty, whether you'd have a word with him, give him a few tips as to where to start, that sort of thing.'

Crusty almost fell off his chair as he beamed with pleasure.

'Give us this day our daily bread,' I said.

CHAPTER 12

Grievous Bodily Harm

It was late August and spring came to town. It arrived as the bearded billygoat thrust for new life and clattered into town on eager, procreation-seeking hooves. It randied its way into the talk and swagger of the young men in the bars. It found expression in a deeper base note to the laughter of the shearers at smoko time. It descended as a sort of aura around every eligible woman and some who were not eligible at all. Manners came back into fashion. Station hands, in town to replenish their stores, opened doors for the women with exaggerated courtesy. And blushing adolescents became painfully aware of what nature was doing to their bodies, and in trying to hide it, drew attention to themselves. And, so help me, it even found a target in the most unlikely person that I knew.

I had long resigned myself to the fact that there are some folk that, try as you might, you just cannot make any headway with. The one big thorn in my flesh was still Ferret. I ran into him from time to time and did my best with a few cheery 'hellos', but there was always frost in the relationship. He barely deigned to speak to me. It seemed to me that there was deep down such great hurt that it would take a miracle to do anything about it. I had always said to the church folk that nothing was impossible for God, but secretly I wondered whether even He could melt the man.

One day I was doing what I had been called to do when I was ordained, namely the visiting of the sick. It was my habit whenever I was in town to do the rounds of the local bush hospital, visiting those who had been brought to my attention and naturally having a word with those others in the various wards that I visited.

I was halfway down the main corridor when I ran into nurse Margaret Arnold. Since I was such a regular visitor there I had got to know the small nursing staff fairly well and we were all on first-name terms. It was common for me to get a good-natured hail from inside one of the rooms where the nurses were attending to a patient.

Margaret was a good sort in every meaning of the word. She was efficient, good at her job, young, pretty and with a personality that I am sure hastened the healing process in everyone she tended. She gave me a big smile and a bright hello as she was coming out of one of the single-bed rooms. Then she turned her head and said to the occupant, 'Here's Brother Mark come to visit you.'

I went to step into the room and as I crossed the threshold I saw that the patient in the bed was none other than Ferret. But it was a different Ferret from the one I had ever encountered before. He looked at me awkwardly and I could see he was a little ill at ease. His face was pink and I realised that he was blushing. As he looked after Margaret's retreating figure it occurred to me that Ferret was more than a little smitten. He greeted me with fumbling words that were the most affable he'd ever sent in my direction and it was a few moments before he regained his composure. But it wasn't for long. The lovely Margaret soon returned with some extra pillows and between us we sat him up whilst Margaret, with a twinkle in her eye said, 'I hear that you're a bit of a hard man. Just you make sure that you are civil to Brother Mark.'

She obviously had his measure, but she flashed him another big smile as she left us to it. The colour flushed straight back into Ferret's face. He looked like a man on fire and gasping for air. I'd no idea what had happened to put him into hospital but could guess that some nasty and unfortunate accident had befallen him. He sat propped up now on the pillows with his arm in a sling and obviously in some pain. His head was a mass of cuts and scratches, some of them quite deep and festering. He looked as though he'd been dragged through a thorn hedge backwards and then, for good measure, forwards again. What appeared to be a largish wound on his forehead had a dressing on it through which seeped a suggestion of good red blood.

It wasn't long before I got the story out of him.

'I was in town visiting Chugger Jones. You know Chugger. He's a mate of mine from way back. It was Friday evening and while Chugger went down the street to get us a few beers I was out in his back garden. It was just about getting dark when someone felled me from behind. I remember getting a great thump across my neck and left shoulder and it must have knocked me over because all I can remember after that was Chugger bending over me as I lay on the ground. He found me lying there when he got back. I must have been out cold for ten minutes or so. I ended up with a broken collarbone and a great gash in my head, which the police said was from hitting it on a bit of garden concrete when I fell.'

'And all those nasty scratches?' I asked.

'You tell me,' he said. 'Nobody seems to have the faintest idea how they came about.'

'Any idea who did it?' I asked in amazement. I knew, as did everyone else, that Ferret was a difficult man, but ours was a pretty law-abiding town and grievous bodily harm wasn't usually on the year's calendar of social events.

'Not a clue,' he said briefly, 'but if I ever find out I'll be waiting for him down a dark alley one night, that's for sure.'

All of that was a pretty long speech for Ferret and we lapsed into an uncomfortable silence. I was about to leave when he asked me with what I thought was rather feigned indifference, 'Do you know Nurse Arnold well?'

'Pretty well,' I said. 'She's been here for a couple of years now. Came here from Sydney for a bit of experience in the bush,' I answered. I could see the cogs turning in his mind as he wondered how best he could use this information. I knew without a doubt that this sudden outbreak of affability was because he didn't want to do anything that she might hear about and turn against him. I was grinning as I said goodbye and left the room.

In the next room I was surprised to find young Glen who had met me at the station when I first arrived. He greeted me with a doleful expression on his face.

'When did you come into hospital?' I asked, 'and what are you in here for?'

'It's me leg, Brother,' he said. 'About six months ago I was unloading some fence posts and one of them slipped and hit me here on the thigh. I didn't think much of it at the time. When you're fencing you're always having these things happen. It came up in a great big lump and a hell of a bruise. But the bump never went away and I went to see the doc when I was next in town. He said he'd keep an eye on it. Sent me for an X-ray and everything, but nothing was broken. It just kept getting worse and I went back to him a couple of times. I'm in for another check-up before he sends me down to the big smoke for some tests in the Royal Hospital. I didn't understand it all, but it's the something or other "ology" department. The doc wants me to go as soon as he's fixed it up.'

'At least they're having a good look at it,' I said. I was conscious of not really knowing what to say. 'I'll pop in again tomorrow and see when you're due to go. Is there anything you need in the meantime?'

'Thanks, Bruv, but no. The doc said he'd be in to see me first thing.'

I left the hospital that day in pensive mood. Here was one person opening up when I least expected it. And there was another in whose presence and situation I discovered that it was I who had nothing helpful to say. My inability worried me. Wasn't I supposed to be the one who could bring help and comfort to the ones in pain and worry?

I popped into the hospital again the following day. This time I went straight to Glen's room to find out what the doctor had arranged for him. I discovered that he was being sent down to the oncology department of one of the big hospitals. He was to catch the train down the following week and check himself in. It had all been arranged. I could see that this news worried Glen even more than he had appeared to be on the day before, and that was understandable. I looked at him and saw a good-natured lad born and brought up out in the bush. He had rarely been down to the city in his life. I didn't know what to say to him about his illness, but at least I could do something practical.

I said to him, 'Listen, Glen, how about I set aside a few days next week and drive you down to the big smoke? I can take you right to the hospital and when they've done the tests it would be better for you to know that you had a lift home again, wouldn't it?'

'Aw, I wouldn't want to be a bother to you,' he said in his slow, decent way.

Nevertheless I could see the relief on his face at the idea.

After visiting Glen I stopped at the nurse's desk and asked Margaret whether Ferret had had any visitors.

'Not one,' she said. 'You'd think that at least one of his so-called mates would have dropped in to see him. He's really not too bad underneath all the outward gruffness. I think he puts it on as a sort of protective shell.'

'Any more news from the police about who might have done it?' I asked.

'Not really. They're a bit baffled, I think. They're treating it as a case of grievous bodily harm. They asked him if there was anyone he knew who might want to hurt him. Well, when they inquired around they were embarrassed with suggestions. What's got me intrigued is all those deep scratches all over his head. How on earth could he have got them?'

'I haven't the faintest,' I said. 'Remind me. When did he come into hospital?'

'It was last Friday evening,' she said, 'after dark.'

I left the hospital again in reflective mood. Something was nagging at the back of my brain. I had seen scratches like the ones on Ferret's head somewhere before, but I couldn't immediately think where.

I wasn't quite sure where Ferret's mate, Chugger Jones, lived, so when I got back to the rectory I made a point of looking him up in the telephone directory. After that, things began to fall into place in my memory. I remembered being out on a property on a visit one day and watching a big old goanna slowly climbing up a gum tree. They are great climbers and go upwards when scared and when they are foraging for eggs out of birds' nests. I remembered remarking to Ron and Elsie, the folk who lived there, as to how slow and ponderous he seemed to be.

'Oh, he's got all the time in the world as he goes about his business,' they said, 'but look out when you're in the way of one that's had a scare. Then they can really move like greased lightning.'

'We had one here in the garden a couple of years ago,' Elsie said. 'Ron came out of the house and found him sunning himself on the front steps. Actually he inadvertently stepped on the end of his tail. Well, you should have seen that lizard go. He ran straight up the nearest thing there was, and the nearest thing was Ron. When he got to the top of him there he clung. He dug in with those long claws of his and he wasn't letting go. Poor Ron had the scratches for weeks. Come in, I'll show a photo we took of him. Ron looked a sorrier sight than that old goanna ever did.'

I went inside and they brought out the photo album. Sure enough there was one of Ron with the goanna on his head and then another close-up of the state of Ron's head afterwards. I wasn't surprised at the mess the goanna had made. They have long, sharp claws which give a marvellous grip when they are climbing trees and the like but can inflict long, raking cuts if used on softer material such as human skin and flesh. After I remembered looking at that photo, I knew without a doubt what had made such a mess of Ferret's head and shoulders.

It was the location of Chugger's house that set my mind racing, and the remembrance of what a goanna can do. A deep and disturbing suspicion was gradually growing in me, mixed with a little guilt. Last Friday evening I had been remarkably close to Chugger's house. What happened was this. I had been visiting one of our older parishioners who lived along the river road near the outskirts of the town. As I made my way along one of the unsealed streets I came upon the local fire truck with a group of some members of our volunteer fire brigade standing around discussing something. I stopped to say hello and to see what was up.

'Where's the fire?' I asked.

'Oh, there's no fire, Brother,' said Nails who was one of their number. 'We're just doing a bit of an exercise in emergency training.'

He looked a bit sheepish as he went on to explain what they were doing.

'Young Peterson's granny lives out this way and she has a bit of a problem. So, I put it to the lads that we help out as best we can. She keeps a few chooks in her backyard, Brother, for the eggs, you know! Well, the eggs have been disappearing of late and she didn't know where they were going until today. She happened to be looking out of her kitchen window and what does she see but a bloomin' great goanna wander in, as calm as you like, and raiding the henhouse of her fresh-laid eggs.'

'I can see that something urgent would have to be done about that,' I said seriously whilst trying to hide my grin. 'So you blokes offered to come and hunt for the goanna and deal with it.'

'Well, you're nearly right, Brother,' said Nails without a hint of a smile. 'Truth is, the old lady took to the thing herself. She grabbed the yard broom and set about the animal. Well, the lizard took off, and who could blame it. It ran straight up this tree.'

He pointed to a youngish but tall tree out beside the street on the river bank side. I peered up into its ample foliage and could just make out the goanna clinging to one of the branches. It was a really big one about six feet from nose to the tip of its tail.

'So, one of you is going up to get it. Is that it?'

'Well, not exactly, Brother,' said Nails. 'It's a darn big lizard and as you know, you don't mess about with 'em if you value your eyes. No, when you arrived Bill here was about to climb part of the way up the main trunk and give it a bit of shake to see if we can dislodge the thing. We should then be able to throw a net over it and put it in the back of the truck and take it out of town well away from Granny's chooks.'

The enterprise looked as though it might be interesting, so I hung around to watch as Bill started up the tree. He was not exactly built for the job. He was a bit tubby and had short arms, but he did have bulk and, if he could get himself lodged in a conveniently placed fork some fifteen feet off the ground, then he might manage to set the rest of the tree aquiver. It was worth a try.

Up he went and eventually managed to wedge his not inconsiderable backside into the fork. He grasped both of the main branches which issued from the fork, one in each meaty hand, and shook them for all he was worth. And the tree, as if it knew what was needed, responded. It was one of those foreign imports that the shire council had been planting along the town streets, not as brittle as most of the local gum trees. In fact Bill had those branches whipping back and forth as if they were thrashing about in a tornado. But all to no avail. The goanna looked down and regarded us all with a baleful eye. However well Bill was wedged in the fork below him, the goanna was more securely anchored above. No matter how vigorously Bill shook the tree, the lizard remained firmly stuck where it was.

Eventually Bill simply ran out of puff. It was time for him to come down and time to try something else. But getting him down was easier said than done. What with his weight and all the bodily exertion, Bill's frame had sort of settled into the tree. It was like the sugar jar when you shake it about. What starts out as a full jar ends up only three-quarters full because the sugar has settled and become compacted. So it was with Bill. The more he shook himself about and the more the tree was contorted as it thrashed about, the more Bill's frame got wedged down into the fork. He tried to get out, but it was obvious that he was jammed solid.

The members of the volunteer fire brigade went into a huddle underneath the tree as they tried to decide what to do. Some were for getting hold of a long pole and pushing up on poor Bill's rump to try and free him. Bill seemed not to be in favour of this. Someone suggested getting out the chainsaw and cutting the tree down. One of the volunteers was a shire councillor and he wasn't at all keen on that idea. The planting of the foreign trees had been a controversial decision at the time and there were plenty of folk in the community who remembered it and still felt aggrieved. To cut one down now would be seen as a shocking waste of ratepayers' money. Someone else interjected that as night was fast drawing on, the temperature would be going down fast and everyone knew that lower temperatures meant that things shrank. If they simply left Bill where he was until midnight perhaps he would have shrunk enough to get himself out of the fork. Another suggested that Bill slip out of his overalls and that might enable him to get unstuck. But Bill wasn't really the right shape for a contortionist and he didn't really take to any of the suggestions.

Then Nails had an idea worth considering. He went to the truck and came back with a length of rope. His plan was to throw it over a branch higher up than where Bill was and get Bill to tie it round himself under the arms. That would give Bill something to pull himself up with and also enable those on the ground to help by pulling on the other end of the rope.

It wasn't easy to get the rope thrown over a suitable branch, but after several throws the feat was achieved. Bill duly tied it around himself and three hefty men pulled hard on the rope. The immediate effect was on the tree. It began to bend over and there was a chance that the branch would break before Bill was freed, but in the end Bill gave a sort of grunt and there was a loud tearing sound as he left the seat of his overalls impaled on a bit of twig that jutted out in the wrong place. The tree flung itself back to its upright position and Bill climbed down to the hoots of his colleagues.

In the general melee everyone seemed to have forgotten the goanna and why they were there in the first place. That was until the goanna made a move. It gave a sudden leap from the branch to which it had been clinging and onto the main trunk. Then it ran up as far as it could to the treetop where the twigs looked hardly able to bear its weight. Dusk was closing in by now and if anything was going to be done about the thing it had to be done fast. Nails was ahead of everyone else in this. He had another idea which for him was going some. You could fairly see steam coming out of his ears.

'That tree seems to me to be more bendy than you might think,' he mused. 'What if we get the rope tied as far up the main trunk as we can, then fix it to the towbar on the back of the truck and gradually inch the truck forward until the tree bends over enough to bring the goanna low enough for us to get the net over it? It would mean somebody will have to be on top of the truck and ready with the net when the goanna gets within range.

Either from desperation or resignation everyone thought this was a workable idea. The truck was duly backed into place. Bill was sent back up the tree with the end of the rope and he reached a creditable height before he stopped and tied the rope's end around the trunk, which was pretty thin at that height. As soon as he had scrambled down Nails gave the rope a turn around the towbar and then to my surprise gave the end of it to the nearest person, which happened to be me.

'It's no good tying it on tight, Brother,' he explained. 'That couple of turns should be enough to hold it, but it leaves us free to let go immediately if the tree starts to snap off. Just stand there and let it go quickly if you hear it creak too much or if there's a breaking sound.'

I did as I was instructed as the truck was put into gear and the clutch let out. It crawled forward and took up the slack on the rope. Then, true to the plan, the tree began to bend gracefully down. Nails, by this time, was on top of the truck with the net in his hands. I was alert and on my toes, acutely aware of every tension in the rope, every little sound and every little movement made by the goanna, which could hardly be seen by now as night gathered its darkness into deep, inky pools on the ground.

Looking back on it afterwards I really do think we might have done it successfully had not Bill decided at that moment that he'd had enough. He looked at his watch and said, 'Gracious me, look at the time. I promised the wife I'd be back before now. We're supposed to be going out and I've got to get ready.' He walked past and behind me and as he went he gave me a playful and hefty slap on the back with the cheery words, 'Hang on tight to that rope, Brother.'

He couldn't have done anything worse. The tree was almost bent double, the goanna was still clinging to it and almost at reachable level and Nails was tensed, ready for the throw. The thump Bill gave me knocked the wind out of me. Worse still, it took me completely by surprise. I still contend that anyone would have reacted the same in that situation. Inadvertently I let go of the rope.

That tree was not only pliable, it was downright whippy. It had more energy stored in it than any longbow of old. It sprang back with a loud *twang* and the goanna did what anything fitted snugly in a catapult would naturally do. The operator of any mediaeval siege engine would not have been more pleased than to observe what happened. To the onlooker it was as if a film was running in slow motion as six feet of flailing goanna left the tree abruptly and sailed in a beautiful arc through the dusky evening air. Nobody saw where it landed – it was now too dark for that – but all of us heard the thud and a sound as if the air was being suddenly forced out of a deflating football. In hindsight I know now that the lizard was propelled in the direction of where Chugger Jones lived.

Most of the volunteer fire brigade were friends of Ferret. I can fully understand their reluctance in paying him a visit. The man was a walking time bomb at the best of times. As for me, I thought it prudent to join their conspiracy of silence. I knew that Ferret's new found politeness to me would only last as long as he was in hospital and while there was advantage to be gained in getting into Nurse Arnold's good books. Once up and well again he would revert to the same old Ferret we all knew. I made a mental note to walk on the safe side. I'll be avoiding dark alleys for the foreseeable future and hoping against hope that nobody ever tells him who it was that let go of that rope.

CHAPTER 13

Return and Farewell

I was true to my word with Glen. The week after seeing him in hospital I drove him down to the big smoke and then into oncology for his medical tests. They admitted him for a couple of days for these. I took some time off, went to a concert and had a look at the tourist sights. Then we drove back up to Blaxford. Glen had been told that the results of his tests would be sent to his local doctor and to make an appointment to see him for a week's time. I offered to put him up at the rectory while he waited.

When it came the news was not good. The knock on his leg had triggered a rare type of cancer, one that was difficult to treat at best, usually impossible. Glen came back to the rectory looking as though he had been poleaxed. I sat him down, made him a coffee and watched as his shoulders began to convulse and great sobs racked his body. I found that there was nothing I could say. Words formed in my brain and then shrank into meaninglessness. We just sat there. Much later on in my ministry I came to realise that there is a ministry of simple presence. There are times when words fail, and if they didn't they were useless anyway. Simply being there with folk in their suffering has a value in itself. But I had not come to appreciate that at the time. Glen felt wretched and I felt awkward and superfluous and inept.

It was the first time in my life that I had lived so close to one who was facing a premature death. I had visited mainly older folk in my parish rounds who had not long to go. I'd prayed with them, listened to them as they shared memories with me, saw how they accepted death as a necessary part of life, even laughed with them. But then I had left them to those who had the daily care of them. This time I was the one who was the carer. If anything or anyone convinced me that I needed some help in how to minister to people in real suffering and need, then it was Glen.

If only Brother Edwin were still around, I thought. He'd have something to say to Glen. He could bring his own understanding into the situation. After all, he had the experience of having a tumour and living through the hopelessness of it all.

There was no hospice care for hundreds of miles and what to do was a pressing and practical problem. The only family Glen had when I had arrived at Blaxford was his old Granny and she had since died. There was simply nobody left to look after him.

We both went to see the doc to find out what we could manage to do to care for Glen in his remaining days. He told us that it was likely to be days rather than months. The cancer had got a good hold and secondaries were evident all over the place. Glen had spent all of his life out in the bush and did not want to be holed up in the local hospital all of the time. Between us we worked out that Glen would stay with me for a while and that Nurse Margaret Arnold would call in each day and dress his thigh, for the tumour there had broken out into a kind of raw ulcer that needed daily dressing. Margaret had apparently worked in the past on the cancer ward of a city hospital. What strings the doc pulled with the matron of the hospital to get one of her nurses released each day to do this I don't know, but he managed it and she was a real godsend. No one else could have cheered Glen up as she did. She was only a few years older than Glen and somehow she managed to combine a fine motherly care for her patient with a sparkling vibrancy of life which seemed to pass right into those around her. The place lit up when she came through the door and Glen responded to it. She had her own very real ministry of presence.

There were, of course, times when I still had to be away for a day or two at a time. The parish still made its normal demands. At such time Glen would spend a day or two in the hospital, but he was always glad to get out of the place.

One night on impulse I rang Brother Edwin up in the Territory. I had let him know about Glen as soon as he got the results of his tests, for Edwin it was who had befriended Glen originally and brought him to a living faith and Edwin it was who had become a real father figure for him.

'I'm coming down,' he said.

'It's a long way. How will you manage it?'

'Well, turns out I've been asked by the local flying club if I can ferry an old Cessna down to Melbourne and then bring a new one back. They've decided to upgrade two of their aircraft, so there'll be two trips out of it, one now and another maybe later this year or maybe next. What's more, there's no rush. I can fly in to Blaxford and spend a few days and then do the same again on the way back.'

'Marvellous,' I said and it was heartfelt. 'When shall I expect you?'

'Day after tomorrow,' he said.

I came off the phone feeling a relief that was beyond words to tell.

I met Edwin at the airstrip two days later. As we drove back into town he quizzed me about Glen and I brought him up to date as best I could.

'He's going downhill fast,' I said. 'He'll be glad to see you. Thinks the sun shines out of you.'

'Have you anointed him?' he asked.

'Yes, did so right at the start, but it doesn't seem to have made any difference.'

'There's always a difference,' said Edwin. 'Only sometimes the difference is not what we think should happen.'

I couldn't argue with that. Edwin had been on the receiving end and knew for certain what God had done for him. No one could deny him his own experience. I mused aloud on that bit of New Testament scripture from James' letter. 'Is any among you sick? Let him call for the elders of the church and let them pray over him, anointing him with oil in the name of the Lord; and the prayer of faith will save the sick man, and the Lord will raise him up.'

'Beats me,' I said, 'why God seems to physically heal some folk and not others when we do that.'

'You think I haven't asked myself the same question,' said Edwin with feeling. Why me and not the next bloke?'

'And what conclusion have you reached?' I asked with interest.

'It's God's world and He can do what He likes with it. As his priest I'm called to obey and leave the rest to Him.'

'And where does that leave me with Glen? He is certainly not getting better but rapidly worse physically. How do I cope with that?'

'Stop being so hard on yourself,' said Edwin as we turned into the rectory street. 'Listen, I've seen hardened men, bitter at the sickness that life had thrown at them. I've anointed them and prayed over them and seen no physical healing but something else given instead, and that was a peace and an acceptance, and seen them die gracefully. That's a kind of healing too, you know.'

We pulled up and got out of the car. I carried Edwin's bag indoors while he went off to the garden at the side where we could see Glen sitting in the sun.

After that it was a lot easier for the next five days which is how long Edwin could stay. He was marvellous with Glen, talked to him like the father in God that he truly was, and seemed to pick up accurately on his every mood. What's more he was able to do what for the life of me I could not do. He began to talk to him about dying. It had to be done and I was failing Glen in my own inability. Young though I was I had already seen the consequences of not doing so. There are doctors and relatives who conspire together when someone is known to be dying. They say things such as, 'Don't let him know. Why give him extra things to worry about when he's so ill?' They think they are performing some Christian act of charity. It never works that way. The sick person almost invariably knows within himself that he is sick unto death and relatives are left with a hefty serving of guilt because their relationship has ended in deceit and lies.

After the first and natural shock of it all Glen was magnificent.

'Good job I've got no relatives, no wife and kids to leave without a breadwinner, eh, Brother? No one to have the heart torn in anguish,' he said to me.

'There is that,' I said carefully, 'but you know there's privilege in being concerned about those we love.'

'Yeah, I pick a bit of that up from Brother Edwin, but you know what I mean.'

I wondered whether I would be so sanguine in his situation. I was still floundering and determined to look around for further help in my ministry when my brotherhood days were up. I'd done four and a half years out of my promised five now and needed some different experience.

There was one other thing which Brother Edwin took in hand and which had simply not crossed my mind. He talked to Glen about making a will.

'I don't have all that much to leave,' was Glen's response.

'You'll probably be surprised when you add it up,' said Edwin.

'Yeah, there's me place with the shed on it for all me fencing stuff, and me ute and the tinnie I use for fishing in the river. That's about it. Oh, and I've still got me mum's engagement ring. She gave it to me before she died. I think she thought I might find a use for it someday.' He gave a half smile. 'Won't be needing that now.'

'It's best to have it down in black and white,' said Edwin. 'Saves an awful lot of arguing about things afterwards. I'll get John Sinclair the solicitor to come in and set it out straight for you.'

Meanwhile the folk in the parish rose to something like saintly status in the way they cared about Glen. There was a regular procession of kindly folk bearing casseroles and inquiring whether there was anything they could do, anything that Glen wanted. Even diminutive little Miss Ridley offered to take Glen into her own home if it would help.

I felt humbled as I received her kind and self-sacrificing offer. I knew her circumstances and taking anyone in would be a huge step for her and a very sick one an almost insurmountable barrier. Besides which I knew that she had, what was for her, a large and demanding project on hand. She was the one person in town whose life was devoted to music. For years she had been the one to whom parents sent their children for music lessons. She taught them piano and, amazingly, the flute as well. She sometimes got together a quartet of budding musical hopefuls in an effort to keep them up to the mark in the basics at least. Now she had had a request to get them together to play at a wedding. It would take all her application and tenacity to do it. And this was not any old wedding but that of a lifelong friend.

The new found friendship between Larry Williams and Ada Pearce had sailed along nicely in a way that astounded everyone who knew them. Larry himself, who at first had seemed to come along to church on Sundays just to please Ada, had moved ahead in leaps and bounds. His former antagonism towards the Christian church and anyone who had any claim to faith in God had now disappeared. Once having made the move towards a faith in Jesus it seemed that some kind of great gulf had been bridged and he now found that life on the other side was not what he had once feared it might be. He was the classic case of a man touched and called by God who had been in rebellion against that call all of his life. Deep down he had known the pull of the kingdom of heaven but was too afraid to commit himself. Once his reservation had been breached he now discovered that it was the most natural thing in the world to accept the call that had long been insistently whispered inside him. Ada had been the catalyst that released him.

I discovered all this as I prepared him for confirmation. Along with his now discovered faith had come a remarkable change in the outward man. His step became more assured, his smile more readily given and his personal appearance more spruce. He had even begun to tidy up the land surrounding his house. No doubt some of this change was not so much an act of faith but a desire to please Ada, but the fact remained that it was now acknowledged with some wonder around the town that Larry was a nicer bloke than he had ever been.

It had been at least two years since the episode with the pig. Larry's daughter Noeline and her husband Barry Dolan were now the parents of a healthy little boy and had settled well out of town on a place along the Wirruna Road next door to that of Alan Hasket from whom Brother Edwin had bought the Tiger Moth. Noeline was now expecting again and the thought of it fair made Larry burst with pride.

Ada and Larry had become such a common sight doing things together that nobody gave it a second thought any more. A couple of months before, they had come to see me, both of them remarkably nervous and shy, and asked if I would marry them. Naturally I was delighted to do it. They both intimated to me privately that this was an act of self-sacrifice. Ada explained that Larry really needed a woman to look after him and Larry had bluffly told me that Ada needed someone who could do the practical things around the place.

'Things like mending fences and the like, to keep pigs out,' I said with a grin.

'Something like that,' he said without taking offence. 'And looking after all those fruit trees she's got,' he added.

It was clear that there was much more to their desire for marriage than these simple practical things. They both knew that they wanted and needed 'that mutual help and comfort that the one ought to have for the other', of which the marriage service spoke. No one who knew them would want to deny them the escape from the loneliness that both had known since the deaths of their respective former spouses.

The wedding date was set for an early September Saturday. It was to take place out of town at the little bush church on Emmy Blade's place. Ada had been born in the house long before the Blades bought it. It was where she had spent a great deal of her growing up years. In the intervening time Ada and Emmy had become close friends and it was part of Emmy's generosity, and also that of her late sister Alice, that Ada had often been invited out to see how the old place was faring and what was new in the garden. It was the obvious choice of place for the wedding. Emmy got more carried away by the prospect than even Ada and Larry themselves and started to make preparations for a grand event.

Brother Edwin took off for Melbourne to pick up the new Cessna. He said he'd be back in about three days, depending on how long the inevitable paperwork took. And the weather would play its part too.

Glen was visibly fading. His spirit was good, but his poor body was closing down on him. I spent as much time with him as I could. Things were easier now that Brother Edwin and he had talked so openly about his dying. That had released the embarrassed tension between us and I sat in his presence, comfortable with the silence and aware that Glen had found 'that peace which passes all human understanding'. He had put his whole trust in a God who would receive him into eternal glory and he was content with that. More than that, he drew great strength from it. The amazing discovery for me was that he passed that strength on to me. I had thought that it was up to me to give everything to the sick and dying. I now realised that this was a mistaken piece of arrogance on my part and that I was receiving far more than I was able to give out.

The sudden move from one set of individuals and into the different emotional needs of another is part and parcel of a parish priest's life. It kept me on my toes, but it was also emotionally wearing. I had an imminent wedding on my hands and also a dying man which spoke of an imminent funeral. I got in touch with Nails and told him about Glen's rapidly deteriorating condition. Nails would want to be as prepared as he could be for the event when it came. He was a compassionate man and was quick to tell me that since Glen had no close living relatives then there would be no charge from him for the funeral. I thanked him warmly. How we were going to pay for Glen's funeral was a thing that had been worrying me. There was one further complication.

Glen had spent all his life in the bush. His folks had had a place out near to where Emmy Blades lived. His father and mother were buried in the little local cemetery under the trees where the magpies carolled to the dawn. It was just down the road from the bush church where Ada and Larry's wedding was to take place so soon now.

'Don't bury me in town,' Glen had whispered to Brother Edwin and I one evening as we both sat beside him. 'Can you put me down right next to where Mum and Dad lie? It's a peaceful place,' he added, then, 'It'll be good to know you'll both be there to wing me on me way.'

We had agreed to do what he asked and we let him talk on about his short life and how grateful he was to have spent it where he did. There was not a trace of bitterness about his few years. He seemed to radiate thankfulness for all the little things that all take for granted, the necessary things of living. There were no tears from him, but I had to leave the room and wept bucketsful.

We were soon into the final week before the wedding. On the Wednesday I gathered the main participants in the church in Blaxford. There were papers to sign, statutory declarations to be made, the usual legal stuff that had to be done before any marriage. The prospective bride and groom, best man and bridesmaid needed to be assembled and walked through the wedding service so that they all knew where to stand and when to answer on the day itself. I was to be the celebrant at the actual wedding, but Brother Edwin, who had flown in again that day with the new Cessna, was rather startled to be asked by Ada if he would give her away. He was clearly moved by being asked and pleased as punch, but he went all coy about it when I later ribbed him about being a father figure to Ada, for all her years.

Glen died peacefully on the Thursday morning. He slipped quietly into the Lord's kingdom with an almost satisfied smile playing on his lips. As it happened there were three of us present at his bedside – Margaret Arnold, Brother Edwin and myself. Instinctively we bowed our heads and Brother Edwin gave quiet voice to God on behalf of us all as he commended him into the Lord's keeping.

Glen's death on the Thursday gave us all a bit of a problem. I had Sunday services to do and then I was due to leave on the Monday to speak at the diocesan youth camp. The bishop had asked me to do this, months ago, and there was no moving it. Brother Edwin had to leave on Monday as well to deliver the new Cessna. The funeral would have to be held on the Saturday, the same day as Ada and Larry's wedding and at the same church. I had a frantic round of phone calls to make. In the end we fixed the funeral for nine o'clock on Saturday morning and the wedding was to be at four in the afternoon.

The church was to be decorated with flowers on Friday and Ada and Larry were only too pleased to share their floral arrangements with Glen for his funeral. They intended to be at the funeral in any case as they had known Glen as he grew up. Miss Ridley was okay for playing the harmonium. Two musical events on the same day was not going to worry her, she said. The real problem was going to be with the food. People in the bush lingered and chatted at the end of every funeral and there was always a mountain of food for them to chew on as they did it. The parish ladies had been standing ready for a couple of weeks to do the catering for Glen's funeral. They were also involved with the wedding catering. To do both on the one day was asking a bit much. Ada was the one who normally took charge for funerals and the like, but she was the one getting married. I put the problem to Emmy and she took over, the light of purpose bright in her eyes.

'It doesn't look as though it's going to be too hot on Saturday,' she said. 'I'll get some of our fellows to mow that bit of grass alongside the church and to take the truck down with some trestle tables and a portable generator. We can manage a picnic lunch after the burial is over. And if you, Brother, can get in touch with Wilma at the telephone exchange and ask her to pass a message along all the party lines asking folk to please bring their own chairs, that would be helpful.'

As expected, Saturday dawned cool and clear. Edwin and I were silent as we followed Nails' old hearse out to the church. Nails had drummed up six pallbearers from his mates in the volunteer fire brigade and taken all round they had all scrubbed up pretty well for the occasion.

Brother Edwin conducted the simple funeral. The congregation would have surprised Glen. There was a fairly large gathering which included many property owners whose fences Glen had constructed and mended. Edwin spoke movingly about a young man on whom he had kept a fatherly eye.

After the service in the church we all followed the hearse the three or four miles down the road to the local cemetery. It was small; a piece of cleared ground hacked out of the surrounding bushland. There, tucked in at the far end, next to Glen's parents' resting place, was a newly dug grave. Little dots of mica in the pile of earth beside it glinted in the sun. A row of honest shovels stood beyond it. We lowered the coffin into the grave while Brother Edwin read the prayers of committal. When all was decently done, the men who were there took off their jackets and, as was their custom, piled the good earth back on top of the coffin. It was when they had completed this and stood aside, slowly arching backwards to ease their lumbar muscles, that the trumpet notes rang out. It was electrifying. Miss Ridley stood out on the tree line and played a slow lament, the notes dropping into the silence like shards of crystal. Into my mind came the words that we had heard in the funeral service: 'We shall all be changed ... at the last trump etc.'

Who would have thought of diffident little Miss Ridley as the angel with the trumpet of judgement. That such a small creature, who looked as if a puff of wind would blow her over, could play the trumpet beggared belief. It was an ending and a beautiful one at that.

As the notes died away the magpies took up the challenge and were still carolling away when we left. Then it was time to return to the tables set out beside the church for cups of tea and sandwiches to fortify us before the second event of the day.

When we got there I noticed with some surprise that Ada had on her apron and was directing operations as the church ladies saw to the provision of the food. To my quizzical look she said, 'The wedding's not for ages yet. I can slip into Emmy's house and get changed after we've finished here. So can Larry.'

Larry was standing at a far table, his sleeves rolled up and doing some washing up of those dishes and cups which had been used by folk who had got there earlier than us.

'Miss Ridley is full of surprises,' I said to the Brother Edwin.

He nodded. 'In all the time I've known her I've never heard her play that trumpet before, although,' he added, 'I think I remember someone telling me that she used to play when she was young.'

Morning soon turned to afternoon and the ladies, having finished at the tables beside the church, drifted over to Emmy's house where all was bustle and action in preparation for the wedding. A large awning had been erected on the front lawn and the men were dragooned into carrying the trestle tables from the church and setting them up under the awning's shade. Many of those who had been at Glen's funeral stayed for the wedding and others were arriving by the carload.

I went into the church to get ready for the wedding which I was to take. I had half an hour's blessed silence in which to sit and get composed after we had buried young Glen. It was an odd interlude and not easy changing gear mentally and spiritually on the journey from one significant event to the other.

First to arrive was Miss Ridley and her quartet of budding musicians. They soon set up their music stands at the front and off to the side. Next came Larry with his best man. I had never seen Larry look so scrubbed. He seemed to have the patina of old polished wood. His best man was Barry Dolan, his son-in-law. He came in with Noeline who was so advanced in her pregnancy that she was glad to sit down straight away.

Soon the little church was packed to capacity and there was a fair overspill outside the back door as well. It was a really nice country wedding. Ada came in on Brother Edwin's arm and Brother Edwin was the one who was blushing. Miss Ridley's music group played without too many missed notes and everything went without a hitch. Soon the newlyweds were walking down the aisle on their way out of church and Miss Ridley was raising the roof with Jeremiah Clarke's 'Trumpet Voluntary'.

It was when we were all safely outside that the drama began. Noeline suddenly went into labour. Amazingly Miss Ridley took charge. She came out of the church and like a field marshall overlooking a battle she took in the situation and began deploying the troops.

'Emmy, can we lie this girl down in one of your spare rooms? And can you find us a waterproof sheet, please?

It was typical of Emmy that she had a waterproof sheet. It was even more typical of her that she knew exactly where to find it in a crisis.

'And Nurse, I shall need your help,' continued Miss

Ridley as she turned to Margaret Arnold who had been at Glen's funeral and stayed on for the wedding. 'Sharp scissors and sterilise them in boiling water,' she barked.

There was no hint of the slightly fussy and self-deprecating Miss Ridley that we had got to know. Gone was all scattiness, diffidence and loss of memory as she strode purposefully into the house in the wake of those who had escorted Noeline to Emmy's spare room. I was later to find out that forty years ago she had been the district midwife. Some of the older folk obviously remembered and there were some rueful grins as they were taken back in time to when Miss Ridley had bossed them about at the birth of their own children.

This little bit of drama left the wedding guests milling around but provided them with plenty to chatter about. Larry and the expectant father paced up and down, the classic picture of prenatal angst. Ada took Larry's arm and coaxed him into position for some wedding photographs and that inevitable part of the proceedings nicely covered the forty minutes of waiting time until a thin wailing sound told us all that somebody new was alive here on Earth. Emmy came out of the house with the news, 'It's a girl.'

Brother Edwin had been asked to be the MC at the wedding feast. It took him some time to be heard over the general excited hubbub, but eventually folk quietened down and heard his call for them to be seated at the tables. Ada and Larry led a procession and sat down at the top table and the festivities began. There was no doubt that the ladies had surpassed themselves this time as prodigious amounts of their fine food and drink sank without trace like a ship in a storm.

It was just before the speeches were due that Emmy appeared with a white bundle in her arms all wrapped up in a fine lace shawl (and where had she dug that up from?). She marched up the aisle between the flanking tables and handed the bundle over to a beaming Larry.

'Here's a little wedding present for you, Grandad,' she said and everyone naturally cheered and stamped their feet.

'At least it isn't a pig this time!' someone called out which made Ada blush.

All in all it was a day to remember.

Later in the evening cool as we sat outside the rectory I mused aloud. 'What a turn-up for the books Miss Ridley proved to be.' And then, after a pause, 'Birth, marriage and death. It's the stuff of life, isn't it?'

'The stuff which we as priests are called upon to share in with people,' said Edwin. 'I never lose my sense of wonder at it all, nor the sense of privilege at being there.'

'But, thank heavens, not usually all in the one day,' I said, laughing. 'Mind you, there's one thing that my ministry with Glen and many others here has taught me and that is that I don't know half I as much as I thought I did. I came here fresh from college and found that I was suddenly the expert to these folk. People here have come to me for advice about their lives, the education of their children and all sorts of vital things. I wouldn't let a trainee dentist near my teeth, but these folk have entrusted me with their lives.'

'So, what are you going to do about it?' asked Brother Edwin.

'I've found out about a two year course in pastoral care that the chaplaincy department of a major Melbourne hospital is running. I've applied to do that when I leave here and my five year brotherhood time is over. I'm hoping that will help me to talk more helpfully to people like Glen.'

On the Monday morning both Edwin and I were up very early. We both had hours of travelling ahead of us. Before I left I took Edwin out to the airfield. There was the new club Cessna gleaming in the morning light. He was in for a less bumpy ride than I was. He stowed his gear and was about to climb aboard when he stopped and said, 'I may as well let you know now before the solicitor rings you. Glen left his place to his cousin, the one who lost everything when the house burned down last year. He left his ute to me, but I can't use it, so I'm leaving it here for the use of the parish. Margaret Arnold gets his mother's engagement ring, and he left his tinnie to you.'

'A boat,' I said. 'What on earth am I going to do with a boat?'

'I'm sure it'll turn out useful for something,' he said over his shoulder as he climbed into the plane.

CHAPTER 14

Homesick

There was no doubt about it. After the death of young Glen and Brother Edwin's departure I was feeling pretty low. I had ministered to many families in grief at the death of a loved one, but somehow this was different. Most of the folk I had buried had been those who had died full of years and the grief of their families was tempered by the knowledge that they had died at a good old age. The death of younger folk was a different matter and Glen's death hit me hard.

'What you need is a decent break,' I was told by Margaret Arnold one day whilst I was visiting at the hospital.

'How long is it since you had a holiday?' she continued. 'I've seen you always running hither and yon to deal with some person or other. Come to think of it, when did you last have a day off? The Good Lord created heaven and earth in six days and rested on the seventh. Who are you to go one better?'

'She's right, Brother,' said Peter Limson who was delivering prescriptions to the hospital and had joined us in the corridor. 'Look, Glen left you his aluminium boat and outboard. Why don't you take a couple of weeks and head off to the coast? Do some fishing, forget all about the parish and relax.'

That gave me something to think about as I proceeded down the corridor and into a room where lay Mrs Ezekiel. She was in for a couple of days to have some small surgery done on an ingrowing toenail. I knew that this could be painful, so we prayed for an absence of pain and a rapid and full recovery.

'Thank you, Brother,' she said, 'but I do hope that this procedure won't dampen down that toe's usefulness. It's my right big toe and, laugh if you like, but that one always tells me when it's going to rain.'

'Must be very useful, having your own portable barometer with you wherever you go.'

'Oh, it doesn't work like that, Brother,' she said. 'It only works here. I was born here and have always lived here. I suppose it has got used to this particular geographic spot.'

I went on my way smiling at the quirks of nature which seem to be in us. I also got on the phone as soon as I could and talked to Miss Vercoe. She was the local fishing expert and I wanted to know about the nice little place down on the coast that she always went to for her holiday. If I was going to take a break soon I needed to organise things straightaway.

It took a few days, but eventually I got away. I hitched the boat trailer to the car and drove away from it all for two weeks. Between them Margaret Arnold and Peter Limson had managed to make a wise decision for me. Away from the parish things took on a different perspective and I was able to relax. It was an opportunity for me to test out Glen's boat and to get used to handling it. I used it to do a little fishing and also to meander up and down some coastal lagoons where I could watch and photograph some of the bird life there. Being out in the fresh salt breezes gave me a healthy appetite and cleared my head which, I guess, is what a holiday ought to do.

When I returned I was surprised to see frenetic activity on the final approaches to the town. No matter from what direction you approached Blaxford there was always a bit of an incline in the road. Over the years the town had suffered many floods and long ago had been surrounded by levee banks. Trees and shrubs had grown to cover the sides of the banks and eventually they blended into the landscape. What we all experienced as we drove in was a long and gradual incline and then another long and gradual decline, a sort of massive speed hump. Other than where the railway cut through, the whole place sat inside a veritable wall of earth. Now as I came into town I could see tractors and bulldozers working on the levee, putting the banks in order and piling fresh earth on the top.

'What's going on?' I asked Peter Limson as soon as I saw him.

'Flood's coming,' he said.

There was no sign of rain even, yet alone a flood. The sky was blue, not a cloud in evidence.

'How do you know?' I asked.

'Well, for one thing, Mrs Ezekiel's toe is throbbing with pain. And she's never been known to be wrong.'

'Surely you're kidding me,' I said with some conviction until I saw the expression on his face.

When I got home the weather forecast confirmed the prognostications of Mrs Ezekiel's toe. A great weather system had moved in from the sea and reached far inland. So far it was situated way up north, but even I knew what that meant. Huge dumps of rain meant full rivers and, even if the weather did not move south, the water would. In a few weeks we could expect a flush to come down the river and from the forecasts there would be huge volumes of water, enough to spread out and flood the surrounding plains and more.

I could understand the urgency as everyone tried to be ready for the worst that nature could throw at us. But all of the weather systems were hundreds of miles away from us. Why was Mrs Ezekiel's toe sending out its warning? She had told me that it only operated locally.

The sky continued cloudless for days as if to defy Mrs Ezekiel. I knew from experience that defying Mrs Ezekiel was a risky thing to do. Even the weather would surely rue the day it went against her.

Then suddenly it all changed. We awoke one day to just a few wisps of clouds in the sky. The wind changed direction and by midday great piles of clouds were multiplying like huge galleons driven before the wind with all sails set. There must have been thousands of tons of water in them and there could be no doubt that much of it was going to fall on us.

Mrs Ezekiel's toe was right. Rolls of thunder made the windows rattle. Lightning flash photographed everything in its violet light. Then came the rain, torrents of it. The drought-cracked earth almost sighed with pleasure as it received the needed moisture. Amazingly, within minutes, frogs were everywhere. From old dead logs, from under stacks of wood, from inside downpipes they emerged, thin from long dehydration. But soon they grew fat as they sponged up the blessed water. All day and all night the air was filled with their various calls, everything from a deep, resonant thump like the sound of an empty drum being struck, to croaks and whistles and a hundred variations.

After three days it stopped. The town steamed in the aftermath. People breathed deeply, filling their lungs with air washed clean from the usual, ever-present hanging dust. Gardens began to bloom and all looked well.

But there was inevitably one result that wasn't so good. The river came down eventually, full and insistent with all that water gathered from its long journey south. Since the land around us was now already soaked from our own local rain it had no capacity to soak up any of the fresh water. The river rose and rose and soon spilled over and spread far and wide as it flooded the land for further than the eye could see.

Out on the stations most folk were as ready as they could be. Many of the flood-prone homesteads already had their own levee banks in place. Graziers had moved their stock to any patch of higher ground that was available. Extra food had been ordered in to enable families to sit out the time when roads were inevitably cut by the muddy water. Nonetheless there was a steady stream of calls coming over the two-way radio at the emergency centre and voluntary workers were kept busy.

Nails came round to see me. He was not only the fire

brigade captain, he was also the co-ordinator for emergencies. He wanted the church hall as a sleeping centre for anyone who needed it. He also wanted me and my boat.

'Come with me, Brother.' The invitation brooked no refusal. 'Let's hitch up your boat and trailer and I'll tell you where we're going on the way.'

The aluminium boat was soon hooked up to the car and a can of spare petrol went in with it for the outboard. As we headed for the boat ramp that ended near the top of the levee on the river side Nails told me what was on his mind.

'I'm a bit worried about the Farrs. They live on that old place down the river. It's been there since the first settlers. Its earthworks kept out even the big flood in the 1890s. Bill and Louise wouldn't leave earlier because they've seen off every flood since they've been there, but I reckon this one's the biggest ever and they could be in trouble.'

I knew the Farrs. They were in their early eighties now and only came into town about once a month. Bill was an upright man in every way, decent, honest and he still stood tall in his soldierly way. When the First World War broke out he was one who went to Britain and enlisted in the British army. He went in as an officer trainee, survived the war and stayed a few extra years in the army after it. He rose to the rank of brigadier.

At the war's end he met and married Louise in Britain who came from a well-heeled family and was, it was said, the niece of a duke. She had that aristocratic way of looking at you as if she was sizing up horseflesh at a yearling sale. She did not suffer fools gladly and could be cutting when she spoke. She was no harridan, but as she got older she seemed to get more and more impatient with people and could be quite sharp with them at times.

When she came to Australia as a new bride she brought some of the family valuables with her. She especially prized some very nice and very rare pieces of Delftware that had somehow survived the rigours of transport and then a family of several children. They were a tangible link with her original ancestral home and perhaps that was why she valued them so much.

Nails and I soon launched the little boat and he sat amidships whilst I started the outboard and steered out into the wide brown flood. I was glad I had Nails with me. Steering a course downriver in normal times was bad enough, but now there were no guides as to where the banks were, or even as to which direction we were heading. Nails was amazing. He was able to pick out the line of riverside trees and eventually a collection of roofs came into view which was the Farr's homestead and sheds. And Nails had been right in his concern about this particular flood. Water was spilling over the levee banks of the homestead and silently filling up the last few inches of the space inside.

We managed to get the boat over the banks. On the top there wasn't much depth of water, but Nails got out and waded and pushed until we were over the bank. He carried a load of glutinous mud on his feet as he got back into the boat and we were soon floating alongside the house walls. We called out to see whether the Farrs were still inside and got a hefty answer from Bill. I steered the boat to the back door and managed to pull open the screen door, but the inner door was shut and the handle was well under water.

Nails came to the rescue. That longer right arm of his had its uses. He reached down and found the handle and gave it a turn. Slowly I nudged the boat forward and the door gradually opened, heavy against the press of the water. Inside, on two chairs which had been placed on top of the kitchen table, sat Bill and Louise. The floodwater was nearly up to their knees. All around them, floating on the water, swirled various items of household furniture and effects. Saddest to see were the books, limp and falling apart.

It took a bit of careful handling, but eventually we got the old couple into the boat and edged our way out of the door. As we went some of the flotsam tried to follow. We pushed most of it back into the room hoping that it could be recovered later, but there was one blue and white jug that refused to go. It bobbed away every time we lunged towards it. Louise recognised it as a piece of her precious Delft and told me in no uncertain terms what she thought of my efforts to try and retrieve it. That darned jug had a mind of its own. No matter what we did it just wanted to get out into the swirling flood.

Seeing my chance I edged the boat obliquely into the doorway, intending to trap it between the boat and the door itself. I got it trapped all right, but as Nails leaned to catch it I must have given the outboard just a bit too much throttle. Wedged now between door and boat the jug broke clean in half with an audible crack and the two pieces sank beneath the rich brown water.

We got the boat successfully over the shallow water on top of the house levee bank and then we puttered uneventfully back to Blaxford where we were able to deliver

Bill and Louise safely into the hands and home of Bill's sister-in-law.

'I really think we could have died from the cold and the wet, let alone being drowned.' Bill was almost in tears as he expressed his heartfelt thanks to us.

'Even if it was so clumsily done.' Louise was looking at me as she spoke, and she couldn't resist adding, 'That jug was original Delftware from the eighteenth century.'

'Don't take too much notice, Brother,' said Nails to me as we drove back to the rectory. 'She's upset and will soon forget.'

I wasn't so sure. But I soon had other things on my mind. I hadn't long been back from the whole incident with the Farrs when the phone rang. It was Mildred Turner telling me she had flood trouble. Mildred was a widow who lived in town, so I was surprised that she was apparently having trouble with water inundation. As far as I knew the levee banks had held and the water outside was at last going slowly down.

I got into the car and drove round to Mildred's house, but not before putting a shovel into the boot as well as a pair of gumboots. Something told me I might need them.

Mildred was a bit of a drama queen. There was always something happening to her that required involving the neighbours and her friends. She was getting on a bit in years and as thin as a wand. Her fingers had taken on the look of the underlying bones; indeed her hands looked like an X-ray of themselves. Her wedding ring now hung obliquely and loose like an overly large quoit on its peg.

Some months before, she had decided to make her

declining years a bit more comfortable, so she installed an inside loo with a septic tank in the back garden. At first she was very proud of this fine new addition and invited everyone she talked to into her house to see it and admire the overhead cistern and its brass chain with the porcelain handle, even to sit and test out the seat.

Her opinion of it all changed dramatically one day when she was cleaning the new facility. While vigorously using the toilet brush she lost her wedding ring. It slipped off her emaciated finger and lay gleaming at the bottom of the toilet bowl, inviting immediate recovery. But Mildred, unnerved by the fact that something she had worn for over forty years had made its bid for freedom, went to straighten up and stumbled in the process. She put out a hand to steady herself and inadvertently pulled on the chain. The cistern emptied in a great rush and when she looked down again the ring was gone. The plumber was called and he spent several hours digging up and disconnecting pipes, but the ring could not be found.

When I got to Mildred's house she wasted no time in showing me the source of the problem. The council had recently done some roadworks behind her house. In the course of this they had created a slight embankment, no more than a foot high, but it was enough to form a wall that held back rainwater which was draining from several house blocks around. The water had now broken out and was pouring across Mildred's back garden and under her back door. That, however, was the least of her worries.

She took me inside and showed me to her new loo. It was everyone's worst nightmare. Muddy water was welling up through the toilet bowl and spilling out over the floor. Worse still, it brought with it the offerings of past days, things which Mildred never hoped to see again. The stench was awful.

I went outside and grabbed the shovel. What had happened was that the septic system had been put in while the ground was bone dry. As soon as the earth got soaked it expanded and pushed the septic tank up and out of line. The whole thing had cracked open. Water was pouring into the septic tank through the cracks and out again into the pipework. The whole system was working in reverse.

I got to work with the shovel and diverted the main flow away from the back of the house and down the side driveway. This was remarkably effective and it didn't take long for the flow through the loo to abate. I was glad I'd brought my gumboots as I set to work to clean up the stinking mess all over the floor. I sloshed in and out of the house dumping several bucket loads of mud and filth onto Mildred's garden. Then it was time for the hose and after that much wiping and drying with some old towels that Mildred dug out of a cupboard.

The job was finally done and I straightened up, glad to get it behind me. You'd have thought I was the Archangel Gabriel the way that Mildred went on. But that was only the beginning of her praises.

I went into the loo and took a last look to make sure all was well. In the loo the remaining water was the colour of weak tea. Something small was there too. I grabbed the loo brush and snared the object against the side and carefully pulled it upwards. It was a ring, Mildred's lost wedding ring. It must have been snagged on some irregularity within the S-bend and then dislodged and washed back by the reverse flow, a small miracle in Mildred's later life. She gave a whoop of delight and kissed me on a muddy cheek. Once more, words from the Book of Job came into my mind. 'The Lord gave and the Lord hath taken away'. Only in this case the sentiment was reversed: 'The loo hath taken away and now hath given back'.

Next Sunday, after church, Mildred was all smiles and happiness. Nothing could contain her joy as she moved from person to person showing them her recovered wedding ring. It did seem to have an extra gleam as it sat lopsidedly on her skinny finger. She was indefatigable in telling everyone how marvellous Brother Mark had been and, if it hadn't been for him, she wouldn't have got her ring back. She even insisted on kissing me on the cheek again. I blushed with embarrassment and not a little pleasure.

The pleasure was short-lived. Out of the church came Louise and she was telling everyone in a loud voice how clumsy Brother Mark had been and, if it hadn't have been for him she would still have her precious Delft jug. I met her in the street the next day and once again she gave me a right roasting about it.

'Don't think I'm not grateful for being rescued from the flood, Brother,' she said as she stopped me in my tracks, 'but there is such a thing as respect for people's property as well, you know. I consider that you were far too careless. I'll never be able to replace that jug.'

The floodwaters took the best part of ten days to go

down. There was a massive amount of work to be done in the clean-up that followed. The shire workmen cleared the roads and hosed off the mud, the PMG department got teams out and restrung various telephone lines where flood loosened poles had weakened and tilted sideways. Life soon got back to normal.

As soon as the road was open I felt duty bound to drive down the river road to visit the Farrs, who had returned to their property. I knew there would be plenty to clean up there and wanted to help if I could. Truth to tell I felt a bit guilty about that Delft jug and wanted to make amends in some small way.

When I got there I found that the place was humming with activity. Various neighbours had come over and the clean-up was well under way. Piles of furniture were out on the lawn gently steaming dry in the sun. Floors were being hosed clean of mud. Walls were being washed down. I rolled up my sleeves and got stuck into the action.

Late in the afternoon everyone downed tools and took a break for a cuppa. As Louise poured me a cup she apologised for the crockery.

'Sorry about the mismatched cups and saucers. I'm afraid we're a bit limited in the crockery, Brother. Most of the valuables haven't yet been washed.' She looked meaningfully at the Delft pieces on a side table and I knew she hadn't yet forgiven me.

Later, Bill found me working away from all the others in a quiet corner.

'Don't be too upset about that jug, Brother. It's had a hairline crack almost right round it for years and we've all thought it couldn't last in one piece for much longer. It's a miracle it didn't leak. It just went on and on.'

'Like a homesick heart,' I added as gently as I could.

CHAPTER 15

White Spirit

I had been tying off the ends of various things in preparation for my departure. Brother Edwin would be back in a month's time on his way back to Melbourne to pick up the second Cessna. There remained, however, something that I dearly wanted to get to the bottom of, one little unsolved mystery that hovered in the background in the parish. It had all begun some months ago out at the Kidds' place.

Sam Kidd was a nice young man with an engaging smile. It was always a delight to catch up with him whenever I visited his parents' sheep property, way out west beneath a ridge of outcropping stone known as Dromedary Ridge. The homestead sat on the plain below the ridge and by means of an ingenious series of earthworks, drainage channels and culverts, it received just about every drop of run-off from the ridge itself whenever it rained, which was seldom. There was also a windmill which dragged water up from a deep bore which sat alongside the house. All of this meant that the place sat within a veritable oasis of green garden. Sam's mother, appropriately named Gardenia, or Denny for short, was a keen gardener and somehow managed to coax the very best out of the sandy soil. She grew lots of vegetables and her flower garden was often a riot of colour when everywhere else was dust, dry leaves and general desiccation.

The property had not always been a sheep station. In the nineteenth century it had been a camel breeding station, from which I guess the ridge got its name, that and the fact that the ridge had a very pronounced hump in it. In those days the wool of the district was hauled to town by bullock carts, but in that sandy country it made more sense to make use of the ship of the desert. Afghan camel drivers with their camels came into the district and what was now the Kidd property had been the place for breeding up the engine power for hauling everyone's else's wool bales. With the advent of motorised transport the camels and bullocks disappeared, but the Kidds were left with the cunning and very useful water collection system put in place by the Afghans of old.

Young Sam was best described in the more forgiving language of former times as being a bit simple. I found that his so-called simplicity went with a forgiving nature and also with his own sort of cleverness. He was, I guess, what these days would perhaps be called a savant. He could tell me the name and habit of every plant that grew in the vicinity and his knowledge of the animal and bird life was incredible, far surpassing any other sixteen year old. He had even memorised the Latin and Greek scientific names of most of the species he encountered. He used to wander, especially at night, and he saw and heard things that most folk never experience. He was, you might say, a natural born naturalist. And he had a sense of humour.

His parents encouraged his interest in the natural world.

They were both keen themselves and the house was full of books on natural history. On a previous visit I had noticed and remarked upon their possession of a copy of Eugene Marais' *The Soul of the White Ant*. I should have kept my mouth shut, for this led into one of the difficult and age-old questions.

'Do you think that animals have souls?' It was Denny who posed the question.

'Let me tell you a story,' I countered. And I told them of an old man I had known. He was in the last years of his life and he was still angry at something that had happened to him when he was only ten years old. It had coloured his view of Christianity all his life and got in the way whenever anyone around him raised the matter of belief.

When he was ten he had a much-loved pet dog which died. As a child he asked the local Scottish minister if he would come and bury the dog in the back garden. The minister was of the severe old Presbyterian kind and curtly told the boy that animals don't have souls and therefore didn't get Christian burial. In that one sentence he trampled all over the lad's budding faith and caused damage ever since to any attempt to reconcile the old man to his God. 'So that's why I tread cautiously whenever anyone asks me the question,' I said to Denny.

'So, does that mean that you believe that animals have souls or not?' asked Denny.

'No, it means that if you get into a certain way of thinking about souls it can lead you to the point where that old Scottish minister was,' I said. 'You are asking a loaded question.'

'In what way?' she countered.

'Well, the question assumes that a soul is something you have, rather than something you are,' I said. 'Let me explain,' I added as I saw her wrinkle her brow. 'The whole idea of soul came into Western thought originally from the ancient Greeks. It was the psyche, the very breath of life, all that was not physical, and included what we would call the mind and spirit and consciousness. It described the essential being of a person. So, we still talk of someone being the life and soul of the party. But gradually people began to assume that a soul was a sort of extra bit that humans had in their make-up. They split the human personality into bits as if the pieces could exist separately. They began to talk about *having* a soul rather than being one. Eventually missionaries, for example, were sent out to save the souls of non-believers. It was as if they believed that people had a sort of spiritual black box and that was the only bit that God was interested in retrieving at the end of a human life. These days, thank heavens, we now talk again about the whole person. We think not so much in terms of saving an extra spiritual bit called a soul as bringing the whole person as a believer into the Kingdom of God.'

I was being very careful with my words as I put it to her. This was a topic that had got me into hot water before now. I had once discussed the same ideas with another parishioner, a jolly old lady known to all and sundry simply as Aunty Rene, who saw the funny side of most things. I had said to her the same thing, only the words I used had been, 'it's not so much that we have souls it's more that we are souls'. And then for good measure, so that it sank in, I was daft enough to repeat it. 'Not that we have souls, it's that we *are souls.*'

Aunty Rene threw back her head, slapped her hands onto her thighs and laughed out loud as she replied, 'Oh, Brother, I didn't know that you clergymen were allowed to use language like that.'

Denny, I could see, was itching to get a word in on this subject, so I paused and listened.

'But we do pray in our Book of Common Prayer, Brother, right in the middle of the Communion service, the words "that our sinful bodies may be made clean by his body and our souls washed through his most precious blood". Doesn't that imply that we have a body and that we have a soul?' She had a look on her face as if she thought she'd played a trump card.

'Exactly,' I said. 'Such thinking was rife at the time the prayer book was compiled in 1662. That is one of the reasons why liturgists and theologians in our church are working right now at updating the prayer book and removing such a split in our understanding of a human personality. My guess is that within the next ten or twelve years we shall have a new prayer book, written in more up-to-date language and more in keeping with our understanding of the wholeness of a human person, that a human being can best be described as a soul, in the sense that such a word is all-inclusive of us – a body, mind and spirit – and that we stand as a total package before our God. It is not that we have a sort of spiritual bit added on.'

'So, where does all of that leave the animals?' she asked.

'Good question,' I said. 'The trouble is nobody knows what

it is like to be an animal. We don't know what a dog or a bird or an elephant is thinking or how far their consciousness of things extends. We call humans "souls" as a way of summing up the completeness of what it is to be fully human, our bodies, minds and spirits, our consciousness of self and the world around us, our understanding of a vast range of things and our ability to come to a belief in God and to respond in prayer and praise and the dedication of our lives. But, if they are honest, nobody really knows what goes on in an animal's consciousness. We can respond to our God because of who we are and that gives us certain responsibilities. Who knows what responsibilities an animal is conscious of having? Most people suspect that the consciousness of all creatures other than human doesn't go anywhere near as far as ours does. But nobody knows for sure by how far we are different.'

'Okay, so we call ourselves souls because we can respond to God.' Denny was sticking with this until she'd got it worked out to her satisfaction. 'Where does that leave us in understanding God's relationship to animals?'

'We're on more solid ground here,' I said. 'There are words of Jesus and others in the New Testament that tell us about that. Remember the sayings of Jesus: "Look at the birds of the air: they neither sow nor reap nor gather into barns, and yet your heavenly Father feeds them." Then there's that bit about the lilies of the field being gorgeously arrayed by God. And in St Luke's Gospel: "Are not five sparrows sold for two pennies? And not one of them is forgotten before God." Jesus gives us a picture of God as caring very much for all the plants and birds and animals. And the Bible tells us clearly that we humans have a responsibility of care for them all too. So, although we are not in the habit of calling them souls, nonetheless we are to reverence life in all its forms because God loves everything he has made.'

During our conversation Sam had come into the room and he sat quietly listening. I wasn't sure what he had heard or how much he had taken in until he chipped in with his contribution.

'So, we're called souls and other animals aren't, but God loves everything he made.'

That just about summed it up neatly.

I was invited to stay the night with them, which was usual this far out from town. After a good meal Bill Kidd and Denny were sitting on the veranda and I was lying face up on the lawn trying to spot some of the new man-made satellites that were now circling the earth. It was a good time of quiet relaxation at the end of a hot day.

There came the click of the wire gate into the garden and Sam slid into view. He had been out and about in the dark on his wanderings. He had certainly mastered the art of silent travel. None of us heard him approach before the gate clicked.

'See anything interesting?' I asked him.

'Heard an owlet nightjar,' he said, but there seemed to me to a bit of evasiveness in his voice. '*Aegotheles cristatus,*' he added. 'It means crested goatsucker. People used to believe they sucked the milk of goats at night. But they eat insects.'

'Too dark to really see anything,' I rejoined.

'Well,' he said slowly, as if he really didn't want to tell us. 'I did see something, looked tall and white and moved with a drifting sort of movement. Don't know what it was, unless you believe in ghosts. Looked like a ghost ought to look.'

'Probably a big old man kangaroo,' said his mother.

'Never seen a white kangaroo before,' Sam said in his solemn way.

I left the next morning wondering what Sam had seen. It must have been three weeks later that I heard from another parishioner, who had heard it from his cousin out in the scrub, that a drover had told him of an eerie looking apparition which appeared out of the timber alongside where he was camped with a mob of sheep he was taking north. 'Long, thin, waving sort of thing,' he said, 'and white. Stood out in the moonlight.'

'Probably had a few too many at the Goolga Bridge Hotel,' was the common view of that one.

But the story wouldn't go away. Over the next couple of months, as I travelled round on my visits, I began to hear more of such incidents. And with the stories there grew an edge of fear. Folk didn't like going out at night. And children at school began to tell increasingly lurid tales to one another, each trying to outdo the other in what they had seen or imagined or simply made up for the prestige of the thing.

This wasn't the only ghost scare of recent years. Only two years before on the Parkins' place, only twenty miles down the road from the Kidds, there had been an incident at night. It wasn't really a ghost sighting, more like one of Old Nick himself. The Parkin homestead was an old one, one of the first to be settled in the district, and it had been in the same family from the beginning. It was old, slightly run-down but had a sort of nostalgic charm about it; all, that is, except for the bathroom and toilet arrangements.

A good old-fashioned dunny out the back with the traditional long drop served to accommodate any call of nature. A wooden cover dropped down by means of some fairly fancy old brass hinges and covered the hole when not in use. It kept the bush flies out, mostly! This dunny had character. It was a little termite ridden, but it stood within reasonable walking distance from the house and over the years there had grown up beside it a big untidy pepper tree with long branches hanging down and sweeping little circles in the dirt as they moved in the wind. It was a fine place to sit and meditate on a warm day, for the breeze got in and the bite of the sun was tempered by the dappled shade.

The tree afforded a degree of privacy too, which was just as well for the door hinges had long ago come adrift and the door, or what remained of it, sat tilted sideways and leaned against one of the walls. Nature called and in return the sitter felt surrounded by nature's wonders. Birds hopped in and out and the odd little lizard or two scurried busily across the wooden seat and disappeared between the cracks in the walls.

It so happened that an old friend of Mrs Parkin was up from the big smoke. She was a rather fastidious spinster and never could really understand why her friend had married and opted to live so far inland and away from what she saw as the delights and blandishments of fine city life. She had certainly never encountered a long drop dunny before.

One evening the Parkins invited the Kidds over for a

meal so that the old friend could meet some of the locals. Sam, of course, went with them. It was a beautiful night with full moonlight and, after the meal, the friend felt the call of nature and ventured outside whilst the others sat round the table and yarned. It was a night to cause anyone to stop briefly and wonder at the stars and the pale beauty of a moon-washed landscape. Even the dunny under its dappled moving shade had a sort of ethereal look. The friend took it all in and breathed with a pleasure that she had never felt in her usual city landscape. The pleasure did not last long. As she approached the throne sheer terror took hold of her.

There, sitting on the cover in horned majesty, complete with pointed beard, was the devil himself. She gave a half stifled shriek and bolted back into the safety of the house where she was received with bemused incomprehension by the family. It took them a while to get any sense out of her. She was obviously in shock, but eventually she managed to tell them what she had seen. It was Sam, with his natural curiosity, who went outside and discovered that the billygoat had broken out of his pen and taken up temporary residence in what it must have thought was a superior residence. He came back in and reported in his own special way what he had discovered.

'*Capra hircus*,' he said. 'Common domestic goat, now reclassified as *Capra satanica*,' he added with a grin.

The story went round the district like wildfire and the friend felt that she had to return to her city home earlier than she had originally intended. Nevertheless the ghost stories didn't seem to go away. They died down for a while, but every now and then an account would reach town that somebody had encountered something at night that they couldn't explain.

Stories like that were a part of bush life. If it wasn't ghosts talked about around the camp fire it was the ever present one about a big cat, usually a black panther-like creature, caught momentarily in the headlights or of its spoor seen imprinted in the sand. Whether it's the yeti of Nepal or Bigfoot in America most countries have some such tale. Once started they seem to generate their own momentum. So, I didn't take a lot of notice. I thought that most likely the tales would soon die down until something else stirred the public imagination.

My composure was disturbed a little when Emmy Blades came into town one day and confessed to me that she had seen something the night before as she drove home. She couldn't say what it was, but she had been aware of something out on the periphery of her vision that seemed pale and had loomed for a moment out of the surrounding darkness. Emmy was normally the most level-headed and sensible person I knew, so I agreed with myself that I would keep an open mind on the subject.

Not long after talking to Emmy Blades I got a phone call from Mrs Ezekiel asking me what I was going to do about all these stories of a ghost being seen. I thought that she was telling me that I should stand up in church on Sunday and scotch the rumours. It was soon evident that she was on the opposite tack altogether.

'Doesn't the church have a service for exorcism?' she asked.

'It does,' I answered somewhat warily.

'Well, couldn't you use it or something like it on Sunday?'

I fended her off. 'That would be difficult,' I said. 'That service is only used in homes and places where whatever is disturbing the peace is known and clearly identifiable as some unquiet spirit. We don't have anything like that, just some rumours and tales about what people might have seen, or imagined, and the stories are not confined to one place. It's not as if any one person or house is felt to be haunted.'

Eventually she calmed down as I explained the situation to her, but I did take up her suggestion that at least on the coming Sunday we should sing John Bunyan's old and famous hymn, 'He who would valiant be'. It was rather dated with its quaint line from the seventeenth century when beliefs were differently expressed: 'No goblin nor foul fiend can daunt his spirit', but I managed to convince her that that would cover things for the present. She tried once more, but I drew the line at her suggestion that we should include in the Sunday prayers the old Cornish imprecation: 'From ghoulies and ghosties and long-legged beasties, and things that go bump in the night, Good Lord deliver us'.

It was not that I was denying the possibility of spiritual evil somehow being made manifest. There's far too much in the gospels about the Lord casting out evil spirits from people, not all of which can be explained away by modern psychology. People still experience their demons, only they talk about them in a different way these days. Something told me that, whatever it was out there, it was not some supernatural manifestation. And then I saw the thing myself.

I came across Pepper O'Neill on one of my evening trips home. He was standing beside the road and leaning rather awkwardly against a wire fence. I pulled over and asked him if he was okay.

'Er, a bit sore really, Brother Mark.' He grimaced as he said it.

'What's up?' I asked, 'and where's your ute. What are you doing out here all alone in the wilderness?'

He grinned sheepishly. 'Well, Bruv, me and some shearing mates was having a few beers at the pub down the road and they was tellin' me that one of them had seen a ghost up among the sandhills between here and Blaxford. I didn't believe him, so I thought I'd play a bit of a prank, more fool me. But I'd had a few beers, you understand, so I wasn't thinking things out too well. Anyway last night I thought I'd get meself up all in white and, when they come out of the pub I'd stand off at a bit of a distance among the trees and give 'em a bit of a scare. Which was okay as far as it went, but I hadn't counted on that rabbiter who had a shotgun in his ute and he took a pot shot. I thought I was well and truly out of range, but the blighter was one of those keen blokes who make up their own cartridges. He put a bit of extra powder in and used bigger shot than you usually find, so I got a few bits of lead in my behind and, well Bruv, it's a bit hard to sit down let alone drive to town. I wonder could I lie down on the back seat and you could give me a lift into the Blaxford Hospital.'

I got out and with extravagant gesture motioned him into the back seat where he half sat and half lay as he tried to get comfortable.

The day was wearing on and long before we got back to town the dark curtain of night dropped before us as we went east. Despite the pain in his fundament Pepper O'Neill fell asleep and was now emitting various snores and grunts.

As the dark closed in I got that familiar sense of loneliness at being the only vehicle on a deserted road and I knew I wouldn't see the light of any dwelling until I was nearly into Blaxford again. My headlights carved a long tunnel into which I was driving. The bush on either side receded into the dark and I was alert for anything that signified movement. I didn't want to hit a kangaroo at this late stage of my time at Blaxford. Simmo had already had enough to do over the years repairing the parish car from a variety of encounters with wildlife and the odd slide into the trees on loose gravel.

At a place where the road formed a series of long switchbacks over red sandhills my lights picked out something white ahead. The hairs on the back of my head prickled and I was all too conscious of the stories of the ghostly thing seen hereabouts. As I got nearer and nearer whatever it was appeared to be bigger and bigger. Someone has hung something long and thin from a tree branch was my first thought. And then the thing moved. It swayed sideways with a strange undulating movement. I could see why folk had been puzzled and scared. I had heard of Fisher's ghost, which apparently used to appear near a bridge down on the coast. I was open to the fact that sometimes the dead don't lie down in peace and gave credence to some of the tales of haunting that I knew about.

By the time I came near to it the thing was shining a

ghostly white and seemed all too real. It was very tall, much too big for a sheep, much too big to be a horse. It had two very long legs and appeared to be headless. My rational mind told me that there must be an explanation, but something deep and primitive in me seemed to want to take over. I wasn't exactly in a cold sweat but not far from it.

And then it turned sideways and lifted its head. I let out a small breath of relief. Nonetheless I couldn't believe my eyes. It was a camel, a pure white albino camel. Until it turned I had been looking at it from behind and its head had been down. I had stopped the car by this time and I wound down the window. The animal picked up its heels and trotted away, swaying, into the darkness. Pepper O'Neill kept snoring, so I was denied the corroboration of a witness.

As soon as I hit town I drove straight to the hospital and delivered a blushing Pepper into the capable hands of Margaret Arnold who, it seemed to me, nearly choked with suppressed glee as she gathered swabs and tweezers for the job in hand. I had just enough time to get myself a hurried meal before folk started to arrive for a parish council meeting. When I told them what I had seen, in an effort to dispel the rumours of the supernatural, I was met with disbelief.

'A camel,' they said. 'They died out round here years ago. You must have been seeing things. Are you sure it wasn't a white horse?'

A week later I was vindicated when Bill Kidd shot the beast. Denny went out one morning and found that something had blundered its way through her garden. Whatever it was had left huge rounded footprints in the dug earth. Bill tracked the animal and discovered the camel had got bogged in a muddy dam, part of the old Afghan waterworks on the side of the ridge. He took one look and knew what to do. The animal was obviously old and very scraggy. Its white flanks bore many scars from past bullets and it was clearly on its last legs, so rather than put a rope around its neck and trying to haul it out with his tractor Bill gave it a mercy shot. Even then he had a tough job hauling the camel out onto dry land and then burying it. He dug a huge hole in a great sand drift along Dromedary Ridge itself, not far from the hump, and hauled the animal into it before raising a mound over the site of the burial.

It wasn't until I was talking to the Kidds after the event that I remembered my momentary feeling when I was camped with Brother Edwin on one of my first trips out with him nearly five years before. I thought I had seen something move just at the edge of vision from the camp fire. Could this camel have been what I almost saw, all those years ago? If so, why had it only just cropped up in people's recent experience? It was possible, I thought, that it had wandered far off into the centre of Australia where there are still plenty of wild camels, descended from escapees from old camel farms such as the Kidds'. I wondered what had brought it back into the district after all this time. Had it some deep animal memory of where its predecessors had come from and had it deliberately eventually wandered back to die there?

Sam insisted that he show me the spot where the camel had been buried on the side of the ridge. As we walked towards the spot he said to me, 'Would you say a prayer or something over the grave, Brother? Seems a pity that any creature should be buried without someone at least saying "thank you" for its life.' Then he looked me in the eye and added with a grin, 'Right to give a decent burial for the poor soul.'

I noted the word 'soul' and knew where Sam stood as far as animals were concerned. So, that is what we did. There's the miracle of life in all of God's creatures and the only response to that is gratitude.

At the end of a short prayer of thanksgiving Sam took a wooden, T-shaped notice that he had made and stuck it firmly into the sand above the grave. On it he had burned with a hot iron in fine legible letters the simple inscription: '*Camelus dromedarius*'. On the other side he had inscribed: '*umbra alba interioris*' which means 'white ghost of the inland'. I couldn't have put it better myself.

As we left the spot we took a long look back at the ridge, its extra hump quite evident.

'Bactrian Ridge now,' said Sam.

CHAPTER 16

Out With a Splash

I'd been in Blaxford for nearly five years and my time with the Brotherhood was almost complete. My application to join a two-year course of pastoral training with the chaplaincy department at St Martin's Hospital in Melbourne had been approved. It seemed to me the sensible step for my next years of ministry. God and his people in the Blaxford Parish had shown me where the gaps were in my ministry to them.

Throughout the whole of those five years there had been one piece of community service that had constantly kept me busy. When Brother Edwin originally handed the parish over to me, just after I arrived, he had, as it were, thrown me in at the deep end of the proposed town swimming pool. For nearly five years I had chaired the committee that was working towards building a pool so that town families could swim in safety instead of diving into the river, the steep and muddy banks of which were only the first of many hazards encountered alike by those whose ambition was to swim for Australia and those who simply wanted to cool off on a hot summer's day. Submerged tree branches and other hidden snags had resulted in a regular procession of the walking wounded to the local hospital suffering everything from cuts and bruises to broken limbs.

At the regular monthly meetings of the committee, held at the rectory, we had organised fundraising events and thrashed out details of what was required to complete the project. In the last few months I had learned what it was to hire earthmovers and contractors for pool and buildings. I had wrestled with the complexities of local planning regulations and spent endless hours trying to cool things off between committee members and to smooth the ruffled feathers of those who couldn't get their own way. Now, at last, the whole project was in the final stages of completion and we were looking at how we should celebrate on the day that the pool was to be opened.

At the start there had been friction on the committee. Nobody had had any experience of this sort of thing, so we were all on a steep learning curve. For me it had begun with Brother Edwin's final words as he stepped into the old Tiger Moth to fly off to his new work in the Northern Territory.

'By the way,' he had said as he climbed in, 'I've told the shire president that the new swimming pool committee can meet in the rectory. Said that I'm sure you won't mind.'

'That's fine by me,' I had innocently replied.

'Oh, and I also told him that you wouldn't mind being the chairman.'

'Thanks a lot,' I had said without conviction. The only experience I'd had as chairman of anything was running the dance committee when I was at college.

The first meeting of the committee had seen an

assemblage of ten folk who had signified an interest in the project. They were a motley lot, mothers who were concerned that their children should have a decent facility, schoolteachers who wanted somewhere for the school swimmers, shire councillors who thought that it was time that the town was brought in this respect into the twentieth century.

The meetings had got off to a good start, but it wasn't long before we struck rough water. The one causing the most splash was a woman called Wendy. Now, you never saw a more unlikely Wendy in your life. Up to that point the name had conjured up for me JM Barrie's little friend of *Peter Pan*. This Wendy was six feet tall, angular and awkward on top and the proverbial six axe handles across the bottom. Perhaps as a result of this she was also aggressive. She dressed in the brightest of primary colours which often clashed. You needed sunglasses to look in her direction.

In the meetings hardly a suggestion went unchallenged by her and the most carefully thought out submission was not immune from jarring interruption. Not only did she put the knife in, but she was happy to stir the entrails until all was sufficiently laid bare to her discerning eye. In short she was a pain in the neck on good days and in the other end on bad ones. She did, however, have two saving graces. In the first place she was as keen as mustard on the project. She had, so she told us many times, been quite a good swimmer in her school years down in the big smoke on the coast and had represented the state at junior level in the backstroke. The second thing she had was an amazing understanding of matters financial. She kept the books for the committee and they were always up to date. She knew which side of a quid was the one that mattered and could always tell where it was best to invest the funds.

Over the years we had wrestled with many problems. Most of these were concerned with fundraising. We'd had barbecues, sponsored walks, a beard growing competition, innumerable dances, concerts, sing-a-longs and every conceivable variation on raffles and fetes. We'd ploughed up the land on both sides of the local airstrip and put in a wheat crop, in the one good year when it rained enough to get one. Lots of folk had donated sheep or cattle at sale time and some said they'd be willing to throw in their spouses as well. In short, everyone had worked their socks off and there came the time at last when contracts could be called to put the pool and its facilities on the block of land donated by the council for the purpose. Once that had all happened, progress seemed remarkably swift and it really looked as though the whole thing would be ready for opening before I was due to leave.

I was tremendously satisfied about that. It would be, I thought, a fitting end to my time among these hardworking and (mostly) good folk. As I travelled the parish saying my goodbyes to all and sundry, there welled up in me a great sadness to be leaving. These people had been so good to me, so patient with my blundering ways.

We were sitting now in the rectory living room, we being all the old committee except Wendy. Some months before she had chucked a mental about a trifling matter where she couldn't get her own way and walked out telling us all where we could put our precious swimming pool. She wanted nothing more to do with it. After a moment's startled silence most of the committee were optimistic.

'Don't worry, Brother. That's Wendy for you,' said Robert, a retired schoolteacher who had seen every shade of frustrated behaviour in his time. 'Gets all overwrought and chucks it all in one minute. She'll be ringing up soon all apologetic and we'll carry on as usual.'

Robert's words were too optimistic. In fact Wendy had walked out on us and out she resolutely stayed. I made an attempt to coax her back, not in the remote hope of an easier life on the committee but because she had all the financial matters at her fingertips and it was going to be a nuisance getting someone else up to speed on that side of things. It was no good. She had her dander up and was very firm and clear that she wanted nothing more to do with the project. Worse than that, she went around airing her hurt with anyone who would listen. Wendy being Wendy and Wendy being well-known by all and sundry, she didn't get very far in influencing most folk.

There was, however, one other relevant thing and that was that Wendy was married to the newly elected shire president and the new shire president was booked to be on hand and to play an obviously important role when the pool was officially opened.

The plans were ambitious. The local member of the state parliament had been invited to say a few words but not to do the actual opening. That was to be done by the shire president, as befitted local pride. The state member was a short, citified man more at home dodging the traffic in the inner metropolis than mixing it with folk who had a different rhythm and wisdom, hundreds of miles inland from the salt blown coast. He spoke a different language from the locals and was awkward amongst them. Though they had elected him they didn't take to him once they got to know him. The federal member would have been a better choice, but he was abroad on what he called 'a fact finding mission', which was political speak for a taxpayer funded holiday.

Music was to be provided by a brass band from one of the military bases too far away for them to know what they'd let themselves in for. And for the authentic touch we had managed to persuade one of the top Olympic swimmers to come and do a celebratory lap of the pool before it was thrown open to the public.

A couple of days before the great event Brother Edwin flew in on his way to picking up the second plane for his aero club and, in the process, taking me down to Melbourne to take up my new appointment.

At last the day of the new pool's opening dawned fine and clear, the sky with a thin line of pink and yellow on the eastern rim which was the promise of fine warm conditions for the ceremony and celebrations. I made sure that I was at the new pool bright and early. There were late preparations to be made and everything needed checking so that all would go well. This was to be a big day out for the town and it was also to be my swan song, the last thing to finish before I flew out the next day.

Nails had constructed an impressive podium at the deep end of the pool. He had covered its board floor with bright green raffia matting. I noted that it was the same sort of thing that he used to put around his freshly dug graves. Around the sides was draped some multicoloured bunting and the whole thing looked good as well as being functional. At the front of the podium we set up a sturdy microphone stand with wires out to four speakers. Nobody was going to be able to complain after the event that they couldn't hear what was being said.

At the other end of the pool was erected a large marquee with a clear sign advertising refreshments, tables of food at one end and benches for dispensing the liquid kind at the other. Tables and chairs were arranged outside so that families could sit together as they ate their lunch.

At the time of the official opening all seemed ready. The sun shone, the band played and just about the whole town and district seemed to have gathered. As Chairman of the Organising Committee I led the assembled civic guests to the end of the pool and those who were to speak came up onto the podium with me. When all were settled, I signalled to the band to stop playing for a while and was making my way towards the microphone to welcome everyone when I was brushed aside by an apparition, a very large apparition who seemed to be dressed in the rainbow. Wendy, wife of the shire president clad in colours that would take your eye out, reached and grabbed the microphone in front of me and took charge of the proceedings.

'I'm so glad that you all could come,' she said, and I could hear the slightly delayed echo coming from the most distant of the speakers. 'Our committee has worked long and hard to make this pool possible. We have felt so privileged to do so.'

Since Wendy had walked out on the venture so many months ago, this was a bit rich. I saw a few surprised looks on the faces of quite a few folk, for it was common knowledge that she had quit. Mrs Ezekiel and Emmy Blades looked downright angry.

There was no stopping the woman, so I let her have her day. I would pick up the pieces and get the introductions back on track when she had finished.

I sat back and took in the scene. Over at the refreshment tent I saw Dougal, the man on whom the wall had fallen five years ago. He had his dog Jack lightly held on a leash while he was making the most of the opportunity to quench his thirst. The sun was hot and I guess he might have imbibed a fair drop. I saw his head gradually nod forward and he was soon asleep. His body relaxed, including his grip on the dog's leash. Jack was certainly not asleep. He knew an opportunity when it came along and he was up and away trailing his leash and chasing errant sweet papers and the like. And then the cat appeared.

Jack was in his element. He streaked after the moggie all the way down the side of the pool. Wendy gushed on, oblivious of any impending doom, whilst the chase came nearer. The cat ran right round the dais, but the dog did not deviate. Before you could say 'woof woof' it was up on the platform taking the direct route to cut off its intended victim. The dog made a beeline for the assembled dignitaries. Someone made a half-hearted lunge at the trailing leash, but it wasn't me. Once bitten twice shy with that animal. The dog veered expertly away from the lunge and ran under a chair and out the other side when it seemed to change its mind and doubled back on itself. In so doing it shot between Wendy's legs one way and then round her left ankle and back between them again. The end of the leash got caught in the leg of the chair, so this effectively hobbled poor Wendy. She was leg-roped as expertly as any contestant in the local rodeo ever leg-roped a heifer. Naturally, feeling a tug on her ankle, she put out her right foot to steady herself. But here she was out of luck, for as she did so the heel of her expensive new stiletto shoes found a worn patch in the raffia matting underneath which was a gap in the planking, so, far from saving her, that threw her even more off balance. Desperately she flung out her arms to grab hold of something more firm than the microphone stand and what is more she found something. Unfortunately that something happened to be the fine cut lapels of the local member's pinstriped suit.

So it was that, as it seemed in slow motion, the three of them – Wendy, the MP and the dog – described a most beautiful arc through the air before they all hit the water at the same time, but not before we all got more than a passing glimpse of yet another item of Wendy's special wardrobe for the day. This was as fine a pair of amazingly bright scarlet knickers as anyone was ever privileged to see and which seemed to blaze even brighter once they reached the water and got soaked.

Meanwhile the champion Olympic swimmer at the other end took it all in and with remarkable alacrity dived into the pool and fairly scorched down its length as he tried to come to the rescue. Of course it was part of his training to be quick off the blocks, but he was impressive nonetheless. The assembled crowd rose to the occasion and stood up and cheered him on, or maybe they cheered to encourage Wendy and the local member who seemed to be doing some kind of intricate water ballet with the dog. The cheers and general hubbub almost drowned out the sterling tones of the military band whose conductor brought them into play right on cue as the Olympic swimmer dived in, as they had been instructed to do. All the youngsters, who had been eagerly waiting in their swimmers for the opening ceremony to end so that they could at last get a go and actually use this fine new facility, now joined in the fun. If the adults were using the pool why shouldn't they? So, in they dived.

Dougal, now shocked awake by the sudden din, realised that Jack was no longer with him. He staggered to the edge of the water and reached down to grab Jack's leash. Jack had got himself free from the general melee and was doing a nice dog paddle on his own. It propelled him fast enough for Dougal now to feel the inevitable tug as he took hold of the leash and in he went. He was soon pulled out by a dozen willing hands.

In the general hubbub there remained one island of calm. The podium, built so carefully to hold the visiting dignitaries, was now deserted except for the microphone and myself. The shire president, forgetting his main role as the person who was actually to declare this new swimming pool open, had stepped down in some vain hope that he could help his wife who trod the water so professionally. She was now swimming on her back with the terrified local member clinging desperately to her arm as if she were a life raft in a stormy sea, a part she played with stark realism. With great presence of mind her husband grabbed one of the flotation rings which were installed for safety purposes on posts around the pool, and threw it with commendable accuracy to those struggling in the water. He scored a bullseye on the local member's head, who, not surprisingly, let go his grip on Wendy's ample arm and slipped noiselessly and unconscious beneath the water just as the Olympic champion reached him, dived and pulled him to shore like so much sea wrack caught in a fishing net. In the act of throwing, however, the shire president took a tumble on what was by now a very wet and slippery pool surround made of highly glazed tiles. In the event he was stretchered off by an all too eager band of St John's Ambulance volunteers and, as I later heard, was not able to walk for the next two weeks.

It seemed the natural and only thing to do. As I stood looking down upon the chaos, I grabbed the microphone and bellowed into it the cheery message, 'It seems that most of our guests feel that it's too hot for speeches and the only sensible thing to do is to get into the water, so it gives me great pleasure to see you all enjoying yourselves so much and the only thing left to say is that this pool is now well and truly open and may future folk enjoy it as much as we do today.' This was greeted with a mixture of laughter and cheering as the onlookers left the children to it and made a surge towards the refreshment tent.

Much later I sat in the shade of the tent with a shandy in one hand and a sandwich in the other. Around me were seated the familiar faces of men and women who I had come to know and respect. Most of them were still grinning at the events of this momentous day.

I saw Dougal weaving his way towards me. He and his dog had been home and dried themselves. I felt a glow of pleasure when I realised that he had returned just to be able to say goodbye to me. He came over to where we were sitting.

'Apart from young Glen, God bless him, I was the first person to meet you,' he said with a big grin. 'Ma doggie here was with me too. I just wanted to give ye this and say thank you,' and he handed me over a bottle of the same hard Scottish stuff, the memorable fumes of which I had encountered on my first night in Blaxford. I stammered out my amazed thanks to him, 'Och, it'll keep you warm on those cold nights in Melbourne,' he said as he left and went back towards the refreshment tent.

'Well, there's a first,' said Peter Limson, 'and a sign of your success. Nobody's ever seen Dougal give drink away before.'

Brother Edwin and I eventually made our way back to the rectory. The night was dark and the stars hung low like tempting fruit waiting to be picked. There was time for a last companionable cup of coffee and we collapsed into a couple of easychairs, mugs steaming with a sweet brew.

'Dunno what it is about you, Bro,' said Edwin after a time of ruminating silence. 'Came into this place with a bang and now you are leaving with a splash.'

'What a day,' I said. 'Did you see the expression on Wendy's face as she was heading for the water?'

'I have to admit I wasn't really looking at her face at the

time.' Edwin grinned. 'What an amazing colour. Oh well, red for danger, they say.'

'And that bandmaster was quick on the uptake too,' I said.

'How come?' said Edwin.

'Didn't you notice what the band struck up with as they all fell into the water?'

Brother Edwin looked blankly at me.

'Red sails in the sunset,' I said. 'Couldn't have chosen better.'

Edwin finished his coffee. 'I'm off to bed. Early start in the morning. I'll be leaving for the airstrip just before eight so that I can refuel and check out the Cessna. You can follow later. Take off time is 9.30 am. I've got an ETA logged in at Moorabbin, so don't be late.'

'Don't get your shirt in a twist. I'll be there. Who's taking you out there?'

'Peter Limson, just before he goes and opens the pharmacy. What about you?'

'Simmo's taking me. Reckons he owes me one after all the work I've given him mending and servicing the car over the past five years.'

My last day in Blaxford dawned fine and warm. A light breeze was blowing from the north. Edwin was true to his word, up and breakfasted and off by a quarter to eight. I didn't have to leave until ten past nine, but I was ready long before. I was taking a last look round at this solid old place that had roofed over me for my time there when there came a hammering on the front door.

'Are you there, Brother?' It was the voice of Police

Sergeant Hughes. 'I know it's your last day, but can you spare a minute?'

'What's up?' I asked, looking at my watch.

'It's Steve,' he said. 'He's in the flaming river, says he won't come out, says he's going to commit suicide, says he'll only talk to Brother Mark.'

'It'll have to be quick. I'm due at the airstrip in fifty minutes.' I got into the police car with him. 'Tell me about it on the way.'

'Surprisingly he's not in trouble this time. We went to see him just to get a witness statement. He was an onlooker when Crusty's baker's shop window was smashed last night. I know it wasn't him. It's not his style at all.'

We drove quickly and came upon a scene at the river bank straight out of Breughel. Half the town seemed to be there looking on, offering advice.

'What's all this about, Steve?!' I called down to him. He was standing with water up to his chest, shivering in the cold river but looking defiant.

'I'm not going with him, Brother. I'm not going in them cells again. I done nothing wrong. They's always trying to pin things on me. I'll drown meself first.' Then as if to assure himself of his intention, 'I'm going to end it, Brother.'

I said the first and obvious thing that came into my head. 'Look at yourself, Steve, standing there in the chilly water. You'll catch your death of cold if you stay in there.'

A squall of understanding seemed to hit him. He shook his head and a slow grin spread across his face. I wasn't sure whether up to that moment he had been playing a part for the crowd's sake, and the policeman, or whether genuine and sudden realisation came upon him.

'Oh yes, Brother, could be dangerous, eh?' And, with that, out he came slipping and sliding up the bank, dripping muddy water, reaching for my hand.

'You're not in trouble, Steve. The sergeant here just wants you to tell him what you saw last night. He doesn't think it was you.'

'You're a good man, Brother,' said Steve as a farewell benediction. 'Gonna miss you, that's for sure.'

'Me too, Steve,' I said and meant it. 'Stay out of trouble. Be a good example to the young fellas. They depend on you, look up to you.'

'Try to,' said Steve, grabbing my other hand in a vice-like grip.

'And thanks, all you good folk!' I yelled to the assembled throng.

'Three cheers for the Brother!' someone shouted out. And to that mighty acclamation I left them to it.

Simmo and I arrived at the airstrip just a bit after nine-thirty. Edwin was standing by the plane, which had its engine running ready for take-off.

'Where on earth have you been?' he asked as he took my suitcase.

'Saying goodbye to Steve. It's a long story. I'll tell you later.'

'We've got another passenger. Hope you don't mind. She said she was going to Melbourne, so I offered her a lift.'

'It's your flight. You can take who you want. Who is it?' I asked as I tried to look up into the plane. But the morning sunlight was reflecting off the window and I could see nothing.

'You'll see,' said Brother Edwin with one of his mischievous grins.

Oh, please Lord, not Mrs Ezekiel all the way to Melbourne. It was an unworthy prayer.

I opened the door and climbed in. There sat Margaret Arnold looking crisp in a smart linen skirt and a pink, open-necked shirt. She was grinning from ear to ear.

'Bit of a surprise?' she said.

We took off against the breeze at ten to ten and circled the town. I looked down and mentally picked out the houses of all the folk I had come to know. A long, wide ribbon of green stretched for miles on both sides of the river. The recent flood had left lush grass and the season would be good for those who ran sheep and cattle in the district. It seemed to me a kindly benison upon those who had fed and sheltered me over the past five years.

'Not to worry,' said Edwin. 'We've a tailwind and should make up the lost twenty minutes easily.'

'So,' said Margaret with interest, 'what is it for you now, Brother Mark?'

'Not "Brother" any more. Mark will do fine.'

'Mark,' she said as if tasting the name for the first time, like butterscotch rolled in the mouth. 'Okay, Mark, now that you're released from the brotherhood rules, are you going to swing the other way into wine, women and song?'

'I might sing a bit,' I countered.

'Hope that word's got a G on the end of it,' cut in Brother Edwin.

'What about you?' I asked her. 'You off to Melbourne for long?'

'Oh, like you, I thought it was time to move on, advance my career. I'm off to pick up another nursing certificate. I'm going to do obstetrics.'

'That takes a whole year, doesn't it? Where will you train?'

'Saint Martin's Hospital,' she said.

'Same place as me,' I said.

'So it seems,' she said, and she flashed me her dazzling smile, long fingers smoothing her skirt.

We flew on into the day, the morning sun coming at us hot through the windows on the left, the air as clear as ice, the future beckoning as we set our course south.

I dread to think what Ferret said when he got to hear about it.

ACKNOWLEDGEMENTS

I would like to thank my wife Barbara for her infinite patience and understanding as I spent time writing this book. Thanks also to Pamela Harvey, author, mentor and critic, who was generous with her time and who read every chapter as it was produced, made helpful comments and encouraged me to keep on writing. Annette Hansen, the chief editor at Sid Harta Publishers, earns my gratitude for correcting my mistakes. For any errors which remain I crave the reader's indulgence.

ABOUT THE AUTHOR

Richard Stamp is a retired Anglican priest. He was born in 1936 on a farm in the English midlands before the family moved to Plymouth in Devon, where they survived the nightly bombing of World War Two. He spent his National Service as a medic in the RAF before graduating from Durham University in 1960. After completing Theological studies he felt called to Australia to join one of the Anglican Bush Brotherhoods. His first parish covered around 25,000 square miles of outback Australia.

Much of his ministry has been in rural parishes but he has also been a hospital chaplain and spent six years as chaplain/teacher at an Anglican boarding school.

In his youth he started rock climbing in the English Lake District and later climbed in the New Zealand Alps. He has travelled widely and once spent a week adrift in the Pacific Ocean after a ship caught fire.

He is married to Barbara and they have two adult sons and three grandchildren. Now living in rural Victoria, he describes himself as spending his time growing his own vegetables, watching birds and photographing them, still walking the hills, writing the occasional short story and mediocre poetry, and permanently painting the house.

So Far
& So Good
Denis Charles Petmezaki

DEMONS
AT DUSK
MASSACRE AT MYALL CREEK
PETER
STEWART
Foreword by Peter FitzSimons

"Absolutely BRILLIANT. Superb. Hilarious, too."
Bruce Beresford
REAL AND REEL
The education of a film obsessive and critic
BRIAN
McFARLANE

love under occupation
A PERSONAL JOURNEY
THROUGH WAR, MARRIAGE
AND WHITE AUSTRALIA
Christine de Matos and Noel Huggett

An
UNQUIET
STATE
RUTH CARSON

In a vast and unforgiving land,
only one man can uncover the truth
Billy Two
Garry Boyd

BEST-SELLING TITLES BY KERRY B. COLLISON

Readers are invited to visit our publishing websites at:
http://sidharta.com.au
http://publisher-guidelines.com/

Kerry B. Collison's home pages:
http://www.authorsden.com/visit/author.asp?AuthorID=2239
http://www.expat.or.id/sponsors/collison.html
email: author@sidharta.com.au

Purchase Sid Harta titles online at:
http://sidharta.com.au

NEW RELEASES... ALSO FROM SID HARTA PUBLISHERS

Made in the USA
Lexington, KY
06 December 2011